Sarah had heard enough.

"You are such a...dunderhead! I'm done here," she shouted at Luke as he took a breath before his next tirade.

Luke took a step back. "Dunderhead?"

Sarah spun around and tromped back down the hill toward her friends. She realized the children were staring at them, cramming popcorn in their mouths faster than they could chew.

She had never been this angry at another human being in her life, and she didn't like it. It burned like battery acid in her stomach. She didn't know how Luke dealt with the seemingly perpetual anger he harbored. Was it like this for him all the time? Was this what he meant when he said anger was eating at him? That's what it felt like to her.

Suddenly, she realized she was empathizing with him. Now she knew his kind of anger. She understood precisely what Luke was experiencing....

Dear Reader,

The inspiration for my Shores of Indian Lake series came right out of my own life when I returned to my hometown after thirty-five years of living in big cities like New Orleans, Houston, Los Angeles and Scottsdale, Arizona.

It has been a revelation to me that the lives of those in small towns are filled with just as much pathos, romance, chaos and eternal struggle as people in glamorous cities.

Love Shadows and the characters in it, Sarah and Luke, sprang to life from my own grief after losing my darling sister, Nancy, to cancer only four years ago. Sarah and Luke must deal with so many emotions after the death of a loved one. They both discover that coming back to life is a road embedded with razor-sharp impediments, but that ultimately, life is meant to be filled with joy and happiness. It is the human condition to want and need love. For Sarah and Luke, personal illumination is primary. Only after they come to terms with their own demons can they surrender to each other.

The Shores of Indian Lake is filled with endearing, haunting and oftentimes seemingly eccentric characters who will steal your heart. The next book in the series features Sarah's best friend Maddie Strong, who is faced with impossible choices of her own career dream-making when her first love, Nate Barzonni, returns to Indian Lake in pursuit of his fast-track goal of becoming head of cardiology at a major Chicago hospital and finds himself face-to-face with the one woman he'd left brokenhearted…and very angry.

I would love to hear from you and what kind of story you would like to read about along the Shores of Indian Lake. You can write to me at cdlanigan@aol.com and visit my website at www.catherinelanigan.com. I'm on Facebook, Twitter and LinkedIn, as well.

Catherine

HARLEQUIN HEARTWARMING

Catherine Lanigan

Love Shadows

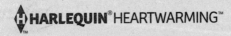

Recycling programs
for this product may
not exist in your area.

ISBN-13: 978-0-373-36672-9

LOVE SHADOWS

Copyright © 2014 by Catherine Lanigan

Printed in U.S.A.

www.Harlequin.com

CATHERINE LANIGAN

knew she was born to storytelling at a very young age when she told stories to her younger brothers and sister to entertain them. After years of encouragement from family and high school teachers, Catherine was shocked and brokenhearted when her freshman creative writing college professor told her that "she had no writing talent whatsoever" and that she "would never earn a dime as a writer." He promised her that he would be her "crutches" and get her through his demanding class with a B grade so as not to destroy her grade point average too much, *if* Catherine would promise never to write again. Catherine assumed he was the voice of authority and gave in to the bargain. For fourteen years she didn't write, until she was encouraged by a television journalist to give her dream a shot. She wrote a six-hundred-page historical romantic spy-thriller set in World War I. The journalist sent the manuscript to his agent, who then garnered bids from two publishers. That was nearly forty published novels, nonfiction books and anthologies ago.

Books by Catherine Lanigan

HARLEQUIN MIRA

Dangerous Love

Elusive Love

Tender Malice

In Love's Shadow

Legend Makers

California Moon

HARLEQUIN/SILHOUETTE DESIRE

The Texan

Montana Bride

This book is dedicated to my sweet, much-loved sister, Nancy Jean Lanigan Porter, who died May 7, 2009; to my mother, Dorothy Lanigan, who died June 12, 2011; and to my loving husband, Jed Nolan, who held my hand through all of the shadows that descended upon us and who will always hold my heart.

CHAPTER ONE

SPRING EXPLODED OUTSIDE Sarah's kitchen window as pink crab-apple blossoms unfurled their petals along a crooked branch. A thick, undulating bed of apricot and orange Parrot tulips swayed in the early-morning breeze and nuzzled against thick masses of purple Muscari. The newly mowed lawn was a lush carpet of a green so rich it did not look real. A midnight rain had gently showered the forsythia and bejeweled an intricate spiderweb that connected two rosebushes near Sarah's back door. Rosegold dawn rays, like the fingers of a divine hand, touched every tree, house and object in Indian Lake with the promise of a new day.

"What a beautiful morning." Sarah sighed after she breathed in the fragrance of lilacs from the open window. "This was Mother's favorite time of year." Sarah smiled wistfully. A now-familiar pang in her heart—though not as painful as her sorrow had been two months ago when her mother died of cancer—plucked at the open wounds in her psyche.

The grandfather clock in the hall chimed the hour. Sarah used to love the burled walnut clock her father had given to her mother on their fifth wedding anniversary, but now its sound was that of an echoing gong throughout the very empty house. Sarah's father had died three years ago and now her mother was dead, too.

Two years ago, Sarah had given up a very successful career as a commercial interior design architect in Indianapolis when she had learned of her mother, Ann Marie's, diagnosis. Sarah knew she'd have to return home, so she applied for and landed a job in Indian Lake at Environ-Tech Design Studios, owned and run by Charmaine Chalmers. The job had been perfect for Sarah's needs in that when Sarah had to take her mother to chemotherapy or stay at home during Ann Marie's last four months and work at her drafting table in her father's study, Charmaine had graciously given her the time off, though she continued to work on her designs from home.

Sarah's move back to Indian Lake also contributed to the eventual breakup with her high school sweetheart, James Stanwyck, an investment banker whose fast-track career was stuck in warp speed. Sarah had not realized how unfulfilling her relationship with James had been until she'd moved back to Indian Lake. They'd dated during high school, college and grad school, and once they'd both begun their careers, their romance had languished until Sarah realized she couldn't breathe. It was Sarah who put an end to *them*. James moved to Chicago, which was only an hour away from Indian Lake, but after sending him a thank-you note for the flowers he sent for her mother's funeral, Sarah had not communicated with him. James had been equally silent.

It didn't take long after her breakup to realize she didn't miss James. She recognized that their long-term romance had been habit more than love, or even *like*. She wished him well, but he seldom entered her thoughts. That was why she found it odd that she ruminated on him today.

You're just lonely, Sarah! she scolded herself, grabbing a bag of salad out of the refrigerator. She stopped midmotion as the fridge door slowly closed. Her stomach roiled as if she was hungry, but she'd just consumed a power bar and slugged back a few sips of coffee. The churning she felt was the same reaction her body always foisted upon her when she was assaulted with the truth.

Since Ann Marie died, Sarah had come to the awareness that she had a fear of being alone. All her life, Sarah had family she lived with and friends she filled her afternoons and evenings with. Even her romance with James, to a great degree, was a convenience for her. She told herself that her life was just ducky. Dandy. Because she had somebody. It didn't matter that he wasn't the right guy for her. It mattered that *they* were a couple. These past months, her loneliness had grown longer, darker and more infinite, like a great yawning abyss that frightened and immobilized her. Though she had many friends in town and most she'd known since high school or even longer, she now had new friendships with her coworkers. It was easy to convince herself that her life was functioning properly.

"I don't have time for all that today," she shot back at her reflection in the small, gold-framed mirror on the wall.

Sarah shoved her emotions back into her mental hiding place and put the salad in her insulated lunch sack. On the kitchen table sat her purse, cell phone, car keys and her battered leather portfolio containing the blueprints and very detailed architectural drawings for the renovation of a strip center on the north side of Indian Lake. Sarah had worked painstakingly on this project, pushing herself nearly to the point of exhaustion with late nights at her drafting table. She should have been excited about this morning's presentation to Charmaine, but she wasn't.

She was worried.

Charmaine was an architect and interior designer whose perfectionist and exacting, creative eye saw shadows and light in spaces that most of her competition routinely missed. Charmaine saw potential for greatness everywhere she went. Broken houses, dilapidated commercial centers and desecrated public buildings were her favorite challenge because she believed she could fix anything. Sarah had never met anyone like Charmaine. Even when Sarah was in college at Indiana University, her design and art professors had not exhibited the kind of peerless inventiveness and vision Charmaine possessed. Sarah could only hope to be half the artist and designer that Charmaine was.

Sarah had just taken a huge gulp of her coffee when the telephone rang. She checked the caller ID and smiled.

"Hello, Mrs. Beabots. How are you this morning?" she asked cheerily of her octogenarian next-door neighbor.

"Fine. Fine, dearie, but you better corral that dog of yours."

Sarah instantly looked over to Beauregard's breakfast bowl and saw that it was still full. Her one-hundred-and-twenty-seven pound golden retriever had not touched a bite, which was very unusual. Frowning, she glanced at the back door. It was still open halfway, just as it was each morning when she let the dog out to do his business. Beauregard always let himself back in, finished off his breakfast and then plopped himself down on his green-and-blue-plaid doggie bed.

Sarah looked at the empty bed. "What about Beau?" she asked, going to the door and opening it all the way.

"I'm looking at him from my bedroom window," Mrs. Beabots continued, "and he's digging a hole at your back fence. From the looks of it, pumpkin, he'll hit Shanghai in less than an hour."

"He's doing what?" Sarah went to the back porch, leaned over the railing and nearly dropped the cordless phone. "I'll call you back, Mrs. Beabots. And thanks."

"Anytime, pumpkin," she said and hung up.

Sarah nearly flew down the back porch steps and across the lawn. "Beauregard Jensen! What are you doing?"

Clumps of mud and dirt sailed into the air and dappled Beauregard's copper and golden fur in a crazy quilt pattern.

Sarah raced up to the golden retriever, still

yelling his name, but he paid no attention. If anything, he dug harder and faster.

A dollop of mud went slinging through Beauregard's hind legs and smacked Sarah in the forehead.

"Beau! Stop it, this instant!" she shouted, wiping the mud off her face.

Beauregard kept digging. He splattered Sarah's freshly dry-cleaned camel-and-black silk suit. Sarah dodged the mud rain and went around to the left of the dog and tried to grab his collar and pull him out of the deep hole he'd dug. Though she tried to steady herself in her tan pumps, she slipped on the grass, which she'd been far too prideful about, and fell rump-side down. She knew she should change out of her business suit in order to avoid serious damage to her clothes, but she'd be late for work if she didn't get Beau out of the hole and back into the house.

"Of all the days in my entire career, did you have to choose today to act like a dog?"

Beauregard paid no attention to her and kept flinging dirt.

"What are you doing? And why are you doing this?" she asked, frustration spiking the edges of her words. Another clump of dirt hit her on the cheek.

"That's it!" Sarah pulled with all her might

and hoisted Beauregard out of the hole and away from the fence.

Beau snarled at Sarah.

She snarled back.

Beau glanced back at the hole and Sarah knew he was thinking about defying her, just like a misbehaving child. "Don't even think about it, Beauregard Jensen. Just look at you! You've made a terrible mess of yourself. It will take me hours to clean you up and I have to be at work."

Dragging Beau behind her, which was a serious feat of strength and adrenaline, Sarah trudged toward the driveway. "You have to have a bath and there's no time left. It's off to the groomers for you!" Sarah pulled on Beau's collar again, but the dog had relented to his fate and now walked, head forlornly hung, next to his master and supposed superior creature.

Sarah ordered Beauregard to sit on the driveway next to her Envoy as she went to the garage, got an old plastic tarp and draped it across the passenger's seat. She stood aside as Beauregard jumped into the SUV.

"The tarp will hopefully keep my car clean, but believe me, it's going to take professional fumigation to get your dirty dog smell out of here!" Sarah slammed the car door.

She went back to the kitchen, grabbed her purse, portfolio and lunch and locked the house.

As she walked around the flagstone path to the front yard, she saw Mrs. Beabots standing on the front sidewalk, hand up to her forehead to shade her eyes from the brilliant morning sun. "Showed him whose boss, din't cha?" Mrs. Beabots asked.

Sarah had lived on Maple Avenue all her life, and for as long as she could remember, Mrs. Beabots had not only lived next door, but she had also felt that whatever was happening in the Jensen household was her prerogative to know. Mrs. Beabots was not a gossip, and blessedly, she didn't share the information. She simply believed she could not help the ones she loved if she didn't know their business.

Unfortunately, Mrs. Beabots never understood that Sarah despised being late to work—or late to anything, for that matter. Mrs. Beabots loved to talk. Talking helped whittle away the hours of her very lonely life.

"I have to get Beau down to Puppies and Paws and then I have to be at work…"

"I know, dearie. I know. You gotta run."

"I do," Sarah said, sliding into the car.

"When you get home tonight, I can help you fill that hole back up. Perfect place for a start of my peonies," Mrs. Beabots offered.

"I just don't know what possessed him to dig like that," Sarah said. "Beau has never been a digger."

Mrs. Beabots turned her thin face toward Sarah's backyard. "Could have been the fact that last night when Beau came home with that dead squirrel, you tossed it over the fence into the old Samuels' yard."

Sarah shuddered as she remembered when she'd let Beau out just before her bedtime. She had been preoccupied with her presentation and last-minute adjustments to her drawings, and hadn't realized Beau was taking an abnormal amount of time outside. As always, she'd left the kitchen door half-open, and when he came in and pushed it open all the way with his snout, Sarah had turned around in time to see a dead squirrel, stiff with rigor mortis, clamped between Beau's jaws. Off her chair in a shot, she whisked a kitchen towel off the countertop, threw it over Beauregard's face and wrenched the squirrel from the dog. She shrouded the dead animal in the towel and immediately went out to the backyard. It was a new moon, black-as-pitch night, but Sarah knew exactly how many paces it was to the north side of her yard, where a six-foot high, white-wood fence separated her property from the Samuels' estate. With one mighty swing of her right arm, she heaved the dead squirrel over the fence.

Turning around, she found Beau standing directly behind her. If she hadn't heard his loud panting first, she would have fallen over him.

"Don't ever do that again, Beauregard Jensen," she warned with a wag of her finger and a steep arch to her eyebrow. Not that he could see her expression in the dark.

Sarah grabbed his collar and yanked him toward the house. She remembered now that on the way back, Beauregard had paused and looked back at the fence. It wasn't until she shouted his name and gave his collar another tug that he followed her obediently.

Sarah knew now that Beauregard had started plotting his strategy for retrieval at that very moment. She wondered if he'd thought about it all night.

Sarah looked back at Mrs. Beabots, who was patiently holding her arms at her sides, the skirt of her black-and-white-polka-dot dress fluttering around her legs. "That house has been vacant for two years. I didn't think anyone would mind," Sarah said glumly.

"You shoulda buried the squirrel out of Beau's sight."

"Why?" Sara asked.

"Because, pumpkin. That critter was his prize.

Dog's always gonna go for his prize. He's a retriever." Mrs. Beabots smiled her thin smile and
nodded.

Sarah watched after the little bird of a woman
who'd always been not only observant but wise,
and somehow invariably managed to make certain she had the last word.

LUKE BOSWORTH WAS lost in thought as he drove
his children—Annie, his eight-year-old, freckle-
faced, redheaded daughter, and his six-year-
old son, Timmy, with the bright blue eyes—to
school.

"Can we go all the way down Maple Avenue,
Dad?" Annie asked.

"Why?"

Annie looked out the window and gazed at
the majestic, hundred-year-old sugar maples for
which the street was named. "I love it. It's so
beautiful this time of year, with all the tulips
blossoming. My favorites are the pink ones."

Timmy gave her a dismissive wave of his
hand. "Aw, Annie. All the tulips on Maple Avenue are pink."

"I know."

"It's okay," Timmy said, sitting up straighter
as they turned off Main Street and onto Maple.
"I like all the big houses. I bet the people who
live here are really rich."

Luke heard his children's chatter as if their words were being spoken under water. They were playing one of their favorite games, where they picked out the "happiest" house.

He barely glanced at the tall "Painted Ladies," the historic Victorian houses painted in pinks, purples, yellows and bright greens. These houses were painted in bright colors during the era when heavy smoke billowed out of the factories in Chicago and steel mills in Gary. The prevailing winds coated the huge homes in Indian Lake with soot, and the bright colors became subtle from grime and pollution.

He frowned and rubbed his aching forehead as they drove past a three-story Italian stucco house with French doors and huge windows.

"That's my favorite," Annie said, pointing at the windows. "Do you like it, Dad?"

Luke wasn't exactly paying attention, so he grumbled, "Hmm." He continued diving deeper into the sea of thoughts about his wife, Jenny.

It had been two years, three months and six days since Jenny died, and Luke felt as if he'd died with her.

The autumn when he and Jenny had first discovered Indian Lake on a weekend trip from their home near Chicago, Jenny had walked up and down Maple Avenue pretending she was house shopping. She chose over half a dozen houses that she liked. She would have loved to raise their children in one of these fine, old homes.

But that was then, Luke thought as he glanced back at the Italian stucco house. *Whoever these people are, they're better off than I am.*

Luke worked as a construction supervisor at a midsize company in town. For four years, since their move to Indian Lake, Luke had been making good money. Because Luke was a former Navy SEAL, with more than one decoration for valor in combat in Iraq, Jenny had urged him to apply for the GI Bill loan to go after an architect's degree at Indiana University-Purdue in Fort Wayne. All their plans were dashed in a single day when Jenny got sick. Very sick.

The doctors told Luke and Jenny that the tumor in her brain was malignant. Inoperable. Terminal. The words still sounded like shotgun blasts. Each time he thought about that day, those words, Luke's head jerked back from the onslaught.

The doctors gave Jenny four months to live. Neither he nor Jenny believed them. They fought back with chemotherapy. They enrolled in an experimental program that administered a new drug right to the brain. It didn't work. Jenny lived six months. She had bought two more months than the doctors had predicted, but their prognosis was still the same. Jenny's time with Luke was flat-out too short.

It was entirely his fault that Jenny died. If he'd been wealthy, he could have flown her to Europe, where doctors were open to alternative treatments for brain tumors. He should have insisted on seeing an herbalist and nutritionist who might have bought them another six months or a year to find a cure. But the cancer overtook Jenny with a vengeance until it finally took her away from him.

Luke had been more than angry at the universe since that day in the hospital when he yelled and sobbed and shouted at the nurses to leave him alone with Jenny's body. He'd held her for hours, watching her turn gray in his arms. He'd been inconsolable. He still was.

He went through his days in a fog, unable to think or respond to his own children. There were times he wished he and Jenny had never had kids. They were always coaxing him back to the present, to the place he wanted to deny. As long as he lived inside his memories of Jenny and the magical love and life they'd shared, he believed he would be saved. She was his savior and his lifeline to sanity. Luke was as helpless and hopeless without Jenny as he'd been two years, three months and six days ago.

Even now, he could hear Annie's voice, prying its way into his inner sanctum of memories, but he didn't know what she was saying. He should pay better attention, but when he did, a burning in his gut ignited and visions of Jenny beckoned him back to the peaceful past.

"Did you say something, Annie?" Luke finally mumbled.

Annie's face was pressed against the glass. "Yeah," she said with a whisper of reverence in her voice. "That's the house I want."

"Me, too," Timmy chimed, looking at his father's mournful expression in the rearview mirror. It was like always. His father wasn't listening to them. Half the time when he did listen, he just growled at them.

Nothing had been good for any of them since Mom had died. Timmy watched out the back window as they drove past the stucco house. *I wish we could live in that exact house someday.*

Timmy realized he'd been making a lot of wishes lately. He wanted a big golden retriever and he wanted a home where everyone hugged each other a lot and always smiled and never frowned as if something was wrong. Timmy didn't think such things were impossible.

That's what wishes are for, aren't they? Timmy thought. *To make dreams come true.*

CHAPTER TWO

LUKE PARKED HIS Ford F-150 smack dab in front of Cupcakes and Coffee Café and turned off the engine. "I'm going to get a quick cup of coffee," he said, turning to his children.

"Okay, Dad," Annie said, unbuckling her seat belt.

"Whoa! Where do you think you're going?" Luke asked sternly, throwing his hand over the buckle.

Annie's eyes flew open with her customary dramatic flair. "To see the puppies. The only thing good about this whole day is that we are going to see the puppies. Right now," she said in that intractable tone that revealed conviction without disrespect. "If we have to go to boring school all day, then we can at least see the puppies."

Luke chewed his bottom lip thoughtfully and rubbed his scruffy, unshaven cheek.

"Please, Dad," Timmy said earnestly.

Peering at both his children, Luke wished he didn't see so much eagerness in their eyes.

It dumbfounded him that dogs could mean so much to them. He'd told them a hundred times that they could not afford a dog. Luke was overwhelmed with all the medical bills that had piled up in the wake of Jenny's illness and death. Luke didn't see how he'd get them paid off even if he had a decade to do so. To make matters worse, both Luke and his boss, Jerry Mason, were very concerned about the slow-down in the construction sector. Jerry had laid off all his full-time crews and used them only on an "as-needed basis."

Luke was the only employee left on salary, and his paycheck had gotten smaller. Still, Luke was lucky to have a full-time job. In order to make up the difference, Luke had been look-ing for weekend work and had cut back on extra household expenses. One of the first luxuries to be eliminated was cable and DSL. In order to use the internet to search want ads, he'd re-sorted to visiting the public library. So far, he'd come up empty.

Somehow, Luke had managed to keep the family afloat over the past year, even with the cutback at work. Although there was some eq-uity in the house that would relieve most, but not all, of Jenny's medical bills, Luke knew that if he were to sell the house, it would be like burying Jenny all over again. He couldn't go through that kind of pain ever again. It was hard enough to live in the hollow space he called his "life" as it was. He had left the house Jenny had turned into a home for them all just as it was on the day of her death. Her clothes were still in the closet, her sweater hung over the back of the kitchen chair and the kids knew never to move it. The house was a time warp, and inside its walls, Luke could pretend that Jenny was alive.

Luke was right, he believed, to deny the kids a dog. A dog required shots and veterinarian visits. They got sick just like kids. There were bills for the groomer. Special diet foods. He knew from his friends and coworkers that owning a dog was as costly as a child, minus the education.

Scratch that. I forgot obedience school.

"You can go look as long as you remember that I'm not buying a dog."

"We know, Dad," Annie answered.

"Annie, you hold Timmy's hand. Don't go anywhere else. I'll only be a sec."

"Dad," Annie said, "we just want to see the puppies. We don't want to run away."

Luke opened the truck door and hauled Timmy out of his car seat, which Timmy despised because it made him feel like a little kid. At least twice a week, Luke caught Timmy weighing himself, hoping he would finally pass the legal forty-pound mark so he could use an "adult" seat belt and not be treated like the little kid he was.

Annie took Timmy's hand, and together they walked up to the bay window of Puppies and Paws, where three two-month-old golden retriever puppies played with each other. They tumbled over stuffed animals and scooted dangerously close to their water bowls, but never splashed a single drop out of the metal containers.

"I like the white one," Annie said. "I think I'll call her Snowball."

"That's a stupid name for a dog," Timmy replied, placing his nose so close to the glass he mushed the end. "These are the best pups Grandy ever made."

"Grandy doesn't make the puppies, she just breeds them. There's a difference," Annie said, though she wasn't quite sure why she was right. Annie just remembered that several years ago, when her mother was alive, they had come to Puppies and Paws and her mother had told her Grandy was a dog breeder.

Puppies and Paws was the best place in all of Indian Lake as far as Annie and Timmy were concerned. Grandy Ipson always had the cutest and cuddliest puppies in the window, and no matter if it was raining or snowing, there was always a new little fellow for them to watch while their dad went next door for his coffee.

"I like the red one," Timmy said. "I'd call him Copper. That's the right kind of name for a great dog like he's going to grow up to be."

Annie smiled at her little brother and slid her arm over his shoulder. She knew Timmy wanted a dog really bad.

Annie looked at the longing in Timmy's eyes. The little red puppy was now licking the glass that Timmy had pressed his face against. The past two years had been very sad for all of them after her mother had died. Annie had often cried herself to sleep, but Timmy had started spending a lot of time by himself. Often, she saw him sitting alone on the back steps of their house, just staring off into the distance. Annie wasn't sure if he was missing their mother or if it was because their father didn't spend time with them like he used to. She knew she couldn't say or do much to make up for their mother being gone, but if she could get a dog for Timmy, maybe then the heavy sadness they all felt might go away.

Right then and there, Annie promised herself that she would find a way to convince their father that dogs could be cheap.

"A DOLLAR TWENTY-FIVE? Since when?" Luke asked Maddie Strong as she handed him the paper cup of robust black coffee. "It's always been a dollar."

Maddie swept a palm over her short, streaked, blond hair, put her hand on her hip and leveled her sparkling green eyes at Luke. "My profit margin decreased when the property taxes went up. Heating bill is through the roof. Water jumped, too. Not to mention there was some drought in Colombia and the coffee beans are sky high. That about cover it for ya, Luke?"

Luke sucked in his cheeks to keep his laughter at bay. "Your face is red, Maddie."

"Gets that way when I'm riled up."

"Sorry I said anything," he apologized, taking a sip. He smiled. "Man, that's good."

Maddie's grin broke free across her face. "I aim to please."

"You want to take a cupcake to your kids?" She leaned a bit closer and whispered so the other customers wouldn't hear her. "Half price."

Luke was tempted as he glanced along the back bar where Maddie kept the instruments of her creative culinary genius. Maddie had invented "Iced-to-Order" cupcakes, an Indian Lake sensation that made Cupcakes and Coffee Café a hot tourist spot all through the summer and fall.

There were six kinds of cakes today, including French vanilla, double Dutch fudge, strawberry, lemon, carrot and red velvet. Once a patron chose the cupcake base she wanted, Maddie added one of nearly a dozen different kinds of icing piped out of thick pastry tubes that hung from a gleaming stainless-steel rack along the back counter. There was chocolate ganache, vanilla butter cream, boiled white non-fat icing, cooked white flour icing, whipped cream icing, Italian wedding cake icing, lemon butter icing and strawberry almond. Luke's mouth watered just looking at the chalkboard list of options. If he had the money, he would buy a dozen cupcakes for him and the kids. "Thanks for offering, Maddie, but the kids are on their way to school and my wife told me it's bad for them to have sugar in the morning."

"Good advice."

"Maybe for a special occasion I could take you up on that offer."

"Sure," Maddie said.

Luke handed Maddie a single dollar bill and counted out two dimes and a nickel. "Thanks for the coffee."

"You take care, Luke."

"You, too, Maddie," he said.

As Luke was coming out of Cupcakes and Coffee Café, a late-model, fire-engine red GMC Envoy screamed up to the curb and parked abruptly. Sitting shotgun was the biggest, dirtiest, happiest golden retriever Luke had ever seen.

The driver's door flew open, and as a young blonde woman stepped out, the dog leaped over the driver's seat and sprang onto the sidewalk.

"Look at that!" Timmy shouted with glee and pointed at the dog. Just as he raised his hand, the dog whirled his head around to see Timmy. Smiling ear to ear, if that was possible for a dog, the retriever shot over to Timmy and stood on his hind legs, placing two filthy, muddy paws on Timmy's freshly laundered and pressed white uniform shirt.

"My God, get your dog away from my son!" Luke shouted as he rushed toward Timmy.

"Beauregard!" the woman yelled, but the dog paid no attention to her. Instead, he licked Timmy's cheek with a long and very slobbery dog kiss.

Timmy giggled and turned his face away, only to be licked on the other cheek. "Hey, he likes me!" Timmy said, putting his arms around the dog's chest and nearly hugging him.

Annie, not to be left out of the fun, sidled up to Timmy and stuck her face close to Beauregard's. She, too, got a wet kiss.

Beauregard lifted a muddy paw and put it around Annie's shoulder as if they were long-lost friends sharing a hug.

"What a great dog!" Annie exclaimed.

"Get your filthy dog off my kids, lady!" Luke bellowed as he rushed toward the scene. "I was up till midnight washing and ironing their clothes!"

SARAH FOUGHT TO grab Beau's leash, but the man's anger was so intense that her hands were shaking. He stomped toward her as she continued to fumble and jerk at Beau's leash, but the dog simply would not take his paws off the two little kids.

"Lady, do something! Doesn't your stupid dog understand commands?"

"Yes, he does," she bit back finally, clutching at Beauregard's collar.

The kids had their hands on Beau's paws and were holding him in place as if they weren't about to let them go.

The little red-haired girl looked up at Sarah with such longing in her eyes that Sarah squinted at her, wondering what kind of game these kids were playing.

"I'm so sorry," Sarah said to the very angry father. His face was red and he looked as if he could bite her head off in one quick motion.

"Just get him off," Luke roared.

"Beau, down. Now!" she ordered her very happy golden retriever.

"That dog should be locked up," the tall, dark-haired man snarled at her as he tried to wipe mud off the little boy's shirt.

"I'm so very sorry. Beauregard never does anything like this. I don't understand what got into him."

"I don't need your life story. Your apology is not going to clean up my children. Now, if you want to miraculously launder their clothes so they can go to school, then I accept your apology."

"I'll pay." She swallowed hard, feeling the heat of his temper bore into her from his narrowed blue eyes. "For their cleaning, I mean. Whatever it costs. I'll even replace their uniforms, if necessary."

The man crouched down as he wiped at the mud on the little girl's shirt, but he only made it worse. Now the streak of mud went up over her shoulder and onto her sleeve. The girl frowned at him, but she didn't say anything.

Sarah noticed the boy was still petting Beau's head, seemingly unaffected by his father's anger—as if he were used to this kind of outburst. Beau jumped up on the little boy again and the boy squealed in delight.

Sarah had to smile. "He really likes you," she said.

"Oh, for cripe's sake," Luke rumbled. "Control your dog. Haven't you heard of obedience school?"

"I said I was sorry."

"Not good enough," Luke bit back.

Anger and frustration uncoiled down Sarah's spine. She hated being angry. Negative feelings served no purpose whatsoever. As far as Sarah was concerned, they caused illness and wrong-thinking. The fact that this man was upset was understandable. If she were the children's mother she would be furious, as well. She cared that her dog was the cause of the problem, but she didn't have time for any of this. Not today.

"I told you. Send me the cleaning bill and I'll take care of everything."

"Yeah, right," the man shot back.

"I'm sorry. So very sorry," she said again, just as Grandy opened the door.

"What's all the ruckus out here?" the stick-thin woman wearing a rubber apron asked. "Oh," she said, looking at the mud-covered golden retriever, "It's you, Beau." Grandy stepped aside just as Beauregard charged past her and dragged Sarah, still teetering in her high heels, toward the shop.

Luke looked at the puppy-shop owner and pointed accusingly at Sarah. "Because of that woman's rudeness, I have to take my kids home so they can change, which will make them late for school and me late to work." Luke didn't notice Timmy's beaming smile.

Annie was keenly aware of her father's fury. She looked at Timmy's happy face and nudged him with her elbow. "Cut it out," she whispered.

Timmy squeezed his mouth into a pucker and hung his head.

"People like that shouldn't be allowed to own a dog if they can't control them," Luke said, looking at Timmy and Annie. He snapped his fingers. "In the truck. *Now.* March!"

"It's okay, Dad," Timmy said, climbing into the truck. "The mud will dry."

"And I'll explain everything to his teacher," Annie offered. "It was just an accident."

Annie buckled herself in and smiled winningly at her father.

Luke growled under his breath, banged the steering wheel with his fist and stifled a string of curses that threatened to explode from his mouth. He turned on the ignition and said, "This is precisely the kind of thing that confirms my feelings about dogs and kids."

"What's that?" Annie asked.

"The two don't mix."

Timmy looked back at the puppies in the window. The little one he'd liked so much was standing on his hind legs with his paws on the windowpane, watching them leave. Timmy felt as if a heavy stone was sinking in his chest. He just knew that little fellow would be a beautiful, great big dog someday like Beauregard, and when he was all grown up, he was going to have a dog just like that.

LUKE DROPPED THE children off at St. Mark's School, kissed them each goodbye and waited until they were in the building before leaving.

He drove back up Maple Avenue and then across Main Street and headed north toward the construction office where he worked.

It wasn't until he was on Indian Lake Drive, which rimmed the north shore of Indian Lake, that he realized his eyes were filled with tears. He pinched them away with his thumb and forefinger. He guessed he was so used to tears now that when they came, he was numb to their presence.

He pulled into the gravel drive of the metal-sided and tin-roofed construction office. Luke threw back the last gulp of his coffee.

Getting out of the truck, he didn't notice the enormous flowering crab-apple tree he'd parked beneath, nor the blanket of pink petals under his truck's tires. He didn't notice the warm spring breeze or the scent of purple French lilacs that formed a screen along the chain-link fence that separated the parking lot from the lumberyard next door.

Luke didn't notice much of any of the beauty around him. All he knew was that he had to face another day of his life without his wife and without the only love he would ever know.

CHAPTER THREE

AFTER MAKING CERTAIN that Beauregard was settled in Grandy's competent and loving hands, Sarah drove toward her office, which sat on a hill across Indian Lake Drive, offering a spectacular view of the lake.

As much as she needed to rehearse her presentation to Charmaine, Sarah's thoughts tripped back to her encounter with the sharp-tempered, currish man she'd met that morning.

Granted, Beau had ruined his kids' clothes, but that wasn't cause enough for him to be so uncivil toward her. She was at fault for not controlling the normally well-behaved Beau, but today he'd been anything but her respectful, intelligent canine companion.

She had to admit Beau's friendly nature had probably ruined the man's morning as much as it had hers.

Can't say that I blame the guy for being angry. But why would he be up late at night doing laundry?

Sarah stopped at the light on Willow Lane

and tapped her fingernail against the steering wheel. Then she smacked her forehead. *He's a single dad! Divorced. That's it.*

The light changed.

His wife probably left him because he clearly doesn't like dogs, not to mention that he's a snarling grouch. What kind of person doesn't like dogs? Sarah chewed her lip and watched the light turn green. She depressed the gas pedal. *Certainly not any kind of person I would want to know.*

As she made her way through town, she looked up at the flowering white almond trees lining both sides of Main Street and thought of her mother.

It was impossible for any of the townsfolk not to think of Ann Marie Jensen when they looked at the beautification projects around Indian Lake. In the past twenty-five years, Ann Marie had been almost solely responsible for the changes that gave Indian Lake its charming, nearly enchanting present look. She'd spent twenty years as a member of the Zoning and Planning Commission, during which time she'd instituted the Downtown Beautification Committee. In the early 1980s, the nostalgia for the forties and fifties that had accompanied the soda fountains, drive-in root beer stands, bike shops, record stores where customers listened to their 45s before they bought them, knitting shops and ladies' glove shops had died. Factory jobs moved overseas, and Indian Lake manufacturing companies shut down. Younger people moved away. Neglect and disuse settled in. The town looked sad, lonely and unwanted, which it was.

Then Ann Marie moved to town, the new bride of Paul Jensen. She was more than a spark of creativity and new life. She was the firestorm Indian Lake needed to ignite the enthusiasm the town fathers had lost and nearly forgotten. She prodded, cajoled and reasoned with politicians and officials until she got the green light she wanted on whichever beautification project she felt the town could not last another day without. "No" was a concept she did not understand. Rarely did Ann Marie reject anyone or any request made of her. She worked long hours—too long, in many cases—for her town and her church. She loved both with all her being.

Ultimately, Sarah believed, her mother's passion for Indian Lake led to her death.

Ann Marie was so used to working hard and sustaining her energy over long periods of time that she seldom slept. The doctors said her lack of rest led to a suppressed immune system. It was Sarah's belief that the decades of putting her family and community ahead of her own health contributed to the cancer that took her life.

Sarah glanced over at the new bay window on Bechinski's Pharmacy, another of her mother's creative suggestions to one of the town retailers. The storefront, with its new, red, wooden door, floated in front of her on a sea of tears.

Exhaling the lump in her throat, she wiped her cheeks.

"Looks great," she said aloud and gave a little wave.

Everything along Main Street looked amazing, thanks to Ann Marie.

One of the reasons tourists flooded to the area in summer and on warm, golden autumn weekends was that time seemed to stand still in Indian Lake. Down Maple Avenue, where Sarah lived, people still sat in wicker rocking chairs on the front porches of their elegant Victorian and Edwardian-style homes in the summer and waved to people as they drove or walked past. They took time to speak to their neighbors as they went in and out of their homes in the winter. They shoveled each other's walks, and they brought a fresh-baked pie when someone died. They cut flowers out of their gardens for each other when news of an illness traveled through the neighborhood grapevine—which was usually perpetuated by Helen Knowland or, to a lesser extent, Mrs. Beabots. Indian Lake was a place where people cared about each other. Sometimes, that caring morphed into being a busybody, but such extravagances of eccentricity were forgiven by the locals. Outsiders or those new to the area didn't understand. They never would, either. That was why they remained outsiders. It took heart to be a part of Indian Lake, and a great deal of courage, determination and persistence. Sarah knew her mother was Indian Lake at its best.

SARAH PARKED HER car in her assigned space, gathered her portfolio and purse and exited the car. She went around to the front of the building and entered through the double glass doors.

Just walking into the reception area of Environ-Tech Design still gave her chills of pride after almost two years. Charmaine Chalmers had carefully laid out the space with the expertise of one of the most illustrious Black Hat Feng Shui Masters in Chicago. The serenity and peace that clients felt walking in the doors was planned, purposeful and dramatic. It was a breath of urban class in a small town, and Sarah loved it. The walls were painted a burned taupe with glistening white crown molding and trim. The floor was bamboo hardwood covered with ancient Persian rugs in muted browns, reds and golds that looked as if they had been dragged through the Sahara to gain their patina. Tall African jars held white bird-of-paradise stalks that Sarah knew attracted aphids like crazy, but Charmaine spritzed the leaves with soapy water and wiped them down one by one on Saturday nights when she had nowhere else to go.

The conversation area was centered with an ink-black mahogany coffee table that glistened like glass and had never once been allowed to display the first fingerprint or speck of dust. The front-desk receptionist, Lou Ann Hamilton, made certain that Charmaine's specially manufactured and painstakingly imported Samoan table was pristine at all times.

The Asian-inspired seating was actually Italian in design and constructed south of Milan, but no one in the office was allowed to give out the name of Charmaine's highly talented, grossly underpaid furniture designer. Charles Vesa was fifty years old, divorced, and other than when he wandered into the Environ-Tech offices unannounced with rolls of design paper under his arm, few people ever saw the man. When Charles showed up, Charmaine always dropped everything she was doing, sat in her conference room and studied his drawings as if they were bits of the Dead Sea Scrolls.

Sarah went into her cubby-hole-size office,

which was only slightly larger than the other offices up and down the hallway. The building, built before the First World War, still had interior doors with walnut bottoms and frosted, "pebbled" glass on the upper half of the door. No one could see in or out. It seemed rather odd to Sarah that, despite Charmaine's intense desire to create a Feng Shui atmosphere in the front of the office and the conference room, the rest of the building felt like the back rooms of an old county recorder's office. The offices were certainly not conducive to creative thought.

Sarah went to her frosted, double-hung window and lifted the sash. A warm, fresh breeze with a hint of lilacs drifted past the sill. She inhaled deeply and sighed.

Just then, her phone rang. She looked at the blinking light. It was Lou Ann at the front desk.

"This is Sarah."

"Charmaine wants to see you in the conference room. Do you want some coffee?" Lou Ann asked sweetly, with a hint of the Southern accent she'd brought with her when she and her husband moved here from Tennessee.

"Sounds lovely," Sarah replied. "I'll be there."

Sarah hung up, looked down at her portfolio and crossed her fingers for luck. *Mom, I know you're up there pulling for me. You, too,*

Daddy. If this goes right today, I could finally get a promotion.

She looked around her office and grimaced. *Okay. That's not likely. But,* she thought, sticking her finger in the air with a bit of anticipation, *landing the client myself would be a huge feather in my cap.*

With one last glance heavenward, Sarah picked up her portfolio and left her office.

CHARMAINE CHALMERS WORE a spring-green, silk sweater set with light beige crepe slacks and low-heeled, leopard-print designer pumps. Today, her jewelry was simple, for Charmaine— a pure gold, diamond-studded chain around her neck and chocolate diamond hoop earrings. She wore no wedding rings, having never been married, and had a man's alligator-banded antique Hamilton watch on her wrist.

No one knew where the watch came from, but Sarah guessed it had belonged to Charmaine's wealthy Miracle Mile entrepreneur father who disinherited his daughter over thirty years ago when she moved to Indian Lake to strike out on her own.

Sarah's eyes squinted together as she watched her boss peer over her drawings for far too long before sharing her assessment.

Charmaine was the kind of person who, if

she liked something, would be instantaneously effusive.

There was nothing coming out of Charmaine's mouth this morning that remotely resembled pleasure—or even mild acceptance.

"You don't like it," Sarah said. If she stated the obvious, maybe the rejection wouldn't cut so deeply.

She was wrong.

"I don't," Charmaine said too bluntly and too quickly. "The reception area is the focal point of all our commercial designs. This is the first impression customers or patients receive. Look here. The counter is much too angular. We have always prided ourselves on our Feng Shui design, and I see none of that here. The client expressly requested that this back wall be a lighted glass block, not this bank of file cabinets and shelves. Also, your color boards don't have the spark I've come to expect from you. Where's your inventiveness?"

Sarah looked at her color boards with their earth tones of tan, brown, camel and brick. Charmaine picked up a swatch of Aztec sungold brocade with turquoise and jet beads and tossed it over the color board. The other colors instantly came to life and radiated energy.

Sarah smiled. Then sighed. "I see what you mean."

Charmaine's expertly made-up eyes glistened with a sheen that Sarah suddenly realized were tears. "I don't know how to say this, Sarah."

Sarah thought she'd quick-frozen her emotions when her mother died two months ago. She was wrong.

Loss and grief had no boundaries.

They just kept rolling on with a vengeance, unmindful of the human hearts in their path.

"Say…what?"

Charmaine exhaled a long, yogalike breath. She folded her hands in front of her, on top of Sarah's drawings. "I want you to know that I hold you and your talent in deep regard. I couldn't love you more if you were my own daughter. Nevertheless, we have to face something here, Sarah…"

"Which is?" Sarah could barely swallow. She looked down at her drawings and for the first time saw them for what they were. Mediocre. She cringed. She felt as small as the tiniest spec in the universe.

"These past months have been difficult for you. No, its more than that. They have been hell. First your father died two years ago, then your mother got sick. You've been her support all this time. I don't know how you've managed to do it, quite frankly."

Sarah couldn't take her eyes off her drawings. "Apparently, I haven't done it."

Charmaine reached out and touched Sarah's hand. "Yes. You have. You do so much. But this—" she swept her hand over the papers "—this just isn't your best work."

"It isn't," Sarah said flatly. She supposed despair would set in later, but for now, she looked up at Charmaine. "You're absolutely right. It's not coming together for me."

Charmaine moved a bit closer to Sarah. "I want you to listen to me. Don't say anything until I'm finished."

"Okay," Sarah replied, her mouth going dry.

"I want you to take a leave of absence. Take a couple of months off."

"What? Now? I can't leave now." A burning sob grabbed Sarah by the throat. Without her work, she would be nothing. Without a project to wrestle with the grief she felt every waking minute of the day, she knew beyond a doubt she would go insane. She was at Charmaine's mercy more than she'd realized. She couldn't imagine not coming to this office every morning and seeing the rest of the staff. The idea was ludicrous. She wanted this job. She needed her work. "You don't understand, Charmaine."

"Yes, I do," Charmaine said softly. "I'm not firing you. On the contrary. I think you have more talent than anyone I've ever met. Given a bit more flair, you could be me." Charmaine tried to laugh, but Sarah's face was stone.

"Okay," Charmaine continued. "Let me tell you a story. A long time ago, I was lost. Truly lost. I had no one. My family had turned their backs on me. I'd lost the one person I thought I loved, but he didn't love me back. I lost my job in Chicago and I thought the world had come to an end. Then I spent a month—maybe more than a month—walking the beach here at Indian Lake. I stood on the shore of Lake Michigan at the beach in New Buffalo and looked across at the Chicago skyline and asked myself what I wanted. Not what my parents wanted for me, which was to live in a mansion on the North Shore and join the Yacht Club and the Sheridan Golf Club. They wanted me to marry an heir to an even bigger fortune than theirs. But I would have been miserable. That's when I decided to pursue my design business right here in this little town. I didn't know anyone except old Hop at the Phillips gas station, who filled my red Mustang tank every Saturday morning. I had to start over. I had to make my own life. And I've never regretted it."

"And you think that's what I need to do? Maybe move away from here?"

"I think you need to decide a lot of things,

and that's one of them. No one can go anywhere around here and not see your mother's stamp. Heck, it's her red velvet cake recipe that Maddie Strong uses at her cupcake shop, for heaven's sake."

"I forgot that."

"See what I mean?"

"Uh-huh."

"Sarah. These are big shoes to fill, and you don't have to do it if you don't want to. You could…"

"Go back to Indianapolis?"

"Well…" Charmaine shrugged. "You were well on your way to an excellent future with Harper Architectural Design when you came here. Maybe you would be happier in a big city." Charmaine touched her gold Cross pen. "Maybe you're only grieving right now. Maybe that's all it is. But I want you to have the opportunity that I had, Sarah. I want to give you the time you need to discover yourself."

"Myself," Sarah repeated, wondering what that meant, exactly.

"You are your own self. Not Ann Marie. Not Paul Jensen. Not even your Aunt Emily. You are you."

Sarah felt a pang a grief shoot through her and it terrified her. "Can I come by and see you? I mean…just to talk?"

"Of course, my dear. I'm not abandoning you. I promise. I just think you need this…time."

Sarah steadied her eyes on her boss. "But you don't want me to work…on this?" Sarah pointed at her drawings.

"No. I'm giving it to Susie. She'll take over."

A knife whipped across the universe from some dark, wicked place and cut a deep, permanent slit in Sarah's heart. "I see."

Charmaine's eyes were intractable and purposeful.

Sarah knew instantly that the conversation was over, so she placed a smile on her lips and rose from the chair. "Thank you, Charmaine. I appreciate your candor and…support." Sarah held out her hand for her boss to shake.

Charmaine did not leave her chair as she held out her hand and shook Sarah's firmly. "You're welcome."

Sarah left the room and did not realize how great her shock was until long after she had gathered her purse and belongings from her desk, gone to her car and turned on the engine. She drove out of the parking lot and got as far as the county courthouse, where she looked at the clock tower and saw that it was not even ten in the morning.

She pulled her car into an empty parking lot across from the Book Nook and Java Stop. Her hands were shaking as she turned off the engine and covered her face. She cried into her hands so that they could keep her sobs from escaping the car.

What will I do for the rest of the day?

She looked at the clock tower and saw the minute hand advance a single notch.

What will I do with the rest of my life?

CHAPTER FOUR

SARAH TURNED THE hundred-year-old doorbell crank in the middle of Mrs. Beabots's heavy wooden door, making an odd, sour, tinny sound. Sarah remembered this particular bell being one of her favorite sounds when she was little. Back then, Mrs. Beabots always baked fresh peanut butter cookies for her. The second the cookies were out of the oven, Mrs. Beabots would call her mother and ask her to send Sarah over immediately to enjoy the warm cookies with the cold milk she had delivered to her front door. Sarah had many memories of Mrs. Beabots, and they were all good.

"Is that you, pumpkin?" Mrs. Beabots asked as she slowly approached the front door, peeking through a smooth section of leaded and beveled glass in an intricate Victorian pattern.

"It's me," Sarah answered. "Are you ready?"

The door swung open with a bit more force and movement than Sarah would have expected.

"I am. I don't like to keep Father Michael waiting on my account."

Sarah bit her lip to keep from smiling. She knew that their priest was a real stickler for starting Sunday services on time. He didn't wait for anyone.

"Oh," Mrs. Beabots said and stuck her arthritic forefinger in the air. "My pocketbook." She turned around and walked over to a marble-topped Victorian entry table where she'd left her purse next to a tall crystal vase filled with white and purple lilacs. The flowers' scent wafted over to Sarah.

"Your lilacs are marvelously fragrant this year, Mrs. Beabots."

"Cow pucky." Mrs. Beabots smiled as she exited the house and locked the front door behind her. "Got it from Angelo Barzonni. He's got plenty on his farm. Manure always makes flowers more fragrant."

"You hate to drive. Please tell me you did not drive out to the Barzonnis'."

Mrs. Beabots took Sarah's arm with her left hand and held on to the black, wrought-iron railing on her cement steps with her right. "Good heavens, Sarah, I wouldn't do that. Angelo had one of the boys deliver it."

Sarah exhaled and dismissed the frightening vision of her less-than-five-foot-tall neighbor behind the wheel of her old Cadillac. It was easily the size of a U.S. Navy destroyer. "The next time you need something like that, I'll be more than happy to pick it up for you."

"Oh, you have enough to do, what with your job and all. I see how late your lights are burning, and I know you're working. Aren't you?"

Not anymore, Sarah thought, but didn't want to get into the subject of her forced unemployment. This was Sunday, and she wanted to enjoy the sunshine and the beautiful day. "And just how would you know how late I'm up, if you're sound asleep like you should be?"

A warm gust shot across their path as they walked north on Maple Avenue toward St. Mark's. Mrs. Beabots reached up to hold her black straw hat on her blue-rinsed white hair. "I should have used my hat pin," she mumbled.

Sarah chuckled to herself. No one on earth still used a hat pin but Mrs. Beabots. Every Friday morning at eight-thirty, Mrs. Beabots had a standing appointment with the hairdresser to have her chin-length white hair washed, colored with blue-rinse, set on rollers and dried under the drier. It was eight blocks to Curls and Combs and no matter what the weather, rain or snow, Mrs. Beabots made the trek—even if she had to dress in rain gear and galoshes.

Sarah had given up trying to drive Mrs. Beabots to the grocery store, hairdresser or the post office. Mrs. Beabots was a walker. In her younger years, she used to ride a bike all over town and even out to the farms to buy whatever vegetables were in season. However, at seventy, Mrs. Beabots was told she had osteoporosis. She was warned that, should she ever take a spill on her bike, her injuries could be serious. Mrs. Beabots chose right then and there to walk. She bought a rolling grocery cart and hauled it up and down Main Street. What she couldn't carry home, she had delivered.

"You look very pretty today, Mrs. Beabots," Sarah said with a smile. "I don't think I've ever seen this dress."

"It's new. I got it at the Goodwill for a dollar. My guess is that the pink rosebuds and apple-green buttons aren't quite the cup of tea for today's fashionable types. But it suits me just fine. One should always wear flowered dresses in the spring and summer." Mrs. Beabots nodded, more to herself than to Sarah. She glanced over at Sarah's ice-blue silk skirt and double-breasted jacket. "You look lovely, as well, dearie," she said.

"Thanks."

Mrs. Beabots looked up at Sarah's face, frowned and then focused her eyes on the sidewalk.

"What's wrong?"

"Well, if you must know, I don't much like your lipstick shade."

"My what?" Sarah touched her finger to her lips reflexively.

"Well, maybe that isn't it, after all," Mrs. Beabots retracted.

"It's not the lipstick?"

"It's you, dearie. I'm very worried about you."

"Why?"

"You're too young to look…well, careworn."

"I look…" Sarah felt the prick of tears at the corners of her eyes. She had no idea her sorrows and fears were this evident.

Mrs. Beabots had always possessed a certain crafty wile. As sweet as she'd always been to Sarah, loving her like a grandmother, she had no qualms about delivering a sucker punch when she felt it necessary.

Sarah was silent.

Mrs. Beabots squeezed her arm. "I think you should take a vacation," she said with conviction. "Always does a body good to get away from the office. Mr. Beabots often said those very words to me."

Sarah rolled her eyes heavenward. "How did you know?"

"Know what, dearie?" Mrs. Beabots stopped dead in her tracks, and with more strength than Sarah believed the elderly woman to have, she yanked back on Sarah's arm, causing her to stumble a bit. "You aren't sick, are you? Real sick? Not like your mother, are you?" Mrs. Beabots asked, fear flinging itself through her words.

Sarah patted her hand reassuringly. "No. No, I'm not sick at all. But something did happen on Friday that I haven't told you." Sarah paused and glanced up to see that they were nearly on the steps of St. Mark's Church. "Apparently, my boss seems to feel the same way you do."

"She fired you?"

"No, but she did give me a forced leave of absence. Essentially, I don't have a job for the summer." Sarah didn't feel the tear escape her eye until it slid off the edge of her jaw. "I have no place to go every day. I won't see my co-workers or have lunch with them. They'll be too busy. But I won't be busy, and I have to stay busy."

"Why?"

The tear was joined by a legion of the same. "Because then I'll have to listen to the emptiness in the house. Then I'll have to think about the fact that I'm all alone."

Mrs. Beabots patted Sarah's hand. "No, you aren't, dear. You have me. You have lots of friends in Indian Lake. Don't forget your aunt Emily and uncle George are here. They're your family. You should talk to Emily. She's always got good advice."

"You think I need advice?"

"I think you need time to sort it all out. Sometimes, pumpkin, we all need to step back and think about what it is that we really want for ourselves."

Sarah wiped her tears away as they started into the church. "Okay, I'll think about it."

Mrs. Beabots squeezed Sarah's arm again as they entered the nave. Lowering her voice, she said, "And get a new lipstick."

ONCE INSIDE ST. MARK'S, Sarah sat up front on purpose. As Mrs. Beabots had once pointed out, no one likes to sit in the front of the church. Therefore, the seat pads in the front pews were used less than those in the back, and were still firm and thick with plush foam and down. Sitting on the green, tufted cushion, Sarah had to agree with Mrs. Beabots.

Sarah found her mind wandering during Father Michael's sermon, and for the first time since she'd moved back to Indian Lake from Indianapolis, she realized that Father Michael's voice did not sound as strong and as vibrant as she remembered. Cocking her head and peering at his face, she saw none of the passion radiating from his eyes that he'd once had.

He coughed several times during his delivery and faltered with his words. Then it hit her. He was sick. She truly hoped it wasn't anything serious.

Father Michael was saying something about not being afraid. Reflecting on her personal life, she realized with a shock that she was deeply afraid. She had no job, at least for the moment, and the idea of her life without her work was absolutely unacceptable. She didn't know how to be on *vacation,* as Mrs. Beabots put it.

I can't vacate my life!

Her job as her mother's caregiver was over, and that meant there was no need to rush home at night after work. There was no one else to cook for or clean up after. There was only her laundry to do and a few dishes to wash. The garden still needed tending, but other than Beauregard, there was nothing that needed her.

And no one.

I have no husband. Not even a boyfriend. No children. There's no one to need me, want me or love me.

She looked down at her folded hands and realized they were shaking. Perhaps Mrs. Beabots was right after all, as she usually was. Sarah was careworn.

Dwelling on her problems caused her to slip into deeper despondency. Sarah had always prided herself on her cheery, happy nature. She'd never been depressed that she could remember. Not even after her breakup with James. Yet here she was, feeling unnaturally sorry for herself.

With her mind wandering, Sarah looked around at her old church, which had been built just after the First World War. It was odd how the windows didn't let in the same sunlight they had when she was a child. The floors and carpets were dull and worn. The plaster on the ceiling was chipped and cracked. The paint on the walls was a murky brown that did little to uplift anyone's spirits. She couldn't help but wonder when or how it had fallen into such disrepair. If the plaster was cracked, what condition was the roof in? Did the brick need tuck-pointing? Her architecturally oriented mind went to work.

As the sermon ended, Sarah noticed how few people were in attendance. She especially noticed the fact that most of the congregation was nearing old age, and there were fewer than two dozen children present.

Sarah wasn't sure if the summer season had brought on this decline in patronage, or if she just hadn't been paying attention all these weeks and months while her mind had been focused on her mother. She guessed the latter.

Sarah flipped her bulletin over and read the

back for announcements. She noticed that the Indian Lake Hospital was sponsoring a free bereavement group on Wednesday nights. The sessions were to last six weeks and were being held in a meeting room at the Indian Lake Public Library. As if a trigger had gone off in her head, Sarah realized the time had come for her to seek professional help. She would go to the counseling sessions and maybe she would find her answers.

In the meantime, she didn't think she could face her empty house all evening. As she and Mrs. Beabots walked out of the church, Sarah asked her friend, "Would you like to come to dinner tonight?"

Mrs. Beabots smiled knowingly. "I'll make my sugar pie. It's your aunt Emily's favorite. I assume you are inviting your Aunt Emily and Uncle George. And Maddie has always been like a sister to you."

"It's not a family party without Maddie. I'll call her."

"Doing for others is always the best medicine, pumpkin."

CHAPTER FIVE

LUKE HELD TIMMY'S hand as they stood with Annie on the dock of Redbeard's Marina, talking to Redmond Wilkerson Taylor Jr., most commonly referred to around town as Captain Redbeard. Well over six-feet six inches tall, Red was a huge man with a barrel chest and hard-as-a-rock barrel belly. He'd tied a leather strip around his full head of flowing red hair—streaked with natural gray "highlights," now that he'd crossed the sixty-five-year marker—to keep it from flying in his face as he sped around Indian Lake in one of the many fiberglass ski boats he rented to tourists and residents by the day or week.

"You sure you don't want to try your hand at waterskiing?" Red asked Luke, squinting his China-blue eyes nearly shut. Red had a craggy face, made rugged from long days in the sun and smiling a great deal. His teeth were even, and as white as the brilliant, puffy clouds above.

"No, thanks, Red," Luke replied. "The kids are a bit young for skis. Besides, skiing is an expensive sport. They just wanted to be on the lake today."

"Purdy day for it." Red laughed as he often did, with an unmistakable explosion of good-heartedness bursting from his mouth.

Annie smiled widely. "That's what I said to Dad. The whole summer will be over before we know it."

Red laughed again. "Well, little missy, since school isn't even out yet, you have plenty of time left."

"I don't want to miss a single second," she replied with a wistful sigh. "I just love the water."

Luke touched the top of Annie's head lovingly. "Yes, you do, don't you?"

"I wish I could be here every day," Annie gushed as she clasped her hands together then dropped them in front of her, striking a rapturous pose.

"You can."

"Excuse me?" Luke cocked his head as he peered at Red.

"I run a summer camp for the kids in town. Five days a week, and the city underwrites most of the cost. I've been doing it for years now. The working parents love it. The kids are outside most of the day. They learn swimming, life-saving, boating, sailing, knot tying, even flag signals. And some things I learned in the rivers in 'Nam."

"Marines?"

"Navy. I was a chief petty officer."

"Not a captain, then?"

Red shook his head. "That's just a nickname. One of my buddies called me that and it stuck."

"I like the sound of this camp. Being a former navy man myself, I want the kids to not just like the water, but to respect it and know how to navigate it."

Timmy was listening intently to the conversation between the grown-ups. He looked up at his father and asked, "You mean we don't have to go to the Lollipop Day Care Center this summer?"

Luke shot a pleading glance at Red. "You got room for two more?"

"Happens I do." Red chuckled.

Annie nearly jumped out of her pink flip-flops. "Yes!"

Luke stuck out his hand to shake Red's. "Then we have a deal."

"We do. And for today," Red said, bending over and picking up two oars. "I'll give you Number Six. It's the blue rowboat at the end of the dock."

"How much do I owe you?" Luke said, reaching for his wallet.

Red looked at the sun and then back at Luke. "A dollar."

"What?"

"Dollar. Looks like high noon. All rowboats rent for a dollar an hour after noontime."

Luke shook his head and took out a single bill. He saw Red glance at his wallet. Not that there was much there to look at.

"Nice doin' bidness with ya." Red saluted Luke.

"Where are the life jackets?" Luke asked.

"In the boat. I had Willie put in two children's and one adult. No alcohol on the lake," Red warned.

"We just brought juice boxes," Timmy said.

"Best you stay around the shoreline so you're out of the way of the ski boats. Their wakes will knock you out of the boat. Some of the drivers are plumb crazy and don't know their safety rules."

"Gotcha," Luke said.

Red looked down at Timmy. "Have a good time out there, young man. Ask your dad to tell you the Legend of Indian Lake while you're on the water. That's always fun."

"What legend?" Luke asked.

"Of Indian Lake," Red replied, looking at Luke as if he was nuts.

"I don't know that one," Luke said.

Red squinted his eyes again. "You're not from around here, are ya?"

"No. We moved here from Chicago just after Timmy was born. My wife didn't want to raise kids in the city. We came here near Halloween that year, and she fell in love with the town. She passed away two years ago."

Red nodded solemnly. "Sorry for your loss."

Timmy pulled on Red's khaki shorts. "What about the legend?"

"Well, son, a long time ago when all this—" he swept his arm over the lake, pine trees and shore "—was Pottawatomi Indian land, the Jesuit priests came from France to convert the Indians. One winter there was an outbreak of influenza or measles or smallpox—one of those deadly diseases. Anyway, the Indian medicine man had done all he could, and still, the villagers were dying by the dozens. Then Father Pierre, who had just arrived at the fur trader's outpost about two miles from here, heard about the Indians dying. He walked in a blizzard across the frozen lake to get to their village." Red pointed to the far side of the lake to a grove of trees and the dozen log cabins that comprised Tall Pines Lodges of Indian Lake.

"Well, sir, it seems Father Pierre went to the village and prayed over those folks somethin' fierce. They say he fasted and abstained for three days and three nights. He carried with him a special cross that had been in his family for a hundred years. They say he touched each of those sick Indians on the forehead with his cross and prayed over them. On the fourth day, they were miraculously cured. When he was walking back across the lake, the ice broke and swallowed him up, cross and all."

"Yeah?" Timmy asked with wide, captivated eyes.

"Some folks say Father Pierre's sacrifice has blessed Indian Lake. From then on, during the worst storms and the most unimaginable disasters, people swear they have seen the image of Father Pierre and his cross. And then, everything gets better."

"What do you think?" Annie asked.

Red laughed. "It's all hooey to me. There's no magic in that lake. Probably never was a Father Pierre, neither. It's just a great story to tell around a campfire."

"What does the cross look like?" Timmy asked quickly, not to be thrown off track.

"Some said it was just wooden. Others said they saw a gold cross studded with jewels. I say it's just make-believe, anyway."

Luke held out his hand. "Thanks for the boat, Captain Redbeard."

"You're welcome."

Luke picked up a zippered insulated bag that held bologna sandwiches and juice boxes for the kids that Annie had put together for them. It was only an hour they bought out on the lake, but it would be good for all of them, he thought. Since Jenny died, Annie had grown up overnight, taking on household chores, preparing lunches and taking care of Luke and Timmy.

Luke grabbed the life jackets out of the rowboat and helped Timmy put his on, then tightened the belt on Annie's jacket. He untied the lines and climbed into the boat, helping both of his children get seated before taking up the oars.

As he rowed around the shoreline, Annie took out two slices of stale bread, tore them into small pieces and showed Timmy how to feed the ducks that had flocked around the tall cattails and grasses at the north end of the lake.

Luke listened to his children laughing and watched enormous white clouds scud across the azure sky. It was a perfect day.

It was the kind of day that should have made his heart sing.

Luke felt that familiar lump in his throat that had been born in the deepest recesses of his soul. For two years he'd been angry with God and the universe and everything that was holy.

He thought it ironic that Red told them an Indian Lake tale that had nothing to do with reality and everything to do with belief.

Belief in what?

Luke had no faith. He lost it somewhere between chemotherapy treatments and Jenny's grave. Luke didn't believe in magical, healing crosses or legends—or much of anything.

"Dad."

Luke heard Annie's voice roll toward him from some distant place. "What?"

"You said you would teach us how to row."

"Right. Okay, today is just basics."

Luke held out the oar and showed Annie and Timmy how to hold the handle and keep a firm grip. He placed Timmy on his lap and held a single oar with his son so that Timmy could get a feel for the weight and length of the oar. Together, they worked the left oar, while Annie sat next to Luke and worked the right. They didn't go very far, and only skimmed the edge of the lake through patches of water lilies, but Luke found himself laughing with his children.

When their hour was up, Luke rowed them swiftly toward the marina. Annie, shielding her eyes from the afternoon sun with her hand, looked up at her father.

"We should come to the lake every day, Dad."

"Why's that?"

"Because you're happy on the lake."

"I am?"

"Yes. You even laughed with us. So if the water makes you happy, we need to be here more and less at home."

"Now that you'll be here every day with Red, maybe we can make that happen," he said.

Annie smiled at Luke, but he pretended to be concentrating on his rowing. Once again, Luke realized he wasn't being the father to his kids that he'd been when Jenny was alive. He remembered laughing and horsing around with them every day. He'd often commented that their house was filled with happiness.

Guilt pressed its iron grip into his shoulders— it had become a familiar pain. Before Jenny died, Luke had been an exemplary father. Now he didn't come close to making the grade.

He'd been blaming the universe for all his anguishes, but his apparent failure as a father was his own fault.

By the time they reached the shore and tied the boat to the dock, Luke's anger at himself seared his insides like a brand. He didn't know how much longer he could endure this kind of torture. And he didn't have a single clue how to deal with it.

CHAPTER SIX

MONDAY MORNING AT the construction trailer brought the usual phone calls from disgruntled customers and demanding suppliers who wanted to be paid. Luke had already been to a small residential jobsite and briefed the crew on their jobs for the morning until his return at noon. At the moment, he was on the phone with the manager of the lumber company who had been shorting them on the deliveries for the past month.

"I'm telling you, the four-by-eights are not here and neither are the two nail guns I ordered. And you never replaced the missing joists from last week. So what's the deal? Your warehouseman can't count? Does he need glasses? 'Cause if he does, I'll personally buy him a pair so we can get this right! Now what are you going to do for me, Mick?"

Just then, Jerry walked into the trailer. Out of the corner of his eye, Luke could see him reacting to the last blast of angry words Luke was firing into the phone. The argument ended with

Luke spewing a string of expletives and cutting off his conversation in midsentence.

Luke stared at Jerry's pursed mouth and troubled expression. "What?"

"You get what you wanted from them?"

"Not yet."

"Surprise."

"What's that supposed to mean?"

"You need to work on your people skills, my man. That, and you need to cool off."

Luke swiped his face with his palm. He was surprised when it came away with sweat. "Guess I got worked up."

"Worked up?" Jerry harrumphed, went over to the coffeemaker and poured them both a mug of black coffee. "We need to talk."

Luke's eyes nailed Jerry's. "You firing me?" Luke's hand shook when he took the mug from his boss.

"No." Jerry leaned against the blueprint table and hoisted one leg over the edge. "This," Jerry said, nodding toward the phone, "isn't about some missing boards." Luke opened his mouth to make a retort, but Jerry held up his hand. "I'll take care of the lumber company. Or the thief in our own midst, if that's the case. But right now, you need to talk to me."

Luke lowered his gaze to the muddy wood floor and was struck by the fact that this company had become more than just a paycheck to him. His work was physical, creative and demanding, and it had kept him from losing his mind over the past two years.

"I don't know what to do, Jerry. I should have pulled out of this by now. I shouldn't be feeling this God-awful ripping and shredding I seem to go through every single freaking day," he said, punching himself in the stomach. "And it's gotten worse in the past six months or so. I think about Jenny all the time. All the time."

"I know," Jerry said, looking down into his mug.

"I'm hurting my kids," Luke continued. "Half the time I don't even know they're around. The other half, I'm barking at them, criticizing them for stupid little things they did or didn't do. They're just kids, for cripes' sake. It's gotten so bad that they're changing their behavior because of my outbursts. They hang their heads a lot and don't look at me. I see Annie giving Timmy hand signals not to talk about certain things when she thinks the subject will upset me. Annie's built this tent in her room out of blankets and chairs and whatnot, where she goes and hides when I get angry or talk about the bills. God. The bills." Luke raked his hair. "You can't imagine how tough it is to make ends meet."

Jerry stood up, put his coffee mug down and reached into his back pocket for his wallet. From underneath his driver's license, he pulled out a crumpled business card. "I've been saving this for you for two years. I knew eventually this moment would come. When you would need help, I mean."

Luke took the card and read it. He burst into sarcastic laughter. "A shrink? I just told you I can't afford peanut butter! Forget it."

"Margot is a friend of my wife's. She runs a free bereavement counseling group on Wednesday nights. I can get all the details for you. It's not as good as a one-on-one, but that can be expensive."

"Free, huh?"

"You'll like Margot. She's brilliant and compassionate."

Luke looked down at the card. "I'll think about it."

Jerry picked up his coffee. "Luke. You can't go on like you've been. I've had complaints from some of the guys in the crews about your drill-sergeant tactics with them. Something has to change, Luke. You have to change. This is eating you up."

Luke's eyes bored straight into Jerry's face. "You're right. That's exactly how I feel. Physically sick inside." He looked at the card. "I'll give her a call."

Jerry walked over to the desk and lifted the receiver, shoving it toward Luke. "Good idea."

SARAH ARRIVED AT the cheery meeting room in the library, carrying a dozen cupcakes from Maddie Strong's café. She met Margot Benner, the counselor who would be leading the bereavement group, a bright, happy-looking woman in her mid-fifties with streaked, blond hair that she wore in a French braid.

"Thank you for the cupcakes, Sarah," Margot said, motioning toward a refreshment table under a bank of huge windows that looked out onto the library's lushly planted gardens. "I provide coffee and tea for everyone, but this is a real treat."

"Maddie makes the best," Sarah replied with a smile.

There were eight folding chairs arranged in a circle. Each held a blue folder with reading materials and book lists. All books, of course, were available in the library.

Within minutes, five people came into the room and introduced themselves to Sarah and Margot. Alice Crane was in her mid-forties and had lost her fiancé in a car accident one week before their wedding. That had been a year ago, Alice explained.

Pete Grobowski's wife died of a heart attack a month ago. She was sixty-three, he said. Robert Bell had been the caregiver for his father through six long years of Alzheimer's disease. Julie and Mary Patton had lost their mother on Christmas Day. Sarah conversed easily with all the people in the group, and as far as she could see, they all appeared to be coping fairly well with their losses. *Or they're darn good actors,* she thought.

Just as everyone was sitting down, the meeting room door opened abruptly. A tall, lean, young man with broad shoulders and thick, dark, brown hair entered the room. He wore a faded blue-and-white-striped, button-down shirt that he'd tucked into his worn-looking jeans. He barely looked at anyone, and went straight to a chair directly opposite Sarah and sat down. He folded his hands and stared down at them.

Sarah recognized him immediately as the angry man with the two children at Puppies and Paws. She was curious as to why he was there. Perhaps he'd lost one of his parents, just as she had. He looked awfully morose, with no greeting smile for the others. She wondered if she looked like that to her friends. If she did, there was no wonder they were worried about her.

The man kept folding his hands one over the other as if he couldn't get it right. Then he clasped them to his thighs and looked up at the people in the room. For the first time, Sarah noticed that he was rather good-looking, with brilliant blue eyes that shot right through her as if he were a hawk seeking out prey. She wondered if he recognized her.

Then he looked back down at his hands, which were pressed deeply into his legs as if he were holding himself to the spot. She wondered if he was angry again.

Margot walked to the center of the circle and introduced herself formally to the group, explaining that she was a psychiatrist who had been practicing privately for over twenty years.

"I conduct these bereavement groups once each quarter, free of charge, because I had a death in my own life that was so traumatic for me, so depressing, that I withdrew from my family," Margot told them. "Frankly, I withdrew from everything. I sat in a rocking chair and stared out a window for over half a year. I went through my days in a fog. I couldn't hear what people said to me and most of the time I didn't acknowledge their presence. If it hadn't been for a friend who happened to be a counselor, who dragged me back to reality, I never would have pulled out of it."

Margot instructed everyone to introduce themselves to the group and mention only their relationship to the person they had lost.

Alice Crane went first. Sarah was next, and explained that her mother had recently died of cancer. Sarah hadn't finished her sentence when she heard a derisive snort from across the room.

Luke lifted his head. "Sorry." He dropped his head once more and then shook it. He stood immediately. "Sorry. I can't do this. My coming here was my friend's idea. This kind of thing isn't going to help me."

Before Luke could leave, Margot rose and placed her hand on Luke's forearm. "What was her name?"

Luke fixed his eyes on Margot's face as he replied with a quaking voice, "Jenny."

He'd said the woman's name with so much awe and love, Sarah knew instantly that he wasn't divorced, as she'd surmised earlier. He was a widower.

"What's your name?" Margot asked.

"Luke Bosworth," he answered carefully.

Sarah noticed that he held his hands in tightly clenched fists at his sides as if he was struggling to control himself from hitting something. Or someone. And when he returned answers to

Margot, the words were pelted through clenched teeth. She glanced around the room and noticed that no one else was as angry as Luke. They look depressed and sad, possibly even in denial, but not raging like he was.

"How long has Jenny been gone?" Margot inquired directly, but softly.

"Two years, four months and five days." He ground out the words.

"And to you it seems like yesterday?"

"Like it was this morning. She was just… here," he replied, his voice trembling with emotion.

Sarah thought she saw a glint of tears in his eyes.

"Tell me about her, Luke," Margot urged.

He smiled slightly and Sarah was struck at how much that tiny bit of a smile lit his face. As he talked about Jenny, his face became nearly rapturous. He'd gone from anger to joy so quickly, Sarah wondered if such an emotional bounce was healthy. But as Luke kept talking, Sarah realized she'd never seen anyone so completely and utterly in love as this man was with his dead wife.

Luke's memories of Jenny filled the room as he expounded upon his wife's talents, her kindness and unconditional love for him and their children. He held the rest of the group's complete attention while he spoke. "Jenny did just about everything. She insisted the kids and I eat healthy food. She grew all kinds of vegetables and herbs in her garden, then all summer and fall she'd freeze and can things. She made applesauce." He laughed to himself. "I was never sure it saved any money, all that work she did, but it tasted wonderful. We never had boxes of any kind of cookies or snacks. Jenny baked cookies and made granola. She sewed, too. She made clothes for the kids and all kinds of stuff for the house. I'd wake up in the middle of the night and find her sewing some kind of surprise for Annie. Doll clothes. A new dress. Secretly, I wondered if she was a magician. She seemed to make beautiful things out of junk and milk pods and pinecones."

"She had vision," Sarah blurted out before she realized she was going to speak.

Luke looked at her and gave her a soft smile of understanding. "Yes, she did. Thank you for saying that."

Sarah could only nod, she was so struck by the sincerity in his voice. She found it odd that this same guy could be hostile one minute and tame the next. To her, he was like Jekyll and Hyde. Which one was the real Luke Bosworth?

Margot's eyes tracked from Sarah to Luke.

"Jenny sounds like an amazing person," Margot said. "No wonder you miss her so much."

Luke's eyes turned stormy, as if Margot had just doused him with ice water. The blue turned to gray, and his face lost all the softness Sarah had seen while he spoke about Jenny. Luke didn't say anything for a long moment, his eyes surveying the room and the other faces looking back at him—some commiserating, some staring blankly.

Then, as if he'd made a decision, Luke inhaled deeply, expanding his lungs with courage or conviction—Sarah couldn't tell which. He clamped his lips shut, as if to stop the flow of words and memories. "Jenny should still be here. It was too soon for her to die. That's what I can't stomach." He slammed his palm on his thigh.

Sarah pressed her body back in her chair when she felt his next tirade coming on. She couldn't imagine having to live with someone so volatile. Sarah had always been uncomfortable with anger. To her recollection, her parents had never displayed anger at each other. They had always had "discussions" and they "worked out their differences." She'd experienced anger at flat tires, impossible government websites and inept retail clerks, but she'd never given or received Luke's kind of intense, blistering anger.

Margot's gentle voice interrupted Sarah's thoughts.

"Anger," Margot said, "is one of the five steps of grief, Luke. It's natural. Understandable. Expected. It just happens to be the step you're stuck on—for the moment. In addition, you're feeling rejected by God."

"How do you know that?" He growled.

"You show it in your every gesture. My guess is that you think God took Jenny, but he didn't take you. You were left here to fend for yourself with your two kids. So you feel rejected."

Luke nodded once, abruptly and affirmatively, but he didn't respond.

"This rejection you feel is a place for us to start, Luke," Margot offered.

Sarah sat up straight when she heard Margot talking about rejection. As she repeated the word in her mind, it was as if a blaring alarm had gone off.

Rejection.

Was that what she was experiencing? Sarah had always had a problem with rejection—or so her mother had told her. Ann Marie often warned her that she was getting overly anxious about her schoolwork, to the point of being a perfectionist. Sarah had been terrified of getting a bad grade. She didn't want to be rejected.

When she broke up with James, she did the breaking up part so she wouldn't be rejected by him. Yet James had rejected her many times—all in subtle ways, tiny snippets of rejection and dismissal telling her she wasn't good enough for him or his wealthy friends.

Sarah had been dealt a double blow of rejection. Her mother was dead and she'd been left to fend for herself. And she'd just been suspended from her job.

Rejection number two.

Sarah sank a bit lower in her chair, wondering if she should extend herself to these strangers. Would this emotional gamble be worth it? She wished she could hide.

Isn't that what I've been doing? Hiding my fears and probably a good amount of my own anger?

No, Sarah thought. *I can't bail. I came here to get better. I came here to make my life the best it can be and not live in the past. I want my future to be a good one. I want so much for myself. I'll stay.*

Sarah watched Margot as she struggled to pry information out of Luke, but he wasn't having it. He was in bad shape, Sarah thought. She was grieving for her parent. Her loss was a nor-

mal part of life that most people knew they'd
have to confront one day. But Luke's situation
was very different. He couldn't have been much
older than her, and yet he had already lost the
love of his life. They'd barely had a chance to
start their life together, and his wife was gone.
Sarah hadn't even thought about a family of
her own until just recently, and she wasn't even
close to finding her soul mate. Her world had
been all about her mother. Yet here was Luke,
nearly paralyzed by his emotions. Sarah almost
wished she was the counselor with all that training behind her so that she could say the right
thing to him. All she could do was remain silent and listen.

Margot was urging Luke to tell her about his
children, but he looked flustered and tongue-
tied. Sarah couldn't tell if he was still angry or
just upset with this dreadful process of spill-
ing his guts.

"Tell me about them," Margot asked politely.

"Nah, I don't think so," Luke said flatly as if
he'd finally controlled his rage. He nodded his
head and pursed his lips as if he'd been in conversation with himself. "I was right about what
I said before. My coming here was a mistake."

Luke stood suddenly, spun on the heel of his
work boots and stalked out of the room in four
long strides. The door slammed hard behind

him, the sound echoing against the walls, rattling the windows.

No one said a word for a very long moment.

Sarah sat up straight. "Do you think he'll come back, Margot?"

Margot turned around and faced her. "I don't know."

Sarah looked past Margot at the closed door. Of all the things she remembered about Luke that evening, the soft, grateful smile he'd given her stood out the most. She'd seen past his anger at that instant, and she felt as if she had helped him, even if it had been in a very slight, tenuous way. "I hope he does. He needs us."

CHAPTER SEVEN

SARAH TOOK BEAU out for his morning constitutional down Maple Avenue, where they both enjoyed the last of the spring tulips. Sarah noticed the spikes of peonies shooting up through the ground. The walk took an extra-long time, as Sarah allowed Beau to sniff all he wanted.

Sarah hadn't been able to get Luke Bosworth out of her mind. She'd never met anyone so tortured. Her heart went out to him because he seemed to be clueless as to how to react to those around him. He was deeply within himself, yet when he spoke about Jenny, he allowed everyone in session access to his innermost fears. Sarah was drawn to his tenderness and depth of compassion. He was an enigma of anger and gentleness. She was already looking forward to the next meeting, when she would hopefully see Luke again and learn more about him.

She was almost embarrassed to be asking for any help at all from Margot, when Luke clearly needed all her guidance and then some. Sarah guessed, from his worn work boots and his jeans and faded shirt, that he hadn't bought any new clothes for himself since his wife died. She remembered him making an offhand comment about medical bills and she could well understand his situation.

Her mother and father had purchased expensive but excellent health insurance a decade ago when Sarah had left for college. Sarah thought it was ridiculous, but Ann Marie had insisted, saying they weren't interested in trips to foreign countries or expensive jewelry or *things* anymore. They wanted to provide Sarah with the education she needed to pursue her dreams, and they wanted to cover themselves in case of disaster. They did precisely that. Ann Marie left only a few thousand dollars in medical bills, and in addition, her mother had prepaid her own funeral and cremation. Sarah had none of the financial problems that she was now realizing a great many people were forced to deal with along with loss and grief.

Sarah hadn't realized that she and Beau had been walking for nearly an hour. When they walked past Mrs. Beabots's house, Sarah could hear her television was turned up, and she could smell the apples, cinnamon and butter that told her Mrs. Beabots had been baking…again.

As Sarah came up the sidewalk to her house,

she noticed someone was sitting in one of the Adirondack chairs on her front porch.

As she approached, the person stood up.

"Miss Milse!" Sarah said with a smile.

The woman, in her mid-sixties, stood nearly six feet tall and was over two hundred pounds of pure-bred German muscle. She wore a very dated, cotton floral house dress with a blindingly white, ruffled apron. The short sleeves revealed upper arms the size of Virginia hams that looked as if she could rip up each floorboard for cleaning and easily pound them back into place.

Her steel-gray hair was pulled so tightly on her scalp and twisted into such a severe topknot that Sarah worried the woman would get a headache.

"I come to clean," Miss Milse announced in her accented, guttural voice as Sarah mounted the porch steps.

When Sarah was a little girl, Miss Milse had been both babysitter and housekeeper for the Jensen family. Sarah knew the woman's ways as well as she knew those of her mother and aunt Emily. Miss Milse could have been a gem for any branch of the United States Armed Forces, which she'd often told Ann Marie that she had longed to do. Miss Milse had wanted to travel the world and earn the nursing degree she dreamed of. But when she had been young, she'd been forced by circumstances to remain in Indian Lake to care for her widowed mother until she died of complications from Multiple Sclerosis.

Odd, Sarah thought. *I know so much about her, but I still don't know her first name. I guess she will always be Miss Milse.*

Because Miss Milse was a force of nature, and truly one on the stormy side, Sarah didn't have the foggiest idea how she was going to turn the woman away. She could not afford a housekeeper right now, especially on a reduced salary. She would have to be very diplomatic if she didn't want to hurt the woman's feelings.

"We need to talk about this," Sarah said, opening the door. Miss Milse bent over and grabbed an armful of her favorite cleaning utensils.

This was going to be tough. Sarah took a step backward to give Miss Milse plenty of room to enter the house. The mop handles clanged against the metal bucket. It was an everyday, ordinary sound that should have gone unnoticed and been absorbed into the walls like any of the other sounds that meander through a house on a given day. But in that moment, the bucket's tinny sound and its reverberation spoke to Sarah like a call from the angels.

The house is empty. Even with me in it.

"I start in kitchen," Miss Milse said, her lips forming a straight, nonemotional line.

Sarah shook her head. "The kitchen is clean. There isn't much to do with only me living here...."

Miss Milse's eyes left Sarah's face and looked past her into the dining room. She frowned. Sarah's eyes followed hers until she saw what Miss Milse saw.

There were no flowers from the garden on the mahogany Queen Anne table. Tall silver vases on either side of the marble-topped hunt board were not filled with English ivy the way Ann Marie had always kept them. A cobweb, glistening in the morning sunlight, stretched between the arms of the Venetian crystal chandelier that had belonged to her father's grandmother. Every generation of Jensens had painstakingly cared for the chandelier and passed it on to the subsequent generation.

The windows had not been washed this spring or summer, and across the wide-planked cherry floor, dust motes spun like fairy sprites.

Sarah looked up at Miss Milse. "I can do this myself," she said in a low voice that lacked conviction.

Miss Milse sucked in a long breath and widened her stance as if she was readying herself for a physical battle. "I clean. I make it like Mizz Jensen always like."

"It's just not necessary," Sarah began but before she could say another word, Miss Milse interrupted her.

"No. I take care of house when your fadder vas sick. Den. Your mudder. Den she die. I not hear from you. I come to you. I clean." She poked Sarah in the shoulder with a stubby finger.

Sarah tried to smile, but lost energy before it landed on her face. "You don't understand, Miss Milse. You see, I, er, lost my job. Well, not really. I hope to go back to my work someday. Soon, perhaps. Maybe when that happens I can call and have you come clean." Sarah looked at the woman's stubborn expression, hoping she'd made herself clear.

Miss Milse looked down the hall at the mirror that had not been dusted, at the chairs that had not been lemon-oiled and at the floor that needed waxing and buffing. She scrutinized the gilt-framed paintings and heirloom family portraits that hung on the wall. She took in the sweeping wood and carpeted staircase that had not been waxed, vacuumed or dusted since the last time she'd been in the house over three months ago. She looked back to Sarah.

"House needs me to clean."

"But I can't pay you what my mother used to pay."

Miss Milse shook her head. "You pay less."

Sarah's shoulders drooped. This wasn't going well. "I want to pay you, but it's just not the right time for me." She looked away, feeling absolutely wretched. "I can't pay you at all."

Miss Milse stood stock-still.

"I'm so sorry," Sarah said and met her eyes again.

Slipping out of the corner of Miss Milse's nearly lashless blue eye was the first tear Sarah had ever seen the woman shed. This huge block of a woman who never understood the first joke Sarah had told her and who almost never laughed or smiled or showed any emotion other than pride in her work, was crying.

"I'm so very sorry."

Miss Milse's chin fell to her neck and she lifted her thick fingers to wipe away her tears. "Don't pay me. I clean. I come be with you." She lifted her head and looked around the house where she had worked for over twenty years. Her tears were careening down her cheeks in rivulets. "I come every morning. I help in house. In garden. I be wit you. I remember your mudder wit you."

Miss Milse wavered like a mirage in the desert through Sarah's tear-filled eyes. She nodded. She understood…finally.

"Yes. Please come every day, Miss Milse. We will work together."

Miss Milse sniffed. "Ya." She trudged off toward the kitchen where Sarah heard her deposit her mops and bucket with a loud clatter.

"Ya," Sarah repeated. The house was less empty now.

CHAPTER EIGHT

EARLY-JUNE DAWN rays glittered amber and gold across the waters of Indian Lake, lighting the path for Sarah and her sculling crew—Maddie Strong, Isabelle Hawks and Liz Crenshaw. As they had done since their sculling days in high school, the women rented a Janousek JS 4x/-long hull, quad sculling boat from Captain Red, who kept the boat in superb shape just for them. All the girls had been on sculling teams in high school and some, like Sarah, had raced in college, as well. Together, they had conquered Lake Lemon, near Bloomington, and raced down the North Shore of the Chicago River. Sarah loved being on the water, skimming along the glassy surface, barely creating a wake and knowing that her body and those of her crew were still able to challenge record-setting times. The white-hulled, fiberglass English Janousek dominated both national and international regattas, and when Sarah was in the stroke seat, she pretended she was once again out there making sports history.

Sarah sat close to the stern, the rest of the crew matching her cadence and movements. The quad and girls shot across the glass-smooth waters of Indian Lake like a summer dragonfly, shimmering, daring and purposeful.

Here on the water, Sarah lost her feelings of sadness and came alive again. She could hear Maddie behind her joking and teasing the other girls mercilessly. Even with their banter, the rowers never lost a second of precious rhythm. They moved as a unit. They thought as a unit. Sarah and all the women knew there were people on shore—picnickers, sun-tan addicts and weekend volleyball teams all stopped to watch them skim the lake as if they were airborne.

LUKE PARKED HIS truck next to the creosote railroad ties outside Captain Redbeard's Marina and looked at the summer dawn as it glinted and shimmered off the lake's smooth surface.

Annie and Timmy climbed out of the backseat and stood next to their father, following his line of vision.

"Wow. Would you look at that?" Timmy exclaimed, pointing an excited finger at the white sculling boat whipping across the center of Indian Lake.

Luke lifted his hand to his forehead and

shielded his eyes. "Sculling. I haven't seen a sculling quad in years."

Annie slipped her hand into her father's. "Did you ever row one of those, Dad? In the navy, I mean."

The corner of Luke's mouth lifted in a prideful grin. "Sure did. Before the Navy and after. Your mom never got the hang of it, though."

"No?" Annie asked.

"She wasn't the athletic type."

"What type was she?" Timmy asked.

"She was every other good type known to man," Luke replied in a melancholy whisper. "Well, come on. Let's get you kids over there."

As Luke walked up to the marina office he saw two dozen children under the age of ten dressed in shorts, sandals and bathing suits, wearing very eager expressions as they listened to Captain Redbeard. "I want all those who can't swim at all to form a group to my right. Those who can swim to my left."

Timmy froze as the kids scurried around to regroup. Luke looked down at his son. "What's wrong?"

"Tell Captain Red I can swim."

"But that's what you're here for...to learn how to do it right."

Timmy's face was filled with fear. "He'll make me wear water wings like the little kids."

"Timmy," Annie said, "you are a little kid."

Timmy pointed to the non-swimmers' group, which consisted of several four-year-olds and one three-year-old still wearing pull-up diapers. "Nah-uh," he said. "*Those* are little kids."

Luke took Timmy's hand. "I'll talk to Red and see what I can do."

"Thanks, Dad," Timmy replied with visible relief.

Annie waved to one of her friends from school. "Dad, I see Madison! This is going to be a great summer!"

"I'll be back at four-thirty to get you guys," Luke said as Annie took off running toward her friend without a second glance back at him.

The marina office was surrounded by a wide, covered porch and from the roofline Red had installed navy blue canvas awnings to shield both the building and large groups of people from the summer sun. Beneath the awning, a few parents sat in rows of folding canvas chairs for this morning's orientation. Luke noticed that two more families arrived late, just as he had, which helped to assuage his guilt somewhat.

Luke realized that the number of children was quickly climbing to three dozen. He spotted two young men, whom he guessed to be sixteen or seventeen, wearing matching white bathing trunks and fluorescent-orange lifeguard sweatshirts. They had the requisite warning whistle on nylon twine around their necks, and they were both deeply tanned, though it was only early June.

Each lifeguard took one of the groups and ushered them toward a newly raked section of beach where they would give the kids instructions.

Red's wife, Julie, sat at a picnic table registering the families, taking money and handing out information packets.

Two fathers came up to Red and began bombarding him with questions. Luke looked at his watch. He needed to help Timmy, but he also needed to get to work.

The sound of a woman's voice calling sculling commands grew louder. Luke looked up and saw that the sculling quad was quickly rowing toward shore. Red looked up at the same moment.

"Hey, Luke!" Red shouted over the heads of the fathers, who were talking to each other and to Red at the same time. "Do me a favor?"

"Sure," Luke replied.

Red reached in his jeans pocket, pulled out a set of keys and tossed them at Luke. "Heads up."

Luke snatched the keys.

"The ladies are coming in from their row.

Would you unlock the boathouse for me and help them put the boat up? I've got my hands full here."

"No problem," Luke said. "Then I need a favor. Timmy wants to be with the big kids."

Red smiled. "I gotcha. Don't worry. I'll take care of it. Tell him to join his sister. I'll talk to Jason, their instructor."

"Great." Luke looked down at Timmy. "You're all set. Go over there with Annie."

Timmy's smile filled his face. "Thanks, Dad." Timmy sauntered off as if he'd just won a sweepstakes.

Luke arrived at the boathouse as the female sculling team rowed up on shore. He instantly recognized Sarah as she expertly lifted her oars and got out of the boat. She was wearing a navy blue swimsuit with white banding, navy lake shoes and a white sweatshirt that she'd tied around her shoulders. Her blond hair was tied up on top of her head, but the wind had blown errant locks around her face and neck. As she walked toward him, the morning sun caught in her windblown hair, creating a halo around her face. It was the first time Luke had actually looked at her. He realized she was pretty.

"Hi, Luke," Sarah said with a tentative smile. If she understood anything about him, it was that he was a tinderbox of anger. She didn't want to do or say anything to set him off. Treading softly was the way to go with temperamental people, her mother had told her. What she didn't understand was the happiness that overwhelmed her, just seeing him. Sarah's heart skipped a beat and she felt a flush fill her cheeks. Why was he here? Had he been watching her? His eyes were steady, measuring her movements as she walked up to him. She couldn't help wondering what was running through his mind. And why, oh why, did his resolute gaze elicit such a thrill?

"Sarah," he said, unlocking the boathouse doors and opening them wide. He walked over to the boat where the other three women were watching him with skeptical expressions.

Maddie was the first to speak. "Luke. What are you doing here?"

"My kids are enrolled in Red's summer camp. He was too busy to help you with the boat. He enlisted me."

Maddie nodded. "He's good at that."

Sarah stood next to tall, willowy Liz with the mane of honey-blond hair. "This is Liz Crenshaw," Sarah said. "Liz, meet Luke Bosworth."

"My pleasure," she said, holding her oars in her left arm and extending her right hand to shake his.

"And this is Isabelle Hawks. We all went to high school together," Sarah explained.

"Nice to meet you, too, Isabelle," Luke said. "And did you all row back then?"

"We did." Maddie grinned. "Sarah was our fearless leader, then and now. She rides us all the time to improve our skills."

"Yeah," Liz added. "We could probably win the Olympics. She's that good."

Sarah shook her head and laughed. "Kidders. They're always like that," she told Luke as they picked up the boat and carried it into the boathouse.

Luke helped hoist the boat onto the rack where it would stay dry and protected.

"Thanks for the help, Luke," Maddie said. "I have to run. I have to make a hundred cupcakes for a wedding anniversary party I'm catering tonight." She elbowed Isabelle, who was gawking at Luke.

Isabelle jumped at the jab to her ribs. "Right. I gotta get to the Lodge. Edgar will have a fit if I'm not there for breakfast seating."

"You work at the Lodges?" Luke asked.

"I'm the bookkeeper, actually."

Sarah chuckled and looked up at Luke. "She's being modest. She does everything there. She's Edgar's right arm, but he doesn't give her enough credit."

"I'm off, as well," Liz said. "Nice weather like this brings out the tourists for wine tastings."

Sarah waved to her friends as they quickly scooted off to their respective cars.

Luke locked up the boathouse doors. Sarah walked back with him toward the marina.

"Luke, I want you to know that I meant it about paying for your kids' clothes. Beau…"

"Forget it," he said sharply.

Sarah was taken aback by his terse reply. She wasn't sure if he was embarrassed because they'd been at a counseling session together and she knew some personal details about his life with Jenny, or if maybe he just didn't like her.

"It's just that I feel awful and I wanted to apologize."

"Sarah," Luke said, stopping. "I was a jerk to you, okay? I'd like to forget it. Can we just put that behind us?"

"Sure." She smiled up at him.

"Good," he answered and began walking again.

"Well, I hope your kids like Red's summer camp. I did when I was a kid. Of course, I was older than they are. You know, Red was my trainer for sculling. He coached me all through high school. He's really great with kids. Plus, he has a built-in audience for all his stories."

"I'm not worried about Annie fitting in. She loves everybody. If I know my daughter, she'll have the entire camp reorganized by next week." He laughed.

"She likes things orderly?"

"She's compulsive. She's the first one up. Annie insists on making all our lunches. I can't talk her out of it. She even counts out milk money for her brother. She has lists everywhere. It could make you nuts."

"Sounds like my kind of girl," Sarah said. "I can't live without my lists—both on paper and computer."

Luke took out his car keys and pointed to his Ford F-150. "This is me. Have a good day, Sarah."

"You, too," she said and went to her red Envoy and got in. She waited while he backed out and drove away. She noticed that he gave her a wave. She lifted her hand in return.

Glancing back at the beach as the instructors began handing out water wings, Sarah spotted Annie holding her little brother's hand and talking to him. He seemed upset about something but he listened intently to his sister's counsel.

Sarah remembered Luke telling Margot that he wanted to join the counseling group because he was trying to be a good dad to his kids. She had to admire that. Even if it had been at the urging of a friend, Luke had taken the big step to seek help. There was still a chance he'd never come back to the group, but Luke impressed her as the kind of guy who was driven to do the right thing, even if it meant swallowing his pride.

She had encountered Luke Bosworth three times now, and each time she'd seen a different side of him. The first time he'd been, in his words, a jerk. The second, he'd been emotionally shredded, angry at God and the fates. The third, he'd been a regular guy, just taking care of his kids. A guy who had planted hopeful seedlings in Sarah's fertile, romantic mind. Although Luke was a puzzle to her—one with severely jagged edges—she liked that he'd set down roots in her thoughts.

CHAPTER NINE

LUKE SCANNED THE want ads on one of the computers at the public library. He'd sold his laptop right after Jenny died to help pay for her funeral. Slowly, he'd begun selling more and more things to the local pawn shop and to one of the antiques dealers on Main Street. He and Jenny didn't have much, but there had been some china that her grandmother had given her and a few odd pieces of sterling silver they'd received as wedding gifts. The kids still didn't know about the sales he'd made since most of the items had still been packed in boxes in the attic. However, Luke's stash of cranberry cruets, crystal sugar bowls and silver candlesticks was running dry.

Lately, he'd been looking for carpentry and handyman jobs he could do on weekends or evenings to shore up his sinking paycheck from Jerry. But as he scrolled through the ads, his eyes kept wandering over to the meeting room where he'd attended his first counseling session last week. He still had mixed emotions about the value of therapy. He'd never had any therapy after Iraq. He'd had Jenny and all her love. Whatever holes he'd had in his heart, she'd filled them up.

No matter how strenuously Luke tried to block out the session, he couldn't forget Margot telling him she believed he was mad at the universe for leaving him here on earth to take care of his kids without Jenny. Was that what this burning ache was? Self-pity? Had his sadness brought him this low?

Sure, he was ticked off about the bills and not having enough money to buy the kids what they deserved, and he supposed, if he was really honest with himself, he'd become absorbed in his financial struggles. It was his anxiety over money that had caused him to be short and even distant with his kids.

And that was not Jenny's fault. It was his.

Raking his hand through his hair, he remembered far too vividly how he must have looked and sounded to Sarah that day at the groomers'. Even now, he could remember the angry fire that had exploded inside him when he saw his kids being muddied by her dog. Now she was part of his counseling group. What were the odds?

Jenny used to say that there were no such things as "accidents." She said everything happened for a reason. The only reason Luke could see for his encounters with Sarah was that he'd made a complete fool of himself and she kept popping up as a reminder to get his act together. When he'd stormed out of the counseling session last week, he'd planned never to return. He didn't need a shrink telling him how screwed up he was. He was just hurting. But to actually hear Margot tell him she understood his pain had reached deep inside his mind and heart and twisted some key on a door he didn't even know existed. The session had unleashed a longing, a real yearning, to want to be a better dad, a healthier person...just for himself. Luke was still shocked at the enormity of emotions he'd felt that night. He'd been so overwhelmed that he simply couldn't stay there any longer. He would really have made a fool out of himself then.

He'd gone to his truck and could barely turn the key his hand had been shaking so hard. He'd cried his eyes out. Even that had been a revelation. He hadn't expected to cry anymore. He'd cried for weeks after Jenny died. He thought that phase of his grieving was over. Apparently not.

He agreed with Margot that he was mired in a deep pit of angry tar that stuck to every fabric of his being. He'd never been an angry guy before, but he sure was one now. And he didn't like it.

He glanced at the door to the meeting room. He'd intended never to go back to counseling, but as he thought about it now, he realized that if he truly wanted a normal life for himself and the kids again, he was going to have to find the courage he'd relied on in Iraq. He'd faced danger, even death. He could face a shrink and a group of fellow grievers.

As a picture of the group filled his mind, Luke remembered the vision of Sarah and her sculling crew on the lake the day before.

Unexpected. That was the word that came to mind when he thought of her. She mesmerized him. Perhaps it was the strength he saw in her. She was in counseling just as he was, but there she was with friends, laughing and pushing herself to get on with her life. He admired her for that. He might have even been a bit envious.

When she'd walked up to him, he'd been embarrassed about how he'd behaved when they first met, but that had fizzled like steam vapor. She was an expert on the water, and that surprised him. She was a "water person," too. They had that in common. And she was grieving over her mother. He doubted she was as messed up as he was. Was anybody?

He looked back at the want ads on his screen.

There hadn't been anything remotely close to his skillset for weeks. He was more than discouraged.

He peered closer. *For real?*

Luke read the ad requesting a painter for a garage and jotted down the phone number. He couldn't believe how low he'd had to sink just to make money. This wasn't even close to his skills as a fine carpenter. He could make custom-made cabinets, vanities and exquisite bookshelves with edge molding. No one could crown mold a room like he could. His work was precision. When he and Jenny first started out, they'd lived near Chicago where the company he worked for always snagged expensive remodeling jobs in the northern suburbs or in the mansions along Sheridan Drive. He'd gotten spoiled too early on, he figured. He remembered working long hours, but the work had been energizing and exciting.

His favorite job was to restore a neglected old home to its earlier glory. Even though he'd never gone to college, his own bookshelves were lined with architecture texts. It was Luke's bet that he'd read and studied as much as any architect in America. Luke didn't go to movies. He didn't spend weekends working on sports cars or playing golf. Luke lived and breathed architecture. When he wasn't reading a book on the art itself, he read biographies of Louis Sullivan, Frank Lloyd Wright, Le Corbusier, Jean Louis Charles Garnier, Mies Van der Rohe and his favorite, William Holabird, who along with his partner Martin Roche and others, founded the Chicago School.

Luke had dreams for himself and his career, and he'd told Jenny every one of them. He missed having her there to listen to his ideas and plans. He missed a lot of things.

Luke read the ad again. *Garage painting.* It wasn't even a house or its interior that needed a painter. It was just a garage. There was no doubt in his mind that the job would be a pain in the butt, and he probably wouldn't get paid enough to balance out the untold aggravation he'd experience.

But he would take it. He just hoped the position wasn't already filled.

Taking out his cell phone, Luke bounded down the granite library steps and walked toward his truck. His call was answered on the fourth ring.

"Hello," an elderly voice said.

"Hi. My name is Luke Bosworth and I'm calling in answer to your ad about the painting. You said in the ad it's a garage."

"Well, not exactly, young man," the woman said. "It's actually a carriage house."

Luke rolled his eyes. He didn't know if he should be excited or deflated. "How old is it?"

"Hundred and ten."

Luke whistled. "That's old. And what state of repair is the carriage house in?"

"It could use some carpentry work."

"How much?" Luke envisioned walls falling in on each other, a rotted foundation and beams that were dried and about to split in half. He'd called on this type of job before, only to tell the owner that the project needed demolition, not a skilled carpenter.

"A few boards are all," the woman answered.

"When can I take a look at it?"

"How about today?"

"I'm on my way to work right now, but I could drop by this evening. What's the address?"

"Fifteen ten Maple Avenue."

"I'll see you then. Sorry, I forgot to ask your name."

"It's Beabots. Mrs. Beabots."

CHAPTER TEN

LUKE TWISTED THE crank doorbell at Mrs. Beabots's house. He was surprised that he felt a bit nervous about this interview. He'd taken over a dozen carpentry and handyman jobs in the past year, but for some inexplicable reason, this one had felt different to him ever since he answered the ad. He could hear light footsteps on bare wood floors. Now they hit carpet or a rug. Through the beveled glass, he saw a short, white-haired woman coming to the door.

"I'm here," she said with a lilt to her voice. He remembered now that she had sounded quite cheerful on the phone. Perhaps that was the reason he'd wanted the job. Working for someone pleasant was always a plus these days, and not to be taken lightly. The homeowners at his past two extra jobs had acted as if he was ripping them off when he told them the hours he'd worked and total cost of his labor. He'd learned his lesson. He bid the job now, giving a complete estimate prior to beginning the work. People who did not work with their hands seldom truly understood the precision and care that carpentry required. Luke was a perfectionist and he just couldn't do a job if he didn't do it right. He hadn't even seen this woman's carriage house, but judging from the massive Victorian porch where he stood and the four large stained and beveled-glass windows, he felt as if he'd just won the lottery.

He could only hope this employer would pay him.

The door swung open. "Mrs. Beabots?" he asked.

She tilted her head coquettishly. If he hadn't known better, he would have thought she was flirting with him. She smiled at him, and it was a smile so genuine, he felt his misgivings melt.

"You're a handsome one, you are," she said with not a single whit of guile.

Luke dropped his jaw and snapped it shut. He had never in his life heard anyone be so unabashedly blunt. "Thanks."

"Hmm," she said, scrutinizing him from head to toe. "You look trustworthy and that's imperative for this job," she stated flatly.

"Thanks, again," he said, assessing her as critically as she was him. Her eyes were clear, direct and intelligent. They were a deep blue color that had apparently not dimmed with age. He noticed that she wore mascara to intensify her eyes, very red lipstick and a touch of blush on her cheeks. She was dressed in a lime-green summer print dress and a white cardigan. She wore slip-on pink-and-lime-green-plaid topsiders, just like the ones Jenny had worn in the summer. Crystal bead earrings that he thought could possibly be antique aurora borealis dangled from her ears. Mrs. Beabots was clearly fashion conscious and proud of her appearance. Her back was ramrod straight, and she walked with purpose and direction. He realized that she was undoubtedly a woman of many facets.

"Let's go see my little house."

Luke's brows furrowed. "Pardon?"

She smiled again. "The carriage house. When I was a little girl, I always wanted a playhouse. My father wouldn't build one for me. Terrible with his hands, don'tcha know. He didn't have a single skill to say scat about." She took a step toward him, carrying a huge ring of keys. She shut the door behind her.

Mrs. Beabots kept talking as she grabbed the wrought-iron handrail and made her way down the front porch steps. "When my husband, God rest his soul, and I bought this house, I always considered the carriage house my playhouse. I wanted to think my husband was kinder to me than my father."

"I'm sorry to hear that," Luke offered.

"Don't be. My father was all right, I suppose, as fathers go. He just didn't care for children too much." She looked up at him. "You are a tall one, aren'tcha?"

"Yes, ma'am." Luke chuckled under his breath. He hadn't had this much physical assessment since he went to Great Lakes Naval Base for training.

She babbled on as they rounded the side of the house and passed by the hydrangea bushes and leafed-out forsythia. Yellow remains of tulip leaves flopped over river stones that formed the borders of the flower beds. He noticed there were very few weeds.

She glanced up at him as he observed the flower beds. "Oh, those will be planted with my annuals next week," she said, as if she were reading his mind. "I have a boy who does my yard work for me. Lester's his name. He's about twenty now. I'm not sure. I think he's always lied about his age. Came here from Kentucky. Runaway, Ann Marie told me."

"Ann Marie?"

Mrs. Beabots nodded. "Best friend I ever had. She died a few months ago. Ann Marie found him, you know."

"Found him?"

"Wandered into town on foot, he did. That was two years ago. She was out there on the boulevard doing her fall bulb planting. Lester had been wandering around and saw her on her knees, humming to herself. Ann Marie was always singing to herself. Anyway, Lester just stood there watching Ann Marie and when she turned around to grab the tulip planter, he handed it to her. He told her he liked diggin' in the dirt. They worked together all that day, side by side. He had no place to stay, so Ann Marie took him home. Fed him, too. He's still pretty scrawny if you ask me. Ann Marie arranged for him to get a job with Burt Nealy. Burt owns a landscape business and that huge tree nursery on the west side of town. Anyway, Ann Marie talked Maddie Strong into renting that apartment she has up over her coffee shop to Lester."

"Sounds to me like your friend nearly adopted him."

"That she did. She was always like that. Helping folks who needed help. Lester doesn't talk much, but I know he misses Ann Marie something fierce."

Mrs. Beabots continued walking and telling her story. "Anyway, the boulevard was all Ann Marie's idea. She started planting the plums and apple trees out there over twenty years ago. Then she designed those curving beds and planted all the perennials herself. The pink tulips and daffodils for spring. Black-eyed Susans, pink cone flowers, Shasta daisies. Labor of love, if you ask me. Ann Marie always made everything beautiful."

Luke looked over his shoulder at the boulevard down Maple Avenue. "My kids love the boulevard. They make me drive down here just to see the changes in the flowers."

"You have children?" Mrs. Beabots stopped dead in her tracks. Craning her neck, she looked up at him. "So you're married?"

"No. Not anymore," he said with enough sadness that the bitterness of it caused him to wince.

Mrs. Beabots reached out and touched his forearm. "When did your wife die?"

"How could you know that?" he asked.

"It's in your eyes. I can always tell. I see the same look in my own reflection. It's never the same after our precious ones pass away, is it?"

"No, it's not," he replied simply.

"Well, then you and I have that in common," she said and dropped her hand. She turned and started walking again.

The carriage house was enormous. It was over two stories high, with a steep gabled roof that Luke thought could house an attic or valuable storage space. The white exterior paint was peeling, and there were a good many rotten fascia boards. He could plainly see old termite damage. The windows were intact, but the sills were split and most likely could not be filled and repaired.

This job, to be done correctly, was going to take far more than just a couple coats of paint.

"This is some playhouse," he said, looking up to the gutters and rooflines.

"Even as a child, I believed in thinking big." She went to the side door. "I have it padlocked."

Luke thought it a silly thing to do. If a thief wanted anything in the rickety old building, all he had to do was give the rotted door a good shove.

Mrs. Beabots inserted the key into the lock, unhooked the latch and turned the old black doorknob, then stepped inside.

Luke followed her as she turned on several ballasts of overhead fluorescent lights. Slowly, Luke walked around the carriage house and assessed the building. "I'm afraid, Mrs. Beabots, that your playhouse needs a huge amount of work. The foundation boards are rotted and need to be replaced. It needs a new roof. Shingles and new gutters. I recommend downspouts to keep the runoff away from the foundation. I need to brace that top beam up there. It's got two rather large cracks, and I wouldn't want this roof to cave in. So slapping on a coat of paint would be a waste of your money."

Mrs. Beabots smiled brightly. "I knew I could trust you. I knew it when I talked to you on the phone. I felt in my bones. You're hired," she said with enthusiasm.

"You're kidding?"

"No. I know what the carriage house needs. My problem is that this is a small town. People talk about a lot of things. Most of the people who used to talk about me are dead. But some aren't. Every year, I've had workmen come to the door and offer to fix my carriage house, but I've always turned them away."

"You didn't trust them."

"I did not. I can always tell. Every year, the roof gets worse, and now it's imperative the work be done. How much will you charge me?"

Luke looked around. "It will take me a couple days to work up an estimate. There are a lot of materials to consider."

She nodded. "I'll give you my charge card for the materials and arrange for the Indian Lake Lumber Yard to give you carte blanche. You just figure out how much I'll owe you for your labor."

"That's very fair."

"Fair is the only way to live your life, Mr. Bosworth."

"Luke. Please call me Luke."

"Then we have a deal?" she asked.

"Yes."

Mrs. Beabots lifted her dainty hand, spit into the palm and held it out to Luke. "Shake on it."

Luke bit back his laughter, spit into his palm and shook her hand. "Deal."

"Very well, Mr. Bosworth," she said, leading him through the door and carefully closing the padlock.

LUKE PARKED HIS truck at Redbeard's Marina. Now that he was going to be working weekends for most of the summer, he would have to find a babysitter. He knew they wouldn't like going to yet another day care or a sitter's house, but there was no way around it.

He felt terribly guilty that he didn't have more time to spend with his children. This money from Mrs. Beabots would help a great deal in paying off his credit cards and the hospital bills. Once more, he would be able to keep his head above water. But only barely. His main concern was where the next job was going to come from after he finished Mrs. Beabots's *playhouse*.

Luke walked up to the dock and peered down the beach to where Red stood waist deep in the water instructing a group of about eight children. Red had just grabbed Timmy's hand and was using him to demonstrate floating on his back. Timmy was an apt pupil—Luke could tell, even from a distance. He was surprised at the flood of pride he felt for his little boy.

"He's doing just great," a woman said as she headed toward Luke from the Indian Lake Yacht Club. He recognized her as Julie, Red's wife. She shielded her eyes with her hand. "You must be Luke Bosworth."

"I am," Luke said. "And you're Julie Taylor."

She extended her hand and Luke shook it. "I saw you last week on orientation day, but I was so swamped I didn't get a chance to meet you formally," she said.

"Nice to meet you." Luke guessed her to be in her mid-fifties. She was slender, tall and dressed in chalk-white cargo pants and a tangerine-colored blouse that showed off her tan. She didn't have a freckle on her face or arms, so Luke guessed her auburn hair was not her natural color.

"Your kids are terrific. Red has really taken a special interest in Timmy. And Annie, she's a natural for the water, Red says. She's such a chatterbox. Apparently, she believes there is nothing she can't do."

"There isn't," Luke replied and looked back toward the beach, where he saw Annie, wearing her pink-and-purple, one-piece bathing suit and an orange life vest. "She's more grown up than I am."

"You love them very much," Julie said as a statement rather than a question.

"With all my heart," he said. "You have kids?"

"No," she said flatly. "And yes. All these kids become family to Red and me."

Luke smiled. "I understand that. The best part is you don't have to find summer babysitters."

"That is a problem, isn't it?"

"For me, it's a nightmare. I don't know what to do. I was just hired for a summer weekend job, and..."

"I'll take them."

"What?"

"Annie and Timmy. I'll take them. Just on the weekends, though," she laughed as if she had the inside track on her own joke. "I take a few extra kids on the weekends while Red is busy renting boats and giving adult ski lessons and whatnot. Keeps me busy, and I love the children."

"It would help me tremendously," Luke said. "This is like..."

"An answer to a prayer?" Julie offered.

"I wasn't exactly going to say it that way."

"Why not? I would say exactly that."

CHAPTER ELEVEN

SARAH MET MARY Catherine Cook at St. Mark's School on Tuesday morning. Mary Catherine was putting together a children's choir for the church, hoping the children's participation would help bring back some of the parishioners who had slowly been abandoning St. Mark's.

"You play the piano so beautifully, Sarah, and I need the help," Mary Catherine said, clamping her plump hands together. Mary Catherine taught third grade at St. Mark's and had four children of her own. She was barely five feet tall and as round as she was tall. What Sarah liked about Mary Catherine was that she always smiled at everyone and not a single negative remark ever came out of her mouth.

Until today.

"This is very ambitious of you, Mary Catherine," Sarah said, "trying to get the kids together in the middle of the summer."

"We have to do something or St. Mark's is doomed!"

"What are you talking about?"

"I know you've had a lot going on in your own life, but surely you've noticed how few people attend Sunday services anymore. Half the enrollments for the school are not from the church. The building itself needs so many repairs," she said as Father Michael walked in the school doors.

"Father Michael. How nice to see you. We were just discussing…"

He put up his hand. "You don't have to say it, Sarah. Our church is dying."

"Well, I wouldn't quite put it that way."

"Really? Then let me take you on a tour," he said, slipping his arm through hers and leading her to the school's main staircase. "See these stairs? They're not just rickety. They're unsafe. I had Harry Abrams give me an estimate. Ten thousand to fix them. And it has to be done before September, when the children come back to school."

Father Michael coughed and then coughed again, raising his arm and covering his mouth with his sleeve.

"Have you seen a doctor?" Sarah asked and looked at Mary Catherine, who shook her head.

"I had pneumonia twice this winter. This bronchial thing kicked me from here to Sunday." He raised his head and looked at the two women. "I am fully aware, Mary Catherine, that the reason we are losing parishioners is because of my chronic ill health. But I can't help it."

"You could eat better and get more rest," she scolded.

"Has Colleen Kelly been snitching on me again?"

Mary Catherine nodded. "That's why I made the vegetable casserole for you yesterday."

"Hmph," he snorted. "Even my wife couldn't get me to eat vegetables. Nasty things. Come, Sarah, let's go look at the church."

They walked outside and down the cement sidewalk where newly planted petunias were bobbing their colorful blossoms in a gentle breeze. Father Michael pointed to the roof. "It needs new shingles."

Sarah squinted and looked closely at the gutters. "The flashing along the gables needs replacing, as well. Definitely some tuck-pointing on the brick. Looks like some cracks in the foundation over there." Sarah pointed to the corners near the back church doors.

"We need a new boiler and furnace, lights and flooring," Father Michael said.

Sarah didn't need a calculator to know that the repairs were going to cost close to a million dollars. "This is going to be expensive."

"But we can't afford any repairs, Sarah," Father Michael moaned.

"We can't afford to let St. Mark's crumble into a pile of dust, either," Sarah retorted, feeling a wave of pride wash over her. "My grandparents helped to build this church. My mother was devoted to this church. I can't just let it… go away. And what of the school? If the church shuts down, what happens then?"

"The school board is already talking about closing it next year," Father Michael said.

Mary Catherine turned to Sarah. "Now do you understand why I think the children's choir would help rejuvenate things?"

"I do," Sarah agreed. "But it's going to need more than just a few songs on Sunday to tackle this problem."

"Like what?" Mary Catherine asked.

"I don't know. But I'll think of something," Sarah assured them tentatively. Had she just made a commitment? She looked up at the soaring spire and saw another dozen shingles that needed replacing. Her church was broke. They needed her help, but she hadn't the first clue how one went about raising a million dollars.

Rain pelted the hundred-year-old glass windows in the library, creating a cacophony of pinging and tinkling. Inside the well-lit meeting room, Sarah sat in the same chair as last week, opposite Luke and Margot. Two chairs to Margot's right was Alice Crane, who was talking about her fiancé's car accident. "He was coming home from work on a night like this," she said, motioning to the huge window. "The rain was coming down in torrents, and it was very windy. The bridge just south of town had washed out, but he didn't see it. The cops told me there was a mudslide, which made the highway even slicker. His car spun and then flipped over twice. He was killed instantly." Alice started to cry and grabbed the box of tissues on the chair next to her. She blew her nose. "Sorry."

"Don't be," Margot said.

Sarah got up from her chair and put her arm around Alice. She didn't say a word, knowing words would have been too much.

Alice bit her lower lip. "It was so fast, you know? He was never sick. He was just dead. Gone. In a single night. We were supposed to pick out our wedding cake the next day. Burt was looking forward to that. He loved cake. It was the only kind of dessert he liked," she rambled.

Margot's voice was compassionate as she spoke. "And so, Alice, I'm guessing that you feel robbed of that chance that both Sarah and Luke were given to say goodbye. Is that right?"

Alice's face shattered, and tears ran in rivulets down her cheeks. "I was cheated. There are so many things I would have said to him."

Margot took Alice's hand, which had been wadding the tissue into a tight ball. "What's stopping you?"

"What?" Luke barked. "Her fiancé is dead!"

Sarah's head shot up. "You don't talk to your wife?"

He shook his head. "No."

"I don't believe you," Sarah said flatly, staring at him. "In the two years since she's been dead, you haven't told her that you miss her? That you wish she were here?"

"Well, yeah, but…"

"It's the same thing, Luke," Margot interjected. "Alice, for next week, I want you to write a letter to Burt telling him everything you would have said to him if you'd had the chance. Say everything. The good and the bad. Then bring it next week to share with us. Can you do that?"

"I think so," Alice replied with a forced, uncertain smile.

Margot turned to Luke. "I was afraid we scared you away last week, Luke. I'm glad you're back."

"So are we," Sarah piped in with a smile. Alice nodded.

"I hadn't thought I would come back, but I

guess you figured that out already. I realized that the reason I came here in the first place was because of my kids. They're my Achilles heel, I guess you could say. I would do anything for them, but right now, I seem to be alienating them more than being a father to them."

"Why's that?" Margot asked.

"I get angry at the least little thing they do, or I don't notice when they've done something special. This is not fair to my oldest, Annie, especially. She's been the little homemaker for both my son and me since Jenny died. She does half the household chores without my even asking. I don't know why she does that."

"She's assumed her mother's role," Margot said. "Because she loves you and sees your unhappiness, she's taken on the responsibility of your happiness."

Luke's face grew stern and pensive. "This is not a good thing at all. She's just a kid. She should be doing little girl things. Not pretending she's the adult, which she does well."

Margot cast him an understanding smile. "Precisely. All the things you can do to promote her being a child will be invaluable. Can you hire a housekeeper to do the chores?"

Luke looked down at his boots and then lifted his head. "No, I can't."

"I understand," Margot said.

Sarah hadn't taken her eyes off Luke since the conversation began. She could tell he was embarrassed to admit his shortcomings, yet he courageously plunged into his explanations. He wasn't holding anything back. He was earnest in his desire to put his grief behind him. If that were so, then the day would come when he would step out of the shadows of his pain.

Sarah's heart opened to him, and she had to fight the urge to get up and give him a comforting hug. She truly wanted to help him, as any real friend would.

Sarah was so engrossed in what Luke and Margot were saying, she felt as if she were an integral part of their conversation.

"Is it just the grief? Or are you unhappy, Luke?" Sarah blurted her thought aloud.

Luke shot her a piercing look. "Sarah, didn't you say earlier that the grief was heavy on you, like you were being crushed or you couldn't breathe?"

"Yes," Sarah answered.

"It's like that for me, too. But you're right, Sarah. There's something else. It burns like the dickens right in my gut, and I know it's anger. I know this. But I can't make it go away."

Sarah gave him mental kudos for blunt honesty. Few people ever admitted their faults like Luke did. Counseling was important to her because she wanted to be whole again. At first, Luke had fought the help Margot offered. But now, Sarah felt she and Luke had come together across a huge expanse. Their experiences were similar. Through their pain, they understood each other on deeply emotional levels. They were strangers no more.

Margot interrupted. "Luke, think about it. Alice wishes for closure. She feels guilty that she didn't say what she wanted to say when she had the chance. It doesn't matter if we know someone is going to die or not, when they are gone, we all feel guilty to some degree. What did you *not* do?"

Luke's eyes went from Margot to Sarah to Alice, then he looked off to the rain-splattered window. "If I'd had money back then, I could have taken Jenny to the Mayo Clinic or MD Anderson in Houston. I read up on herb treatments and diets, even drugs that might have saved her. I had no power to help her. I had to just stand by and watch her diminish to nothing right before my eyes. That's why I call myself a born-again atheist. Jenny was my gold ring. She was everything any man could want. I was lucky to have even known her, much less be her husband. Nobody gets a shot at the gold ring twice in life. See, my bottom line is that I just want to get through the rest of my life and not hurt my kids in the process," he said, misery permeating every word.

Sarah was stunned at Luke's pronouncement. She'd never heard a heart in as much pain as Luke's, and without realizing it, she was crying for him. Sarah half listened as Margot asked Alice if she had any words for Luke. Alice offered a benign platitude she must have heard a hundred times from the people who'd handed it to her.

"God always takes the angels first," Alice said.

Maybe that saying had meant something to Alice, but Sarah could tell by the forced and very wan smile on Luke's face that he was only being polite when he thanked her.

Sarah realized that Luke had built an emotional blockade around himself, cutting himself off from the pain others might inflict while keeping his torture private and personal. He was the kind of person a thousand counseling sessions would not help. Her heart went out to his children, who had to be feeling trapped and perhaps even scared. Sarah was afraid the only thing that would save Luke was Jenny's resurrection.

Margot turned to Sarah and asked, "Do you have anything you wish to share with Luke, Sarah?"

"I'm so sorry, Luke," was all she could answer.

"Thank you for that, Sarah. I appreciate it," he said with the only warm smile he'd given anyone that evening.

Margot concluded the session and asked everyone to help her clean up the refreshment table as they always did.

While Luke folded the chairs and put them in the storage closet, Sarah wrapped up the leftover cookies she had baked for the evening. "Luke," she said as he opened a garbage bag for the paper coffee cups and napkins. "Would you like to take these cookies home to your kids?"

"I shouldn't."

"It's fine. Really. If I take them home, I'll just wind up giving them to my dog."

Luke looked at her askance and laughed. "You give him your peanut butter cookies?"

"Yes," she replied quite seriously. "I bake them for him every Saturday. He loves them."

"But he's a dog."

"Beau is no ordinary dog. Besides, I only let him have one a day."

Luke laughed again. "God, you sound like Jenny. She was such a stickler about sugar for the kids, and I love baked goods. Always have. My mother baked cookies for me and sent them to Iraq all the time."

Sarah's jaw dropped. "You're kidding."

"No. Is that too much information?"

She chuckled. "Not at all. I just didn't know... about Iraq. Army?"

"Navy SEAL."

Sarah was doubly confused by Luke. He'd just told her he'd seen combat, and probably the kind of atrocities she didn't think the nightly news could broadcast. He was a man of more contradictions than she could count. How was it possible for a man who'd been through so much—war, fighting, killing and who knew what else—to be so debilitated by a single person's death?

And then it hit her.

That's how much he had loved. His capacity for loving had been so deep, so boundless, so all-encompassing that the loss of it was nearly his undoing. Luke Bosworth was no ordinary man. He was the kind of man she wanted to get to know. A man like Luke didn't come around more than once in a person's lifetime. She knew that he felt honored to have even known Jenny.

Sarah felt privileged to know Luke.

Luke cleared his throat. Suddenly self-conscious, Sarah turned away and picked up her red rain slicker from the back of her chair.

"Thanks for the cookies, Sarah," Luke said.

"Oh, you're welcome," she replied. Sarah

fumbled with the zipper as she said good-night to Luke and Alice.

Still struggling with the zipper, Sarah's patience wore thin. "This darn thing!"

"Here, let me help," Luke offered, handing her the plate of cookies and then expertly putting the zipper teeth inside the pulley. As he zipped up the slicker, the fingers of his hand grazed against Sarah's chin. He flung his hand back as if he'd been stung.

Sarah stiffened. She wasn't quite sure what happened, but something had zapped her like an electric shock. She stared at him.

His eyes were locked on hers, but she couldn't tell what he was thinking. His expression was implacable.

She held out the plate of cookies. "Don't forget these. For the kids."

"Thanks," Luke said, then turned toward the back of the room where Margot was turning off the lamps. "Good night, Margot."

"Good night, Luke," Margot said.

He threw Sarah one last look. "Bye."

"Night," Sarah said and watched him leave. She picked up her purse, bid Margot good-night and then left the room. As she walked toward the library's huge doors, she stared out at the rain. All she could think about was the electric shock that had run through her when his hand had touched her chin.

She'd never felt anything like that in her life. It was as if she'd been struck by a thunderbolt. Something had happened to Sarah in that moment, but she wasn't quite sure what it was. She'd felt as if she'd come alive from a long, dark sleep. Vaguely, she wondered if this was like the "kiss of true love" that awakened Snow White.

Sarah's level head and logical thinking told her not to dwell on fairy tales. Certainly there were attributes of kindness, caring, good humor and thoughtfulness in Luke Bosworth, but if she'd scoured the earth for a century there was no doubt in her mind that she would ever have found a more emotionally unavailable man.

However, he had helped her with her rain slicker. *Maybe there's hope there, after all.*

CHAPTER TWELVE

SARAH WATCHED HER fingers as they traveled up and down the piano keys, creating the melodic and moving strains of "In the Garden." The children from the vacation Bible School auditioned for the choir with an eagerness she hadn't expected. Mary Catherine had already chosen nine girls and four boys, including Timmy Bosworth. Now it was Annie's turn to audition.

"May I sing something different, Mrs. Cook?" Annie asked.

"I suppose so, if Sarah knows the song." Mary Catherine looked over at Sarah.

"What is it, Annie?" Sarah asked.

"'Ave Maria.'"

Sarah gaped at the eight-year-old. "You know the 'Ave Maria'?"

"In English and Latin. My mother taught it to me. It was her favorite. She was a really good singer." Annie smiled widely.

Sarah smiled back. "It's very difficult, but if that's what you'd like to sing, I would love to play it for you."

Annie, dressed in a white, cotton summer dress with watermelon slices appliqued on the skirt, nearly jumped up and down with glee.

Sarah began the intro and Mary Catherine gave Annie her cue. In less than one bar, listening to Annie, Sarah got goose bumps—the kind that were brought on when one was moved in both heart and soul. Sarah watched every nuance of the little girl who was as much inside the song as any adult soloist could be. With each chorus, Annie's voice rose in crescendo, matching emotion with words and plucking the heartstrings of her choir director and pianist.

When the song ended, Annie stood radiant.

Sarah sat rigid in shock, but only for a moment. Then she bolted to her feet and applauded. "Bravo! Annie. Bravo!"

She rushed to the little girl.

Mary Catherine had tears in her eyes. "Beautiful. Beautiful."

"Annie, we had no idea you could sing like this."

Annie hung her head demurely. "I've been practicing."

"I should say so!" Sarah couldn't help it. She hugged the little girl.

Annie hugged her back. "Thank you, Miss Sarah. I'm glad you liked the song."

"It's one of my favorites, too. My mother always sang it to me on Christmas Eve."

Mary Catherine tapped her cheek. "That's exactly what we'll do for Christmas. We'll have Annie sing the solo at the Christmas Eve service."

"Wonderful!"

Annie's face fell. "What if my dad won't let me?" she asked.

"Of course he'll let you sing," Mary Catherine chirped happily. "With a voice like yours, you should be on one of those television talent shows."

Annie shook her head violently just as Timmy walked up.

He put his hand in Annie's. "He won't let her sing," Timmy said.

Sarah was aghast. "Why on earth not? You are both very talented children. It's practically his moral duty to encourage you and support you."

"You don't understand," Annie said. "He really won't."

Sarah narrowed her eyes. "You two aren't here without his permission, are you?"

"Not exactly," Annie said. "He knows we're at Bible School and I told him I wanted to be in the choir. But he wasn't paying a whole lot of attention when I said today was the tryouts."

"Does he know how good you are?"

Timmy frowned and pouted his lip. "He doesn't know anything about us anymore."

Annie looked from Timmy up to Sarah. "I don't sing much anymore at home. It reminds him too much of my mom. And that makes him sad."

Sarah stood up and folded her arms across her chest. "So where do you practice?"

"On the beach. Mrs. Taylor thinks I'm good, too," Annie said proudly. "She's teaching me some other songs. I like 'America the Beautiful' a lot."

Sarah looked at Mary Catherine, who gave her a very worried look. "I think we have a problem."

Annie's blue eyes were filled with the pain of rejection. "I was hoping… I just wanted to be in the choir. So does Timmy. He's a good singer, too."

"Yes, he is, sweetheart. You both are wonderful," Sarah assured them. "I'll talk to your dad."

Annie's eyes grew wide and Timmy dropped his mouth. "You will?" They exclaimed in unison.

Sarah hadn't expected such elation and eagerness from them. Her heart soared as she realized that, in an instant, she'd become someone's champion. She hadn't asked for the job—she'd simply taken it on. Just as quickly, she realized she might have made a huge mistake. Luke was a volatile guy, and nobody knew that as well as she did. But as she stared at their eager, impassioned faces, she assessed the situation. She decided that the kids were worth the risk.

Mary Catherine escorted the children out of the church as Sarah gathered her music and placed the sheets in her father's battered briefcase.

She looked around the church one last time before turning out the lights. As she walked down the cracked terrazzo floor and passed the pews with their worn-out pads, Sarah's designer-architect's mind stopped her in her tracks.

"This place needs more than repairs. It needs serious redesign." Sarah scanned the dull, brown paint and cracked, peeling gold leaf. Looking at it with a trained eye, it was no wonder the church was losing people. The place couldn't be more depressing if it was a morgue.

"It needs me," she said aloud, as creative adrenaline spiraled through her body. She, turned off the lights—the ones that were working—and closed the doors reverently behind her. Then she took off in a run for home.

SARAH WORKED ALL night at her drafting table, struggling to put down on paper all her ideas for a complete renovation of her church. She used every medium at her disposal, from charcoals to pastel chalks and even acrylic paints, hoping to get just the right blends that would lighten up the church's dreary interior. The hours passed, but to Sarah they felt like minutes. She was completely unaware of the mess she'd made until dawn seeped through the plantation shutters on the window.

"How can it be morning? I've barely begun," she groaned aloud and looked at her watch. She wiped her hand over her face and tried to bring herself back to reality.

She remembered she'd made only one pot of coffee in her French press, and had consumed it early on in the evening. Around two in the morning, she'd gone downstairs for an apple and a handful of walnuts, but glancing at the side table, she realized she hadn't touched her fruit.

Sitting on her high-backed stool with the pink-and-green-candy-striped cushion her mother had made for her when she'd gone off to college, she looked at the large pile of crumpled papers at her feet. She rubbed her eyes and glanced at the drafting table.

Lying before her were twenty-nine depictions of the renovations she knew the church would need. And she didn't remember creating half of them. *When did I do all this?*

When she'd worked on a particularly demanding project back in Indianapolis, she'd gotten into her creative zone and lost track of time, but she'd always kept a sharp bead on her progress.

Something about this experience was different. Very different.

She vaguely remembered opening all the tubes of oil paints. She remembered the acrylics and then throwing those drafts into the wastebasket. She remembered throwing some pen and ink drawings away, but she was at a loss as to how many drawings she'd completed.

Could this be real artistic inspiration?

Sarah, girl. You are really losing it, she chastised herself. Then picked up the first drawing. *Or...could you possibly be getting it?*

Sarah went through the first stack of sketches, which were all done in charcoal pencil. These were for the construction work she knew had to take place before any other changes could be executed. The largest and most costly alteration would be the removal of the old glassed-in "cry room," which sat off to the left of the altar. Sarah wanted to rip it out and make a new area for the choir. She would keep the choir section on the right-hand side of the altar as it was, but refurbish the pews. The addition of the extra choir area was for the children's choir. She knew it would be a mainstay for years to come.

Sarah saw a new electric piano and an electric organ in the left area, as well. They would need amps, a very good sound system and someone to run it. Music brought joy to everyone's lives. She couldn't help thinking of little Annie and the joy Sarah had felt throughout her body just listening to the child sing.

In the back of the church, where the vestibule flowed openly into the main area, she would partition the vestibule off with columns, wood arches and soundproof glass windows. Fifteen-foot-high, massive, wood doors with brass handles would open to the center aisle. There were matching but smaller doors on the far right and far left where people could enter through the side aisles.

The vestibule would double as a greeting area and as a new cry room for parents with babies and small children. Two rows of comfortable, stackable chairs would be placed in this area, and could be removed for weddings and gatherings when seating was not required.

At some point in the seventies, someone had decided to cover the dull, concrete columns that ran up and down the side aisles of the main area with an even duller beige grasscloth. Tear-ing out the columns and replacing them was senseless. In addition, the columns accented, though they did not support, the twelve arches in the lower left and right aisle ceilings. Sarah planned to remove the grasscloth and have the columns painted in a dramatic and rich-looking dark green with gold marble veining. She realized she would need an expert artist to execute the complicated veining process that would make the columns resemble real marble. If the painting was not executed with precision, a very good eye and steady hand, the result would look more like graffiti than faux marbling.

Around the far back wall of the sacristy and altar area, she designed the faux-marble wall decor that would resemble panels, but would require no wood and thus keep costs down.

The costs! Sarah looked at her work, and for the first time since she started her drawings and plans over twelve hours ago, she felt depressed. She knew enough about construction and design work—the materials and the labor—to realize that her initial proposal would cost upwards of three-quarters of a million dollars.

"Buck up, Sarah. You can do this," she said to encourage herself.

She flipped through the drawings again. She reached over to her paint sample fan decks and started choosing the colors she imagined. Sky-blue for the barrel ceiling. Gold leaf for the arches. Butter-yellow for the side walls, choir areas and the vestibule. A deeper sunflower-yellow for the accent curves. The windowsills and window insert walls would all be that dark blue-green. Jamaican Sea. She paused and looked at the paint swatch. *That's the color of the columns and the new carpet.*

With a deep frown, Sarah wondered how they would repair the rose, gray, beige, black and white terrazzo floor. Suddenly, the phone rang.

"Are you still in your drawing room, pumpkin?" Mrs. Beabots asked.

"How do you know that?"

"Your lights were on all night."

"I was working."

"Sounds intriguing," Mrs. Beabots said. "I just wanted to remind you about tomorrow night. The Arts in the Park."

Sarah scrounged through her brain, barely remembering anything besides her drawings. "Right. I'm driving us."

"That's right, dear. It's the first concert of the season. It will be a virtual festival."

A festival?

Sarah felt as if the clock had stopped.

A festival.

The word conjured whirling visions in her head. *Festival* evoked a scene of Renaissance tents and food wagons, Harlequin clowns and jugglers, puppeteers and actors bellowing lines from Shakespeare. A Midsummer's Eve festival would attract hundreds, possibly thousands of people who would spend money freely in a fantastical setting, Sarah thought.

"Sarah? Did you hear me?"

Sarah snapped out of her reverie. "Yes. We'll leave at six-thirty. Maddie said she'd be here at six. I'm making stuffed green peppers for dinner beforehand."

"I'll bring the wine," Mrs. Beabots said. "Something special, I should think. After all, it's the beginning of summer."

As soon as Sarah hung up the phone, she realized Mrs. Beabots had given her the perfect idea for raising the money for St. Mark's.

"I can do this," she said to Beau, who was watching her with rapt attention.

She would organize a summer festival on the church grounds, and all the proceeds would go to the building fund. She needed a huge extravaganza, which was not hard for Sarah to conjure. She always worked best with large concepts. Skyscrapers. Huge shopping malls. Civic centers. That's the kind of work she'd accomplished in Indianapolis. No wonder she hadn't produced a good design for Charmaine on her last assignment. It was too small. Too utilitar-

ian. She couldn't make her head lower the bar
that much. No, a project like St. Mark's was her
forte. She liked tackling the big whale.

In less than an hour, Sarah had jotted down
all the basics for the summer festival. She would
hold it on the 4th of July, when Indian Lake
was host to an extra twenty to thirty thousand
tourists for the weekend. She would start the
festival right after the huge downtown parade,
which boasted bands, fire engines, dressage and
Western horse teams, antique cars and over a
hundred floats. It was not unusual to have the
governor of Indiana come to the parade. There
was always a flyover by F-16 jets from the Gris-
solm Air Force Base at precisely eleven o'clock.
People would stream to her festival. She would
cajole all the best retailers in town to purchase
booth space, starting with Maddie Strong. She'd
also ask Scott Abbott, who owned the the Book
Shop and Java Stop. The competition would be
good for them. Liz Crenshaw could advertise
her wines, even if she couldn't sell them directly to the public.

And Sarah would plan a children's freedom
pageant, which would entice parents, aunts, un-
cles and grandparents to attend, boosting num-
bers through the gates. Sarah envisioned the
children's choir onstage, each of their eager
faces belting out patriotic songs. She would

feature Annie Bosworth as the star. Annie had said she was practicing "America the Beautiful." She would be perfect.

Suddenly, Sarah remembered what Annie had told her about Luke not allowing Annie to sing. Sarah dismissed the possibility. Sarah believed she knew Luke well enough by now to discuss Annie's participation in the choir and her idea about the summer festival with him.

Her mind reeling with one idea after another, Sarah didn't hear Miss Milse as she came to the front door and let herself in. Not even Beau's barking had broken through the tornado of creativity in Sarah's mind. Her feelings of helplessness floated away like foggy vapors. Her energy spiked. She felt as if an ethereal magician had whisked away the cloak of depression that had wrapped itself around her for months. For the first time since her mother died, Sarah was Sarah again.

Something was happening to her and it was all good. She couldn't put her finger on the exact moment of the alteration. She didn't know if it was the haunting voice of a little girl singing in a church, or a *zing* from a man's touch on her chin, or the spark of an idea that ignited her natural creativity. Sarah was moved to wonderment.

"First things first," Sarah said to herself,

gathering up her drawings for the church improvements. She needed Father Michael's permission. She swallowed hard and paused. Then she shoved her cost calculations into her father's portfolio. *I can do this. And if I don't do this...* She shuddered. The idea of false starts or failures turned her blood cold. She was coming back to life and she didn't want to lose this new excitement.

She would find a way to make this happen. She had to.

CHAPTER THIRTEEN

LUKE PULLED A bag of frozen vegetables out of the freezer and put it in the microwave.

"They take six minutes," Annie said without looking up from the roasted chicken breasts Luke had bought at the supermarket deli. She placed a chicken breast on each of three plates. Timmy poured two glasses of milk for him and Annie and one very tall glass of water for his father.

When the microwave beeped, Luke divided the vegetables among the three plates. Annie carefully put out three red-and-white-checked placemats on the round kitchen table, then folded paper napkins and put them under the forks the way her mother had taught her.

They all sat down, and just as Luke was about to cut into the chicken, Annie said, "Can we say a prayer for Father Michael? He's very sick."

"Yeah," Timmy said. "He's got pneumonia. He's going to die."

"He is not!" Annie argued.

"That's what Miss Sarah said," Timmy rebutted.

"Sarah said he was very sick. Not that he was going to die," Annie shot back at her brother, then put a pat of butter on his vegetables.

Timmy shut his eyes, pursed his lips and shook his head vigorously. "You don't know anything. I heard Miss Sarah tell Mrs. Cook that Father had pneumonia and his heart wasn't working."

"She did not!"

Luke put his fork down, not hearing a whole lot past the mention of Sarah's name. "Hold on, you two. Let's get the facts straight here before we jump to the wrong conclusions. Now, Annie. Who exactly are we talking about? Sarah who?"

"You know, Miss Sarah. She helps at Bible School with Mrs. Cook. And I saw you talking to her at the marina."

"She's Beau's mom," Timmy said, carefully moving the peas away from the carrots and corn on his plate.

Luke nearly dropped his fork. Sarah from his counseling sessions was also his kids' volunteer Sunday school teacher. The woman really got around. "I know who she is," he said.

"I like her a lot," Annie said. "She teaches us how to draw and paint. Well, not really paint, but about colors and fun stuff like that."

Timmy never looked up from his task. "I like her 'cause she's pretty."

"Oh, Timmy," Annie grumbled. "There're more important things than being pretty."

"Like what?" Timmy and Luke asked in unison.

Annie glared at her father and brother.

"I was just kidding," Luke said.

"I wasn't," Timmy said.

All three instantly burst into laughter.

Luke took a long slug of his water and watched his children eat. He was amazed that Sarah Jensen kept turning up in his life as if she'd been plunked in his path by crazy circumstance.

On Saturday, while unloading his tools from his truck, he'd glanced over to the house next to Mrs. Beabots's and had seen a very familiar-looking golden retriever run out of the house and race around the yard. The dog had stopped in his tracks and stared at Luke, but he had not approached or barked. Luke didn't believe in anthropomorphizing animals, but he could have sworn the dog smiled at him in recognition. Luke had rubbed the back of his neck, feeling icy prickles as he realized Sarah Jensen lived next door to his new summer weekend job. It was as if he couldn't escape the woman. Now she was giving his kids art lessons. What was going on? Why would he suddenly keep running into the same woman?

Or had Sarah been around town, in and out

of places where he'd been, where he was, and he just hadn't seen her?

Was that what was happening?

Though Margot was a great counselor, it was Sarah's unbridled compassion that truly made Luke want to continue the sessions. She had a way of listening without judgment, speaking without criticism and reaching out to him, exposing her own flaws, that drew him to her.

She was thoughtful and generous—like the way she'd given him those cookies for the kids. She offered them without thinking. He hadn't seen that kind of graciousness since Jenny.

Sarah certainly had a way about her that snapped him into awareness.

Luke had to admit he'd been caught in a time warp since Jenny's death, and even if he'd run into Sarah prior to that day at the groomers, he honestly wouldn't have remembered it.

Looking at his children, he was taken aback at how much they had grown and changed in the past two years. Some days, he almost felt as if he didn't know them. Annie was nearly nine. Timmy was six and a half. While he had been trapped in a haze of pain and grief, they'd had to march on with their lives without him.

Luke had been chastising himself for being angry with his kids and other people all the time, but what was worse was that he had simply been absent. He went through the motions of everyday life with them, but he hadn't really been involved. Even now, Annie and Timmy were chattering away about something and he wasn't listening.

"I'm sorry, Annie, what were you saying?"

"Mrs. Cook just started a children's choir and she asked if Timmy and I can sing in the choir. So can we, Dad?"

Their faces were filled with so much anticipation, he nearly winced from the force. "That would mean rehearsals," he mused.

"Yesss…" Annie replied tentatively, already feeling his rejection coming on. She had to think quickly. "But you wouldn't have to drive us or take time away from your job."

"How is that possible?"

Annie folded her hands and placed them on the table, prepared for this rebuttal. "Practice this summer is going to be part of our Sunday school sessions. Timmy and I will just stay a half hour longer, is all."

"So I would pick you up then and take you out to the marina."

"Yes," Annie said, glancing at Timmy. He kept his mouth tightly shut as Annie had instructed him to do when she was negotiating for them. Timmy only nodded.

"I suppose it's all right," Luke finally said.

"I have this weekend job for Mrs. Beabots. It's only a few blocks from the church. You guys really want to sing in the choir, huh?"

Annie's face lit up and Timmy grinned broadly. "We do!" they chirped.

"Then that's decided," Luke said and speared a piece of chicken.

Timmy scooped two carrots onto his fork. "Will you come and hear us sometime?" Timmy asked without thinking.

Annie immediately jabbed her brother in the ribs. She remembered her father's vow never to cross the threshold of St. Mark's church after their mother died.

Timmy's eyes flew open as he realized his mistake. He slunk down in his chair.

"Don't push it," Luke replied sourly.

Annie bravely leaned closer to her father and asked, "Will you think about it? Just a little?"

Luke's mind was filled with memories of taking the kids to St. Mark's with Jenny. His gut churned with loneliness, and once again all he saw was the future looming dark, empty and endless in front of him. "I'll think about it. Now eat your peas."

SARAH PUSHED THE doorbell at the rectory at precisely nine o'clock when she was scheduled to meet with Father Michael. Amazingly, she wasn't nervous or timorous. She was confident and excited.

Colleen Kelly, the housekeeper and one of Sarah's favorite people, opened the door. The church council had hired Colleen to take care of Father Michael once it was apparent his health was failing.

Colleen was as thin as a rake handle and as feisty and as loud as a cattle drover. With six children all under the age of twelve, she told Sarah all she needed was one paddle, one bullhorn and a sack of hard candies to keep control of her brood.

Colleen answered the door holding her one-year-old baby, with her two-year-old clutching his mother's leg so tightly Sarah wondered if poor Colleen was going to develop bruises.

"Mornin', missy," Colleen said with a smile as bright as an Irish dawn. Colleen was the daughter of two Irish parents who came to the United States from Belfast and who taught her that life was all about attitude. Colleen believed that being cheerful to others was the only way to live.

"Good morning," Sarah replied. "How is Father Michael today?"

"Father is jes fine. Plenty of my good cookin' is fattening him up. I've been getting him back inta living. Ever since his wife passed, he's been dyin'. Everybody says so. He jes needs my kids around. Ain't nothing that brings life back to a body like children. They keep a body young and they give purpose to every sunrise." Colleen grinned a crooked-toothed smile. Her blue eyes flashed in her freckled, heart-shaped face.

"That's wonderful, Colleen."

"Yep. I got this house running like a top. Keeping them busybodies outta here has really helped. Nobody can get well if they're bein' pressed upon by a bunch of ninnies who can't handle their own lives."

"But that's part of Father Michael's job. To counsel his flock," Sarah said.

"They can flock elsewhere until Father is fit and fine again. Till then, I'm keeping the door shut to visitors," Colleen said, ramming her fist fiercely against her hip and glaring at Sarah.

"I hope I'm not lumped into that group," Sarah said.

"No, ma'am." Colleen beamed and led the way into the living room. Normally, the heavy burgundy drapes were drawn, but not this morning. Sunlight flooded the room, and through the French doors, Sarah could see yellow and orange marigolds had just been planted. Apricot-colored impatiens were clumped next to pink begonias. Sarah turned to Colleen. "You've been busy."

"Sometimes, it's best to feed the soul before you feed the body. Father does it with prayer. I do it with flowers."

"So true," Sarah replied.

"Don't be talking about me behind my back," Father Michael warned, entering the room.

"Anything we said, we would gladly repeat." Sarah smiled.

"Don't," he said, and sat down heavily in his favorite, very worn recliner.

"I'll get the coffee," Colleen said, scurrying out of the room.

Sarah scanned Father Michael's face. "You look good. Your color is back."

"I've been to Hell and back ever since that woman came to roost here with that brood of hers," he grumbled through a tightly clenched jaw.

"Father. How unkind of you."

"I don't care." He slammed his fist on the chair arm. "Do you have any idea what she makes me do?"

"No."

"She's here at six o'clock with half those kids of hers. I hear her ordering them around. Pots and pans are rattling and banging. No one could sleep through that racket. She has the audacity to wake me up and hand me a jogging suit and tells me that I have to go for a walk before breakfast. When I come back she ushers me into the bathroom where she's already got the shower going. Then she marches me to the table and feeds me so much food, I can't move for an hour. Now here it is nine o'clock and she expects me to start taking business calls."

He leaned forward and whispered, "She's trying to kill me, I tell you."

"She's doing just as the doctor told her to. You have to start exercising and eating right."

He frowned and looked at the garden.

Sarah noticed his expression soften a bit. "It's pretty, isn't it?"

"It's exactly the way Mary used to plant that little patio. Exactly."

Sarah allowed him to indulge in his memories for a moment longer. "And by the way, Father, since when am I a 'business meeting?'"

"Isn't that why you wanted to see me?"

"Yes, but how did you know?"

He tapped his temple. "I'm psychic."

Sarah laughed. "And what do you think it's about?"

"I don't know, but I hope it's a strategy to get that…that woman out of my rectory and take her children with her."

"Father, she and everyone else at St. Mark's

are trying to save your life. You aren't dead yet, and since you're stuck here on earth, I want you to have good health while you're here. Besides, we have a lot of work to do."

Father Michael knitted his fingers together in a prayerlike fashion, and cocked his head. "Now what duties of mine are you taking over?"

"Architect. Construction General. Designer. Though I will need the pulpit for ten minutes or so on Sunday."

He shook his head. "Elaborate, please."

"The church is falling apart. So is the staircase in the school, as you pointed out. The school needs a bit of refurbishing, but not as much as the church. The roof needs new shingles. Bricks need tuck-pointing. The pews are wobbly. The terrazzo is cracked, the carpet is worn, the paint is peeling. Here," she said, opening her folio case. "I made a list. Along with drawings for a total renovation."

Sarah stood up and withdrew her poster-size drawings. She'd done her homework and had swatches of pew pad coverings stapled to the sketches. She had paint chips, carpet samples and shingle samples. Carefully, she laid the presentation out around the room, leaning the drawings against tables and on the sofa. Drawing by drawing, she led Father Michael through the steps she would take to renovate the church.

When she finished, Father Michael was in awe. "Why, Sarah, it's just beautiful. I never thought that taking the cry room out would make such a difference. And these colors!"

"I want the church to be happy and to elicit joy. Once the windows are scrubbed clean of soot, they'll sparkle, and the colors will dance around the nave."

Father Michael was so enthusiastic he rose from his chair to feel the fabric swatches. "How beautiful this emerald-green is. And the mustard-gold. How will you ever decide?"

"That's the fun of it, watching the paint go on, and the new lights being installed. When the lighting is in, I'll take the samples into the church and we'll decide."

"It's all so…" he started to say, and then, as if deflating like a balloon, he folded back into his chair "…so expensive. St. Mark's can never afford such an undertaking."

"I think we can," she said, taking out the second set of smaller drawings she had just completed. "We'll start the fund-raising with a summer festival."

She placed these drawings on the floor in sequence, so they could see the festival as a patron would. "On the Fourth of July we have thousands of tourists who come here just for the parade. If we started our festival immediately after the parade before people left town or went up to Lake Michigan, we could garner a good number of those people."

Father Michael nodded in agreement. "Smart thinking. I see here there's a Ferris wheel. How are we going to get a Ferris wheel?"

"I found a carnival company in downstate Illinois that will come here. They only have three rides. Ferris wheel, carousel and a little train ride for toddlers. They'll provide a ring toss, milk bottle pitch and a pick-up-the-duck game. I contacted them by email last night, and they had a cancellation for the Fourth. I'll put up their advance fee, and they will give thirty-five percent of their revenues back to the church. The rest of the booths, we provide ourselves. We have lots of parishioners who would help build the booths and who would want to sell their crafts, artworks and baked goods."

"These booths are beautiful, but how can you get them constructed that fast?"

"First of all, we use folding tables as the basic foundation. I'll have a carpenter build the high framework. Then Mary Catherine and I will paint the booths to look like faux storefronts. I've called the art galleries downtown, and since they're closed on the Fourth, they all told me they'd each buy a booth and stock it with artwork. I think Scott Abbott will put some books in a booth and sell his bags of coffee. He'll work the booth himself. The church volunteers could serve barbecue, hot dogs, fried chicken, corn on the cob and homemade blueberry pies. In the booths we would sell baked goods and Louise Railton's ice cream. There would be handmade items, like the quilts from Mrs. Beabots's quilting group, The Bee. I want unique, one-of-a-kind items. Local artists could sell their paintings and pottery.

"I'll charge the merchants for the cost of a booth. Then a percentage of what they sold would go to the church."

"Do you really think we can raise enough money for the renovations?"

"Not all of it. But this would give us a jump-start. Once we raise this money, we'll build fervor among the parishioners. Hopefully, there will be some who will donate large amounts. If we raise enough money, we might be able to get a loan from the Indian Lake Savings Bank."

He rubbed his forehead thoughtfully. "I don't know. This is so much work. You have to advertise..."

"Here are the fliers. Here's an ad for the newspaper. And I've also decided the church needs a website."

"Website?"

She waved her hands in front of her face.

"Don't think about it. Just trust me. I know how to do this."

"It just looks so overwhelming to me."

"That's because you don't feel well," she offered politely.

He glared at her. "It's because I'm old and don't care anymore. That's what you really want to say now, isn't it, Sarah?"

She sighed. "Yes."

"Well, then. That's cleared up. What would you do if I refused to give my permission?"

She lifted her chin confidently and smiled. "I'd do it, anyway."

CHAPTER FOURTEEN

ARTS IN THE PARK was considered by Indian Lake townsfolk to be the kick-off of the summer tourist season. Every Thursday night during the summer, bands from around the county performed free of charge in the band shell at Lily Park. This tradition began a hundred years ago, when there was only a large, white gazebo down by the water's edge, and the band consisted of only fifteen musicians. During World War II, the city shored up the aging gazebo's foundation and gave it a new roof and shingles, but at the end of the Vietnam War era, the poor thing collapsed. The very wealthy McCreary family donated money to the city for an acoustically designed band shell with a state-of-the-art sound system to be erected across Lily Lake Drive. The band shell would be built on a hill where there was no threat of rising lake waters to destroy the foundation.

It was still chilly this early evening in June when Sarah drove Mrs. Beabots, Maddie, Liz and Isabelle to the park. Each brought her own folding chair, a sweatshirt or jacket, and plenty of bug spray, just in case. Sarah packed an extra cotton throw for Mrs. Beabots—the cold night air seemed to bother her more these past few years.

On this night, easels displayed local artists' works. The Tom Milo Big Band was warming up and testing the speakers. Sarah and her group walked down the pavestone path toward the sloping hills where people were already sitting on benches, blankets, tarps and folding lawn chairs, munching on popcorn that was sold from a red cart. One of the local women's sororities sold homemade cookies, lemonade, iced tea and bottles of water. Another men's club sold saltwater taffy by the bag and chocolate-covered peanut brittle, which everyone knew was handmade by Louise Railton, the owner of the Louise House Sweet Shoppe. The Indian Lake Middle School Art Club kids were going around from group to group selling everything from car wash tickets to slices of pound cake.

As they unfolded their chairs, Sarah offered to treat everyone to popcorn, lemonade and cookies. Maddie bought three bags of saltwater taffy and passed them to her friends.

The sun hung low on the horizon and shot the earth with ribbons of pink, red and purple, and a gentle spring breeze lifted the newly leafed out branches of the maple, walnut and oak trees. Sarah closed her eyes and inhaled the fresh air and listened to the sound of her friends chatting amongst themselves. She had only missed six or seven opening nights in the park in her lifetime, and most of them had been when she was away at college. Her parents told her they had brought her to the park every week for the concerts even when she was an infant. Back then, some of the concerts were pretty amateur, usually due to high school quartets or small bands using the concerts more for practice than performance. There were other bands and even orchestras that had knocked her socks off and made her skin tingle.

Sarah had always loved music, and learned to play the piano when she was six. She was a natural, her mother had told her, but there was more to music than just following notes on a page. She remembered her mother saying, "Sarah, listen while the musicians find their groove. Close your eyes and listen while they step to their path. You can do that, too. Each of us has music of a kind to give to the world. You will find your song someday."

In that moment of memory, Sarah missed her mother so much, her heart ripped just a little bit more.

Only Mrs. Beabots saw her tiny tear. She

reached out her hand while still talking with Maddie and patted Sarah's knee. Mrs. Beabots gave Sarah a side glance and a nearly imperceptible nod, letting her know she knew quite well that Sarah was missing her mother.

Maddie was also aware of Sarah's mood. Always the one to bring things back around to the present, Maddie said, "Hey! I think that's Luke Bosworth over there."

At the thought of Luke, Sarah snapped to attention. "Where?"

Mrs. Beabots watched Sarah. She didn't scan the crowd for Luke as the others did. Mrs. Beabots already knew Luke would attend the concert. She had been the one to give him directions and the other details. She suggested it would be great fun not only for him, but also for his children.

Mrs. Beabots smiled to herself. Things were working out quite satisfactorily.

LUKE, ANNIE AND TIMMY entered the park and sat on the hillside opposite Sarah and her friends. Luke had brought two blankets for them to sit on, windbreakers for the kids and juice boxes.

"Look, Dad! They're selling popcorn!" Timmy piped up.

"We just had dinner," Luke said.

"But we didn't have any dessert," Annie

countered, eyeing the little boy on the blanket next to them who was munching on a cookie.

"Since when do you get dessert?" Luke asked.

Timmy pouted and kicked a small stone. "Never."

Annie walked right over to the little boy with the crew-cut blond hair and the cowlick in front. He had a sprinkle of freckles across his nose just like she did, and very light blue eyes. He was almost cute, she thought. *Almost.*

"Hi, I'm Annie. What's your name?"

"Josh," he said dismissively. He went back to his cookie.

Annie was undeterred. "Did your mom bake those cookies for you?"

"No."

"Oh."

Josh kept eating.

"You don't talk much, do you?"

He glared at her. "I'm not sharing."

"I didn't ask you to. But where did you get it?"

Josh smiled, now that he knew Annie didn't want to take his cookie like his little sister always did. "They sell them here," he said. "Next to the popcorn cart."

"I bet it's expensive."

"No, only a quarter. Or five for a dollar."

"Really?" Annie was delighted. "Well, thanks, Josh."

"They sell saltwater taffy here, too. It's the very best, but my mom won't let me have candy."

Annie's mouth drooped despondently. "My dad, neither."

"Bummer," Josh said.

"Yeah." Annie went back and sat down next to her father, who had his arm around Timmy's shoulder.

"I have a dollar, Dad. Can I buy us some cookies?"

"A dollar. Where'd you get a dollar?"

"I earned it."

Luke's head jerked back. "You what? How?"

"I helped Mrs. Taylor put the supplies away on Sunday afternoon at camp, and then Timmy and I dumped the trash. She gave us each fifty cents."

"She asked you to do chores?"

"No, Dad. We asked *her*. We saw that she has a whole bunch of little kids and taking care of them can really cause a mess. So we volunteered to help her. It was her idea to pay us."

"Little kids?" Luke tried to stifle a laugh. He thought of his own children as *little kids*. They were already thinking of themselves as the *big kids*.

"So can I go buy some cookies?"

"How about popcorn, instead? It's healthier. Your mother wouldn't want you to have sugar this late at night."

"Dad, it's seven o'clock," Timmy argued.

"Precisely," Luke said.

"Okay. Popcorn is better than nothing," Annie conceded. "Could I get the cookies for tomorrow?"

Annie wore a stubborn expression, one he often saw in his own reflection. She was a great deal like him in many ways. Taking charge. Standing firm. Never backing down from a fight. Luke realized he was not going to win this argument. "Sure."

Annie and Timmy scampered off down the hill and onto the walkway that encircled the band shell.

SARAH SAW THE children approaching and stood up. "Hi, Annie. Hi, Timmy," she said with a wave of her hand.

"Hi, Miss Jensen," Annie said.

"You can call me Sarah."

"My dad said that's disrespectful," Timmy said with a very wide grin. "We're going to buy popcorn and cookies."

Maddie stood up. "Sarah, why don't you introduce these children to everybody." She put her arm around Sarah's shoulder and returned a smile to Timmy.

"I'm so sorry. Maddie Strong, Liz Crenshaw, Isabelle Hawks and Mrs. Beabots, meet Annie and Timmy Bosworth.

"Mrs. Beabots?" Annie asked. "My dad works for you."

"Yes, he does. And he's doing a fine job, as well. You can tell him I said that. Do you want to be a carpenter, too?" Mrs. Beabots asked Timmy.

He shook his head. "I'm too young to think about my career."

Sarah burst into laughter. "I totally agree, Timmy."

"How is it you know these children, Sarah?" Mrs. Beabots asked, surprise ratcheting up her eyebrows.

Annie chimed in. "Oh, she helps Mrs. Cook at our Vacation Bible School sometimes."

"Yeah," Timmy said. "At St. Mark's."

"I see," Mrs. Beabots replied with a sly smile. "Sarah, why don't you help the children with their goodies? Surely they can't carry all that themselves. And buy them some lemonade. The money goes to charity, you know," she said, looking from Annie to Timmy.

"I didn't know that." Annie stared at the dollar in her hand as if it now had new meaning.

"We must all do everything we can to support the arts in our town," Mrs. Beabots said.

"Amen to that," Sarah said. "I'll buy you some saltwater taffy."

"Our dad won't let us have candy," Timmy said firmly.

"We're restricted at night, but we can have it for special treats other times," Annie argued, then looked up at Sarah with a broad smile. "That would be very kind of you, Sarah." Sarah bit her bottom lip to keep from laughing again as Annie tugged on her hand.

Next to the popcorn cart were three card tables covered in plastic cloths and dozens of desserts—cookies, slices of pie, brownies, lemon bars, home-made donuts and baklava. Sarah stood in line with Annie and Timmy to make their purchases and she listened to the conversations taking place around her.

"Isn't this fun, Sarah?" Timmy asked, taking her other hand.

"It's one of my favorite things to do in the summer," Sarah agreed. "My parents brought me to the park every week when I was a kid."

"No way!" Annie exclaimed. "This is our first time."

Sarah instantly felt both sadness and glee for the children. Though they had missed out on the wonderful music and fun art displays all these years, at least they were here now.

"It reminds me of a carnival," Timmy said.

"Yeah, it does. It just needs a merry-go-round and a Ferris wheel," Annie said.

"Do you kids like carnivals?"

"Sure do!" Timmy said. "Someday, when I'm really rich, I'm going to go to Disney World and I'm going to ride the roller coaster and all those cool rides till after my bedtime."

"I'd go to Cinderella's castle," Annie said, and started humming "When you Wish Upon a Star."

Sarah looked down at Annie and remembered how beautifully she sang in the children's choir. She watched as Annie closed her eyes and sang the song softly to herself as if she were dreaming about wishes and stars and happy things.

Sarah's resolve to feature Annie as her soloist in the Children's Pageant doubled. She already knew Annie could belt out "America the Beautiful," but Annie also had the ability to pluck Sarah's heartstrings with this touching, hopeful song.

Finally, it was their turn to be served. Sarah had been so immersed in thought she hadn't paid any attention to the line or the fact that Louise Railton herself was standing behind the card table to take their order.

"Louise!" Sarah said delightedly. "You're just the person I want to talk to. Well, one of about a hundred," Sarah chuckled.

"Wonderful. Anytime. Now, what will it be?" Louise asked the children.

Sarah interrupted. "I'm buying. Give them one of everything."

"Wow!" Timmy said. "I want the brownie!"

Sarah looked at Annie. "Would you like a brownie? Or a cookie?"

Annie frowned and shook her head. "That's too much. We shouldn't. Not till we ask Dad first," she warned.

Sarah smiled. "Of course, Annie. We'll ask his permission."

Louise packed the cookies and brownies in a brown paper bag.

"I'll help you carry this stuff back and we'll ask your dad together," Sarah said.

Louise loaded the children and Sarah down with three popcorns, three lemonades, a dozen cookies and brownies. Sarah bought a bag of saltwater taffy for later.

"We're going over to see their father," Sarah said to her friends as they walked past.

"Oh, is that what you're doing?" Maddie asked. She'd been watching the entire encounter closely.

Sarah and the kids continued on around the

path as the musicians readied themselves for the first number. The conductor had just approached the center microphone and was welcoming everyone to the summer concert season.

Sarah followed the children to Luke, who was standing up with his hands shoved in his jeans pockets. "What's all this?" he asked, somber-faced.

Sarah beamed a smile at him, hoping to crash through the granite wall of resistance she had come to expect. "I was helping the kids. They said we had to get your permission for them to have sugar tonight."

"I'd rather they didn't."

"I understand. I thought maybe you all would enjoy the cookies tomorrow. Louise tells me that most of them freeze well. And here, I got you some of her famous saltwater taffy. It's not summer without Louise's taffy."

Luke took the bag of taffy. "Thanks."

He looked at the cups of lemonade, the cookies and popcorn. "Looks like more than a dollar's worth to me."

"Sarah... I mean, Miss Jensen, treated us," Annie gushed.

"I see." Luke shot an incriminating look at Sarah.

"I hope it was okay," Sarah blurted, already feeling Luke's anger growing. Suddenly, she felt the censure the children must feel whenever Luke was like this. She didn't like it one bit, and as far as she was concerned it was unnecessary, if not plain rude.

"Nothing I can do about it now," Luke replied, clamping his mouth shut.

Sarah refused to let him guilt her into feeling bad. She continued smiling at him, determined to win this contest of wills.

Annie and Timmy stood spellbound, watching the exchange.

"I understand this is your first concert," Sarah said in a deliberately friendly tone. "I hope you like it. I come every week."

"I just heard about the concert."

"Really?"

"Yes. Mrs. Beabots told me." Luke glanced over to where Mrs. Beabots sat in her canvas chair, staring at the two of them. "So tell me, Sarah. Do you always pick up children at the park and buy them junk food?"

"It's not junk!" Annie retorted. "It's homemade. Fresh ingredients and all that."

Luke couldn't resist his daughter's naiveté. "I suppose it is," he said. "I guess I'm asking how it is that you picked up my kids."

"I didn't pick them up. I've come to know them pretty well, especially now that they're in the choir."

"I heard about that. But what do you have to do with that?" Luke asked.

"She plays the piano for us, Dad," Timmy said. "She's really good."

Luke's blue eyes were scathing as he looked back at Sarah. "Really?"

"Yes," Sarah answered. Not noticing the storm in his eyes, she rushed on. "I'm sure you know Annie has a very mature voice, and I don't think I'd be going too far out on a limb to say she's quite talented. I've never heard a child's voice quite like Annie's. I was hoping to feature her as a soloist in the choir."

"Soloist?" Luke barked. "She's only eight years old."

"I understand that, Luke, but our oldest child is only ten. The older kids aren't very interested in choir practice. They'd rather play soccer and basketball."

Luke shoved his hands deeper into his pockets. "You can stop with the sales pitch right now, Sarah."

"Sales pitch?"

Luke pursed his lips and whipped his head toward his children. "Kids, I need to talk to Miss Jensen alone. You stay right here. We'll be back."

"Sure, Dad," Annie and Timmy replied in unison, their wide eyes glued on their father.

Luke walked Sarah up the hill to a group of soaring Maples.

"Why don't you tell me what you're up to?" he snapped.

Sarah didn't understand his meaning but she interpreted his tone succinctly. "Why don't you make yourself clear, Luke?"

"Fine." He leaned his face closer to hers, his eyes glaring at her. "I don't like strangers buying things for my kids. I am perfectly capable of buying treats for them myself."

"Stranger? We're in group therapy together, and quite frankly, Mr. Bosworth, we're more intimate with sharing our hearts than most people in committed relationships, if you ask me. I'm not trying to buy your kids, and I'm not trying to insult you. I like your kids. They're great people. Which is more than I can say for their father. I came over here because I believe that your daughter is an amazing talent. I think she could go national. Global, if given half a chance. And I would like to feature her as a soloist in a Children's Pageant I'm putting on as a fundraiser for St. Mark's Church, which desperately needs renovation. But since you haven't been in the church for years, you wouldn't know about that, either, would you?"

Luke's frustration rose like magma in a volcano. He hated that she was making sense, and she'd nailed him on his abstinence from church. The idea that he was refusing to let his daughter's talent be a charitable contribution made him seem as evil as Attila the Hun.

Luke redoubled his attack.

"Annie and Timmy tell me that you're not a music teacher or an art teacher at all. You're just a volunteer. I want to know what credentials you have to be telling my daughter she is exceptional in any way. All you're going to do is build up her hopes for something that will only crush her and break her heart in the end, anyway."

Sarah felt as if she was in the middle of round three of a boxing match, and for once she scripted herself as the scrappy underdog. She wasn't about to let Luke land another punch.

"Okay, so I don't have a B.A. in music, but I'm not deaf, Luke. Annie has something. I would like to help nurture her and encourage her in any way I can. The worst thing a parent can do is stifle a child's creativity and talent. And that's what I see you're doing."

Sarah could tell Luke was barely reining in his anger, and when he spoke it was through clenched teeth. "I'm not deaf, either. I listened to you when you spilled your guts at counseling. I believe you're lonely and that this void you talk about in your life is killing you. I think you intend to use my kids to fill that void. You don't have any kids of your own, so you think mine will do just fine. Well, it's not happening. Got that? You can take your solos and pageants and shove them. Get somebody else's kids. You can't use mine."

Sarah felt as if she'd been slapped across the face. One part of her psyche wanted to analyze his accusations, but the other part wanted to sock him in the jaw. "Since we're being so truthful, then why don't you take a long, hard look in the mirror, Mr. Bosworth. Your kids aren't just growing up, they're growing away from you. They're seeking me out. They're seeking Mary Catherine out, and anybody else who will pay attention to them because they can't turn to their dad. He's spaced out in some dreamland with his memories instead of taking care of them. Annie is sad and unhappy. She looks like she's ready to burst into tears whenever I see her. She keeps her feelings locked inside, and yet she tells me she does everything she can for you, but you never notice. Timmy is totally lost. He has all kinds of dreams and I bet you don't know a single one of them. And a lemonade and a cookie once in a while is not going to kill them!"

Sarah watched Luke's hands as they began to shake so much he clenched them into fists. Determination furrowed a deep rut across his forehead, and his eyes blazed. She'd hit her mark, all right. She could tell he wasn't even listening to her anymore. She doubted he would ever heed her words.

He started to speak and spittle sprayed from his lips. "I have rules in my house and they will abide by them. My kids don't eat sugar at night and they don't need you butting into their lives. We're just fine."

Sarah had heard all she wanted to hear. Luke would continue blasting at her all night long and would never hear her side of the argument, anyway.

"You are such a...dunderhead! I'm done here," she shouted at him as Luke took a breath before his next tirade.

Luke took a step back. "Dunderhead?"

Sarah spun around and tromped down the hill toward her friends. She realized Annie and Timmy were staring at them, cramming popcorn in their mouths faster than they could chew, as if they were watching a scary movie.

"Bye, kids," Sarah said as she marched past them. She put her hand to her cheek and realized it was on fire. She had never been this angry at another human being in her life, and she didn't like it. It burned like battery acid in her stomach. She didn't know how Luke dealt with the seemingly perpetual anger he harbored. Was it like this for him all the time? Was this what he was talking about when he said that his anger was eating at him? That's what it felt like to her.

Sarah hadn't had time to assess the meaning of the encounter with Luke, but suddenly she realized she was empathizing with him. Now she knew his kind of anger. She understood precisely what he was experiencing.

Sarah felt her anger at Luke was justified, however. He'd accused her of things that weren't true, and he'd been insulting to boot. She wondered if she would feel better if she'd actually hauled off and socked him. He had it coming. The worst part was that he was utterly blind to his children's needs. It was a big mistake to turn down her request to let Annie be soloist. Annie deserved a chance to try her wings.

Sarah also realized Luke was mad at the world, fate, God and the universe. He had no one he could punch out. No one to blast with curses and no one who would fight him back.

As Sarah approached her friends and watched their anticipation-filled faces transform to concern and worry, she realized she was taking on much too much of Luke's burden. She'd always had a tendency to reach out to others and try to help when they were in need. Her mother had taught her that. Aunt Emily always did that. She'd never thought that being caring and giving was inappropriate behavior, but in the case of Luke and his children, it clearly was.

Sarah could only surmise that the best cure for the pain in her belly and the apprehension she felt whenever Luke came to mind was to stay as far away from him as possible.

CHAPTER FIFTEEN

SARAH CAUGHT GLIMPSES of the full moon outside her study window. A cloudless, inky-black sky was studded with twinkling stars. Sarah heard her mother's voice, just as it had been when she was a child.

See those stars? Each one is winking at you, hoping you will make a wish on it.

Sarah couldn't stop thinking about little Annie singing about wishes and stars. What was it like for that girl to want something so desperately and not be able to grasp even a wisp of it, all because her father was... *Did I actually call him a dunderhead?*

Sarah plopped her chin in her hand and looked out the window. *Well, he was being one.*

But there were other things Luke said that pinched at the edges of her ego. Was it possible that Luke was right about her? Was she so lonely and so involved in other people's lives that she didn't have the courage to jump-start her own? Was she living vicariously through Luke's kids?

Were they only just another project for her, like the summer festival and the church?

Glancing down at the stack of whimsical booth drawings and the festival layout, she dug deeper into her own motivations. The past two years had been an emotional tempest for Sarah. Breaking up with James was difficult, but not insurmountable. In fact, she'd often admitted to her friends and her mother that she hadn't been all that distraught when she left James. Too often she'd felt she was simply a prop for him—an essential ingredient in his rise to the top of his field. The large financial institutions and corporations he pursued liked their managers and directors to be "settled" and "stable." James had "needed" her, he'd told her. Now Sarah realized just what he'd meant by those words.

Truthfully, Sarah had to admit she missed her architecture work in Indianapolis more than she actually missed James. Perhaps it was because they'd grown apart for so many years that when the final break came, there was no "them" to break. James had been swallowed up by the fast-paced financial world of Chicago. Sarah had started work for Charmaine and was struggling with the fact that her mother's cancer was terminal. Sarah had worried, from week to week, about just how much time they had left.

All those months with her mother had been like sitting on a time bomb with the clock ticking and the countdown continuously being reset. Ann Marie made it through one more weekend. Then one more week. She had a rally. She went into atrial fibrillation and nearly died of cardiac arrest due to a reaction to a new medication. Then she rallied. She went into ventricular fibrillation and they were back in ICU.

Sarah hadn't had time to mourn her breakup with James. Had she stowed her affection for James in some back alley in her heart, only to have it surface now? Was that what Luke represented to her? A substitute for James? Was she really so terrified of a future without her own family that she would want a man who was still so clearly in love with his dead wife and didn't want a thing to do with her or almost anyone else?

Am I really that desperate?

Taking out her charcoals, Sarah worked on her sketches for the festival, trying to quiet her mind, but the effort didn't work. Between sketching a fanciful, 17th century Spanish coffee house booth, which she hoped to convince Scott Abbott to rent for Book Shop and Java Stop, and penciling out the cost of each booth, Sarah had a revelation.

James had always said he needed her. Why

would those words mean more to her than "I love you?"

Truth, when it comes to call is not always a welcome visitor, Sarah realized. And Sarah had always needed to be needed. How could she have missed that about herself?

She had always been the acquiescing girlfriend to James, helping him climb the ladder of success. Even in high school, she'd campaigned for him when he ran for student council president.

She had cared for her mother, but to the detriment of her lucrative and fulfilling career. She had liked the attention she got from people who praised her "sacrifice" for her mother. She had not been rejected. She had been accepted for what she had done.

Luke had seen past her manipulation and had nailed her motivations for what they were. Self-serving.

Sarah didn't like the fact that he saw through her one bit.

She felt like an amoeba in a petri dish, ready for inspection. She squirmed on her work stool, feeling acutely uncomfortable.

This new perspective of herself caused a bit of shock. Sarah's mother was the most giving person she'd ever known, and she couldn't help but wonder if need was what had motivated Ann Marie, as well.

Sarah quickly dismissed the notion. Ann Marie shied away from accolades and thanks for her kind deeds. In fact, she went out of her way to keep her donations to the city and to her neighbors secret. She'd planted flowers and tulip bulbs for elderly neighbors without their knowledge. They would wake up on a Sunday morning and find their hedges clipped and their flower beds lush with annuals. She befriended young Lester MacDougal when he walked into Indian Lake from the Kentucky hills as a runaway from a brutal father. She never asked a thing from Lester in return, though he was always around when Ann Marie was tending the community flower planters downtown. Ann Marie did many things anonymously. That was not a trait of a person who was needy. Her mother's accomplishments brought her joy—just as Sarah felt joy when working with the children's choir, organizing the festival and even building a case for a loan for the money to renovate St. Mark's. Her mother was not a needy person. Ann Marie's motivations had come from a deeply caring and committed heart.

Sarah knew that her mother's shoes were impossible to fill. She was trying with the summer festival, and though she couldn't accomplish what she needed to by remaining anonymous, she didn't think she was being neurotically needy. Sarah only knew that at this juncture, despite the late and nearly sleepless nights she'd spent working on the festival and her renovation ideas for the church, Sarah hadn't been this content in a long time.

Rifling through the pages of her past for hours that night had resulted in one conclusion. Sarah and James were not meant to be. She had no remorse where he was concerned. She truly wished him well, and hoped he found love in his new life.

No, she assured herself. She was not pining for James and she was not using Luke as a substitute. She responded to Luke with emotions she hadn't known she possessed. It was because of her growing attraction to Luke, even though he was angry, that she realized she and James had only been friends. Their relationship was fed by habit. Luke was a man who felt deeply and was compassionate, and when he loved, he loved forever. He was a man of commitment and responsibility—both traits Sarah admired.

Sarah supposed these counseling sessions, their reading materials and even her new creative outlet, were driving her to explore these introspective moments, as painful as they could be. Yet even as she trudged through the muck of her faults, Sarah realized she felt more self-reliant and in control of her life.

The more she thought about it, the more she realized she had not used Annie and Timmy for any ulterior motives of her own. She sincerely liked them both and she wanted the best for them. If there was any motivation for the things she'd said to Luke at Arts in the Park, it was that she wanted to encourage the children. All children needed reassurance and inspiration.

She wasn't being selfish where the children were concerned, and she wasn't pointedly trying to fill a void, though that was happening. Someday, she would meet someone special and she would have the love she wanted for herself. She would have children of her own.

Sarah looked up and saw that a horsetail cloud had swept across the moon and obliterated some of the stars from view. Peeking through the whisper-thin cloud, she saw Venus sparkling as if it was meant for her.

Venus was the planet of love—a big, important star, and just the right one for Sarah's wish.

Sarah stood at the podium in St. Mark's and gave an impassioned plea to the congregation about the church's need for renovations. Surprisingly, she was met with loud applause.

"I have spoken to Father Michael, who has

graciously given his approval. Before speaking to you today, we conducted an emergency meeting of the Church Council, who has also agreed that the renovations are desperately needed."

Sarah had gathered some of her old brass and wood easels from the attic and brought them to the church that morning, setting them up in the vestibule. She placed her poster-size drawings and renderings of her vision for construction changes on a first set of easels. Before the service, she'd already received awe-filled looks and generous compliments on her work. It was a hopeful sign.

On a second set of smaller easels, she placed her drawings for her summer festival concept. The children were more than enthusiastic and she saw that some of the parents expressed delight over her ideas.

"Permission has been granted from both the Church Council and Father Michael to move forward with fund-raising," Sarah continued. "As you saw from my drawings in the vestibule, we are planning a summer festival to be held here at St. Mark's, in the church parking lot and adjacent school yard."

As Sarah described the festival and the practicality of scheduling the carnival immediately after the Fourth of July Parade, she was met with silence.

Surprised and a bit fearful, her only tact was to plow forward in a rush. "I have contacted and hired a small traveling carnival and rented two red-and-white-striped tents. Mary Catherine Cook is now passing out fliers that we'll use to advertise. Please take these to your places of business and post or distribute them to the public.

"I will also need help to draw or even paint the cardboard scenery. Don't worry, it won't be difficult. No more than coloring inside the lines."

Still there was silence.

Sarah swallowed hard and continued. "To do what this church needs us to do, we will all have to work together and work very hard over the next four weeks. I need volunteers for all the committees I've mentioned. I have spent many hours organizing and drawing up a budget for everything we need. Working together is what church membership and fellowship is all about. The time has come for everyone at St. Mark's to pitch in and preserve what our parents and grandparents bequeathed to us in this church that they built over a hundred years ago. This will be the fourth renovation that St. Mark's has undergone, and it won't be the last. In order for our children to come to our church, be married here and bring their children here, this is our mission."

Charmaine Chalmers was the first parishioner to stand up and applaud. Mrs. Beabots would have beaten her to it, but her hips were more than the usual bother to her this morning.

Aunt Emily and Uncle George shot to their feet. Isabelle Hawks and Olivia Melton, Louise Railton and half a dozen of Sarah's friend rose and gave her a resounding applause. Annie and Timmy, who had been dropped off for Sunday services by their father, jumped up and clapped along with the entire children's choir. In fewer than two minutes, every person in the congregation was applauding.

Sarah's face broke into a wide and relieved smile. Mary Catherine rushed over and hugged her.

"Thank you. Thank you all," Sarah said with a lump in her throat. "I'll meet you at the back of the church with sign-up sheets. And thank you all again."

Miss Milse was working in Sarah's kitchen when Sarah returned from church. The fact that Miss Milse had a key to the house so she could come and go when she wanted or needed had never bothered Sarah, but because Sarah had not slept all night, she'd planned to draw the drapes and stay in bed the rest of the afternoon. Sarah had never known Miss Milse to work on a Sunday. Unless there was a very good reason.

"Miss Milse, I'm surprised to see you," Sarah said, petting Beauregard. The dog was vying for all her attention. "You never work on Sundays."

"I come. Your mother's sister…"

"Aunt Emily called you?"

"Ya. She did. You not sleep all night, she say. She say I cook for yew. I make eggs, bratwurst and waffle. Come. Eat."

Miss Milse yanked Beau away from Sarah and walked him over to his enormous doggie bed. Sarah noticed Miss Milse had picked the last of the late-blooming daffodils and put them in a blue vase on the table. Sarah smelled buttery waffles just as the waffle iron beeped.

Miss Milse peeled the waffle from the iron and put it on a plate along with pork link sausages and a huge bratwurst that Sarah knew she'd bought at the butcher shop on Main.

Miss Milse poured the maple syrup that had been heating on the stove into a white china syrup pitcher Sarah's mother had used since she was a little girl.

Sarah's stomach growled. She'd had no idea she was this hungry. She'd been running on adrenaline, caffeine and inspiration all night and morning long. "It smells divine," Sarah said, sitting at the table.

Miss Milse plopped a hunk of butter on the waffle and placed it in front of Sarah. Then she poured a glass of freshly squeezed orange juice.

Sarah crammed her mouth full of waffle. Never had anything tasted this good. She rolled her eyes and thanked Miss Milse, who was scrubbing the pan she had used for the sausages.

Sarah was a good cook, and she'd been taught a great deal by her mother, who was known to have been just about the best cook and baker in Indian Lake, but it would be a tall order to rival Miss Milse's years of experience in the kitchen. "Did Aunt Emily tell you why I stayed up all night?" Sarah asked.

"For the church."

"Yes. That's right. I'm organizing a summer festival. I'll need a lot of help."

Miss Milse crooked her head over her shoulder, and without stopping her scrubbing said, "I come every day. You work. I work here. That is best."

"I'll be having the committee meetings here. There will be a lot of people in and out. They'll need tea and coffee."

"Ya. And strudel."

"Yes. That would be lovely."

"I make for you. I make for the church."

"You mean for the festival?"

"Ya. Aunt Emily asked me to."

"Oh, she did, did she?" Sarah smiled and cut up the sausages. "Well, no one in Indian Lake makes apple strudel like you do."

"And prune. Apricot. Poppyseed. Lemon. Blueberry. Cherry. I make them all. You sell. You make church nice. You make your mother proud," Miss Milse said with a very noticeable clutch in her voice. Sarah felt the anguish Miss Milse had for loving and losing Ann Marie.

CHAPTER SIXTEEN

SARAH SAT IN a white, Adirondack-style rocker next to Aunt Emily, drinking strong coffee laced with heavy cream and two sugar cubes. "This is sinful," Emily said.

"Miss Milse makes it this way every morning. I'll probably have to take up jogging to work it off. But in the meantime, I'm enjoying every sip."

"I don't blame you." Emily laughed. "But you're young. You could probably drink this stuff for about a decade before it shows. I, on the other hand…"

Sarah held up her palm. "Don't even say it. You are not old."

Emily eyed her. "I am and you know it. I try to pretend I'm as young as you and as hardy, and some days I can keep up."

"Aunt Emily. Please. You're up at the crack of dawn every day ready to take on City Hall and push them to make the improvements that keep Indian Lake going. Frankly, I don't see anyone else in town doing that."

"Your mother did. Now it's up to me." She sighed deeply. "All I can say is, thank God we got as much accomplished when she was alive that we did." Emily shared a compassionate look with Sarah. They both missed Ann Marie and that would never, ever change.

"Okay, Sarah. What is it that you want me to do for the summer festival?"

Sarah shook her head. "I didn't invite you for coffee just for that."

Emily narrowed her eyes. "Sarah…"

"I'm really bad at entrapment, aren't I?"

"Terrible. But I've always said that bribery has its points. This coffee is enough of a bribe. We'll skip the apple strudel, please."

"I'll take it over to Mrs. Beabots. She loves Miss Milse's strudel."

Emily leaned down and withdrew her day timer from her overly large yellow purse. "Okay. Let's get on with it. I am assuming you want me to be cochair with you."

Sarah looked down the street at the summer flowers that were shooting up by the day. The zebra-striped African grasses were stretching up and leaning against blue Salvia. Blue French geraniums were already in bloom and the potato vines were leafing out. By the Fourth of July the black-eyed Susans would be vying for center stage. "Mom always said you had a gift for precognition."

"She was being kind. I'm just sharply aware of what you need. And right now, you need me to get my butt in gear and organize the ladies in my women's group."

"I do. You know everybody and they'll do anything for you."

"They won't do *anything,* but they will sew, cook, bake and crochet for me. This is true."

"Good."

"What's your biggest job?"

"I had thought it would be the play. But yesterday I took care of that. I enlisted Debra La Pointe."

"Nationally known playwright, Debra La Pointe? You've got to be kidding," Emily said in a high-pitched, very surprised voice. "She's never done anything in this town that didn't give her a considerable personal kickback. I don't believe it."

Sarah smiled to herself. "Believe it. She's signed on."

"Deb is going to write a play for you? Free of charge? Not possible."

"She's not actually writing a play, but she's going to put together a collage of songs and skits. She explained that that would be easier for the kids."

"And where are you getting the kids?"

"I'm advertising for city-wide auditions. I wanted to use Debra for the casting and she agreed. Actually, we'll both audition the kids. I want the best actors from the high school, and I've already talked to the Drama Club coach, Bill Bartin. He's on board and loves the idea. He said he can cross-advertise his fall production of *Brigadoon*."

"*Brigadoon?* Again?" Aunt Emily moaned.

"I love that musical," Sarah protested.

"You would! So much fantasy and fairy tales." Aunt Emily harrumphed.

"I suppose you'd like *Streetcar Named Desire* or something truly depressing."

"I like tragic love stories. Sturm und Drang and all that. Forget it. Tell me more about Debra and why she's so important to us."

"I do have an ulterior motive." Sarah giggled mischievously. "By using Deb's name, I can get some press from the surrounding towns. I'm shooting for journalists or even a talent scout from Chicago." Sarah crossed her fingers. "I hope. I want this to be bigger than just another stupid bazaar."

"I'm seeing that," Emily said, piercing her niece with a studied look. "You've really put a lot of thought into this. So what's the biggest job?"

"I need to get the booth construction under control. I'll need money for the wood, paint, staples, nails, glue and other supplies. My thought is that if I make the booth fronts on heavy corrugated cardboard they'll be cheap and easy to store for next year."

"Next year?"

"Yeah. I want to do this every year. Even if we do well, we will still have to borrow a good chunk of the restoration budget. To pay back the loan, the summer festival will need to become a yearly fund-raiser."

"I hadn't realized that," Emily replied thoughtfully.

"The way I look at it, if we're successful, the children will want to come again and again. This way, the kids will have a carnival to look forward to every year. And if Debra pulls through for me like I believe she will, this pageant could become a feeder for all those televised talent shows. It's not out of the realm of possibilities for Indian Lake to skyrocket in stature in this state."

Emily watched her niece and realized she was moving past the mind-set of being her mother's caretaker. She was unsure about her career, that was true, but this was a new Sarah. Her niece had a fire in her belly that she hadn't seen before. In fact, she'd never seen Sarah this intense about anything. Perhaps Sarah had been adrift when she first came back to Indian Lake, but something had given her a rudder. Thankfully, she was steering it in the right direction.

"How much do you need to pay for these supplies?" Emily asked bluntly.

Sarah's head jerked up. "Aunt Emily, you couldn't possibly…"

"Who's going to do it? You? You don't even have a job right now, plus I'm not blind. You're paying Miss Milse out of the kindness of your heart. I would bet that you're paying for quite a few of the materials and expenses for this festival already."

Sarah looked down sheepishly. "True."

"That's what I thought. Uncle George and I will give you five thousand dollars to front the festival."

"Oh, that's too generous!"

Emily smiled. "We talked it over last night. If you need more, George will talk to a few of his golf buddies and get them to kick in some money, as well. What you said on Sunday is very true, Sarah. There are times when we are all called upon to help our communities, and this is what we have to do. Some people can donate the sweat from their brow, or their expertise. Others are capable of writing checks. The good thing is that everyone at St. Mark's is behind you. I haven't heard a single negative word since you spoke. We all want you to make this a success."

Sarah threw up her arms and leaned over to hug her aunt. "This means so much to me."

"I know, dearest. I know."

They had just begun discussing how Emily could use her position as head of the Indian Lake Tourism Board to help promote the summer festival when Luke's truck pulled up next door.

Sarah watched as he pulled a battered, red toolbox out of the back of his pickup. He fumbled in the bed of the truck for a tool belt that he slung over his shoulder. He was wearing a navy T-shirt, jeans and his work boots. Sarah noticed that working on Mrs. Beabots's house this past week had tanned his muscular arms, and his nose was sunburned. He took out a baseball cap and plunked it on his head before walking back to the carriage house.

Beau started barking, and in seconds Sarah heard the kitchen door open, followed by Beau racing down the back steps and into the yard. Beau was trained never to leave Sarah's yard, no matter the disturbance. However, the golden retriever went straight to the six-foot-tall hedges that separated her yard from Mrs. Beabots's and barked at Luke as he headed to the carriage house. Once Luke went inside, Beau stopped barking and lumbered over to Sarah.

Aunt Emily's eyes had been glued on Sarah as she watched Luke unload his truck. "Mrs. Beabots is having some work done on her house, I see," Emily commented, a wry smile on her lips.

"Just the carriage house. It was practically falling down." Sarah nodded just as they heard a loud bang.

They got up out of their chairs and walked around to the backyard together. They looked at the carriage house and saw a very tall ladder being placed against the outside and then extended to the second floor. Then they heard the sounds of Luke climbing the metal ladder.

Again, Emily watched her niece with mounting interest. "I was telling George the other day that we need to get our house painted. Do you know anything about him?"

Sarah did not turn back to look at her aunt. "He's got real anger issues, if you ask me. He can really ride that high horse of his!"

Emily's smile broadened with mounting curiosity. "So you do know him?"

"More than I care to mention," Sarah groaned. "I met him at my bereavement group."

"Why is he there?"

"His wife died. Over two years ago."

"And he's still having trouble? That's not good, Sarah."

Sarah turned around to face her aunt. "No, I suppose it isn't. He's got two darling kids, but he doesn't spend enough of himself on them."

"That's really not good," Emily said. "For him or the kids. I hope you are doing all you can to help him."

"Mostly, I want to hit him."

Emily blinked twice. "Excuse me? How well do you know this guy?"

Sarah expelled a heavy breath. "I'm thinking of getting to un-know him."

"What? I'm confused."

"Not as much as I am," Sarah moaned. "I have discovered that when you're in therapy sessions with people, they come to know the real you. It's pretty intimidating. So I know things about Luke that he wouldn't tell anyone else because the counselor is very good and has a way of prying information and feelings out of all of us. The thing is, Luke also knows my insecurities."

"You? Insecure? I don't think so." Emily chuckled. "You're too busy achieving your next goal to have time to be insecure."

"Well, I do have some, Aunt Emily. I've discovered that I've put my own needs and my own life on hold."

"Understandable. You were taking care of your mother. But that doesn't mean you're insecure."

"Luke said I was needy and that I was using his kids to fill the void in my life."

Emily was quiet for a long moment as she surveyed her niece. "Are you doing that?"

Sarah shook her head. "I don't think so. How do you really know? I like his kids. The little girl is heart-stoppingly talented. I can't wait for you to hear her sing. But that may never happen."

"Why not?"

"Because stubborn, self-absorbed Luke won't let her be the soloist in either the children's choir or my pageant."

Emily reached out and put her hand on Sarah's arm. "So you think you're insecure because you're afraid to fight these kids' father for them? You have just as much courage as your mother had. What's the worst thing he can say to you?"

"He already said it."

"Okay, so you've mounted that hurdle. Now, get back in the game and go help those kids. Your mother would."

Thinking about her mother, Sarah's blue eyes filled with tears, but she beat them back as she flung her arms around her aunt's neck. "Oh, Emily. She would, wouldn't she?"

"She never backed down from a fight in her life," Emily said with conviction.

"I shouldn't, either." Sarah looked back at Luke standing on the ladder. "No matter who or what stands in my way."

CHAPTER SEVENTEEN

SARAH'S PHONE RANG incessantly for days after her impassioned plea to the congregation. Though she was thrilled that so many volunteers had come forward, she realized that each time the phone rang, she hoped—and frankly, expected—to get a call from Luke.

It was three in the afternoon when Sarah got a call from Jim Thompkins of the *Chicago Tribune*. He told her he'd received the press release she'd emailed the newspaper. Because he covered theater events in the area, he knew Debra La Pointe's name quite well.

"I know she would be thrilled to meet you," Sarah said, hoping that would be the case. Debra La Pointe was as eccentric as they came, and media coverage that was good for the festival might not be quite so good for Debra. It was a children's pageant, not the kind of Broadway-style play Deb had been awarded for in the past, and critics were always hard to win over.

Sarah realized it was now imperative that Annie sing one or two solos for the pageant.

Taking Aunt Emily's advice, Sarah tossed caution aside and doubled up on her courage. She called Luke at the number the kids had given her when they signed up for the choir.

Her call went to voice mail, and Sarah recognized Annie's voice.

"Hi, Luke," Sarah began her message. "This is Sarah. Jensen. Would you please give me a call back? I wanted to talk to you about Annie singing solo in the Children's Pageant. I just got a call from a journalist at the *Chicago Tribune* who is going to be at the festival. I'm really excited about this opportunity and what it could mean for Annie." Then Sarah left her number at home and her cell. She didn't want to miss his call.

For the next two days, she still didn't hear from Luke. She called his house again and left a second message. Then she waited.

ANNIE WAS SWEEPING up sugar that Timmy had spilled on the kitchen floor when she heard the answering machine pick up the incoming call. She knew her father was in the living room going through the mail and complaining about the bills as usual. She wondered why he didn't answer the phone.

Annie put down the broom and headed toward the living room. Then she heard Sarah's voice on the machine.

Annie stood in the doorway and listened. Her mother had always told her it was rude to eavesdrop on other people's conversations, but since her mother's death, Annie knew that if she didn't eavesdrop and spy on her father, she would never know what was really happening in their house.

Just the sound of Sarah's voice put a smile on Annie's face. Sarah had taken extra time with Annie, teaching her how to improve her voice—even if she'd made her practice very boring, repetitious scales. Sarah had taught her how to project with her stomach—her, diaphragm, actually, and how to get more volume out of her voice, which Annie knew for a fact was already stronger than any of the other kids' in the choir.

What Annie liked best about Sarah was that she treated her like an adult, not like a child. Sarah pushed Annie to do better, and even when Annie didn't feel like it, she pressed harder, just to see if she could do it. Sarah talked about things like doing "her personal best" and "self-satisfaction" with her performances.

In just a short amount of time, Annie's voice had improved. She now had a new understanding of music, from the intent of the lyrics to the emotion of the melody. Most of all, Annie knew that Sarah respected her and her talent. Annie was thrilled that Sarah was her personal coach.

"I've left several messages for you, Luke, but you haven't returned my calls," Sarah continued on the answering machine. "I hope you're getting them. This is the number Annie and Timmy gave us on their choir sign-up sheets. I'd like to talk to you about Annie. The bottom line is that I think she is incredibly talented—as I've told you. Please reconsider allowing her to be a soloist for the Summer Festival Children's Pageant. Thanks, Luke."

Annie listened while Sarah started to leave her home phone number. Then she watched as her father quickly rose from his chair. The bills and papers that had been sitting in his lap flew to the floor as he went to the sofa table and snapped off the recorder. He erased Sarah's message before she finished giving her number. "Shut up," he snarled at the machine.

Long-kindled fury spewed through Annie's veins. "What are you doing?"

Luke glanced at the kitchen door. "How long were you standing there?"

"I heard Sarah's voice. I wanted to know why she called."

"Well, now you know," he said dismissively. He stooped to pick up the bills.

Annie stood firm, her hands clenched into fists at her side. "I want to be in the pageant, Dad."

He stood and gave her a compassionate look. "Annie, there will be years and years ahead of you for you to sing on a stage. Don't rush these years, sweetheart. This kind of thing isn't good for a little girl."

Her face pinched into a tight mass of controlled emotion. Her father was not only going to keep her from singing in the pageant this summer, but for many years to come, too. "But I'm really good *now!*"

Luke took a deep breath. "I know that. But you're just too young."

"I am not too young. I'm nearly nine. Lots of talented kids my age have agents and managers!"

"How do you know that?"

She looked at him as if he were the single most stupid person on earth. "I can read, Dad."

"Don't get smart," he warned.

Annie backed down, but only a trifle. "I have been practicing for a long time."

"You only started in the choir this summer," he argued. "I don't think you're prepared for the kind of audience this festival thing could draw."

Annie ground her jaw, trying to hold back her irritation. "Don't you pay any attention to me at all? Mom used to teach me how to sing along with the songs on her iPod. We sang all kinds of songs. She told me I had a beautiful voice. She wanted me to sing as loud and as often as I could. She told me that."

Annie saw tears fill her father's eyes. He nodded. "I remember now."

"Mom would have wanted me to sing."

"Yes," he agreed, and cast a stern look at his daughter. "But I also know that if Mom were here, she would tell you the same thing I'm telling you. Singing in the children's choir is one thing. Being a soloist is another."

Ire erupted within Annie like a volcano. "No, she wouldn't!" Annie nearly screamed.

"Yes, she would," Luke replied in the low, authoritarian tones that usually ended every disagreement they had.

Annie stood her ground. "Mom told me the same thing that Sarah tells me."

Her dad's eyebrow cranked up, and a suspicious expression filled his face. "And what is that?"

"That I'm special. My singing is special. I should be allowed to use it and share it."

"Oh, ho! With the whole world, I suppose?" He chortled.

"You're making fun of me," Annie gasped. Tears filled her eyes, but she choked them back.

She felt as if she were facing the greatest threat to her future she'd ever known. She didn't care that she was only eight years old. Annie knew this wasn't a life-and-death situation, but at this moment, her father was the only obstacle between her and her dream. Her mother had always told her to do everything in her power to always believe in her dream and to make her own dreams come true.

"Not the whole world, Dad. Just Indian Lake. I don't believe anything you're saying. I think you're trying to stop me because you don't believe in me. Sarah believes in me. Mrs. Cook believes in me. I want to sing in the pageant and I will. I don't care anymore what you say! If you loved me, you would give your permission to Sarah!"

The tears that Annie had held back shot to her eyes and flung themselves down her face. She couldn't stop their fury. She couldn't stop the broiling anger that flamed her cheeks. Her father was the enemy, the dark side of her world. Annie raced out of the room, bounded up the stairs and rushed into her bedroom. She slammed the door and immediately scurried into the tent she'd made out of blankets and chairs. It protected her from all evil, all imagined monsters. Tonight, her father had become a real monster.

GAPING AT THE STAIRCASE, Luke watched Annie disappear into her bedroom. The slamming door echoed horribly and assaulted his ears.

In all the years he had lived in this house, there had never been a door slammed in anger. He and Jenny had never fought—at least not that he could remember.

How was it possible that in fewer than two months, his world had tilted off its axis and deposited him into some foreign, emotion-filled land? These days he barely knew his own kids. He didn't know what they needed or wanted. He wished he could put them in glass cases and keep them just like they were on the day Jenny died. He didn't ask for this kind of struggle and he didn't feel he deserved it, either.

When he was in Iraq, serving his country, he'd learned to compartmentalize his emotions. He put his loneliness and longing for Jenny in a box and shoved it into a sacred vault in his heart. He kept his mind sharp, followed orders and executed the kind of missions that kept him and his men alive. He learned not to think about death. Since Jenny died, he couldn't think of anything else.

Tonight his daughter had looked at him as if she could kill him. She had that look in her eye that he'd seen before, but only in Iraq. He was nothing to her. He was an obstacle. A thing.

An entity, but not a human being. Least of all her father.

Tonight, he'd lost his daughter.

Luke also believed most parents experienced the same thing when their children became defiant. It was a parent's duty to watch out for their kids' well-being and to keep them safe.

Luke believed he was protecting Annie from pain. This was all due to Sarah's meddling— putting visions of stardom in Annie's eyes. Sarah both confounded and frustrated him. He'd never met someone as combative as Sarah was when she was fighting for something she believed in. Admittedly, when Luke wiped his emotions from the tally slate he kept, he had to give Sarah credit for being so caring about Annie that she would go toe to toe with him over it. Sarah didn't appear to have the first fear when it came to taking him on. If her only motivation really was to encourage Annie and her talent, Luke was touched. His concern was that if she froze onstage with a large crowd watching her, she would never get over it. Such an event could scar her for life. She could regress, become a recluse like weirdo Austin McCreary, who was said to sit in his Maple Avenue mansion counting his money and antique cars, seldom communing with a soul in Indian Lake.

He had to make Annie understand that his decision was for her own good.

Luke wiped his face with his palm. *I hated when my dad used to say that to me.*

He climbed the stairs two at a time and went to Annie's door. He knocked gently. "Annie, can I come in? I want to talk to you."

"Go away! And don't ever come back!" she yelled.

"Please?" Luke pleaded through the door.

"You don't love me anymore! Just go away. Leave me alone!"

Luke bowed his head, trying to think of his next move. The door to Timmy's room opened. Timmy stepped out into the hall wearing his dog-print cotton pajamas. "She won't talk to anybody when she gets like that, Dad."

Luke blinked at his son. "I've never seen Annie get this mad."

Timmy shook his head. "She's mad at me at least twice a week."

"Really?" Luke walked over to Timmy and lifted him up so that they were face-to-face. "I'm sorry she's been mean to you."

Timmy smiled wanly. "Mostly, I deserved it."

"How's that, exactly?" Luke asked as he carried Timmy to bed and tucked him in.

"She asks me to do stuff, but I don't do it on purpose. I know that's not the right thing, because then Annie has to do all the work." Timmy looked earnestly at his father. "She works really hard around here, you know," Timmy said, crossing his arms behind his head.

Luke sat on the edge of the bed, pondering all that Timmy was saying. He smoothed the hair from Timmy's forehead. "She works too hard for a little girl, huh? Making our lunches. Cleaning up the kitchen."

"I should help her more. I should be a better brother to her," he confessed solemnly.

Luke fixed the collar on Timmy's pajamas and let his hand rest on his son's chest. He could feel Timmy's heartbeat. His eyes focused on the golden retriever printed on the pajamas. "Just why do you want a dog, Timmy?"

"Because then I'll have somebody to love," Timmy replied with such cutting honesty it made Luke wince.

Luke felt as if the hands on the clock had stopped. His children didn't know he loved them. Annie had turned to her talent to comfort her. Timmy wanted a dog.

Luke knew he hadn't paid enough attention to his children, but he hadn't realized his negligence had caused this rift in all their lives.

He was responsible for this dilemma. No one else. Only he could fix the problem.

"I love you, Timmy," Luke said in an emotion-filled whisper. He kissed Timmy's cheek.

Timmy flung his arms around Luke's neck and hugged him tightly. "I love you, Daddy."

"You get some sleep. Maybe tomorrow Annie won't hate me so much," Luke said, though he didn't believe a single word he was saying.

Luke went to the door and looked back at Timmy. "Good night, pardner."

"Dad?"

"Yeah?"

"The other day Sarah brought her dog to choir practice and she let me pet him and play with him for a really long time. Do you think I can ever get a dog like Beau?"

"Sure. When we can afford it," Luke replied with a smile.

Timmy frowned and rolled over and whispered, "That means never."

CHAPTER EIGHTEEN

ON SATURDAY MORNING, Sarah waited until Luke withdrew all his tools from his truck and went down the drive to the carriage house before she donned her Cubs baseball cap and stuck her feet in her running shoes.

Sarah knew that Luke was avoiding her calls about Annie, which meant her only course of action would be to confront him face-to-face. She'd rehearsed a dozen different scenarios to convince Luke to allow Annie to sing.

Sarah marched out the back door with Beau following her. "Stay, Beau," she ordered, but Beau only looked up at her and continued trailing behind.

Sarah noticed Beau's determined expression was almost a carbon copy of her own.

Luke was wearing a pair of work jeans and a navy T-shirt with the New York Yankees logo emblazoned on the front. He was holding a heavy electric drill attached to a long, orange extension cord.

He glared at her as she flounced toward him.

This wasn't going to go well. Sarah gathered up even more courage. She wasn't about to let Luke win this argument. She felt imbued with self-righteousness. She came to an abrupt stop and Beau nearly slammed into her. He stood on all fours, facing Luke.

"You are purposefully avoiding my calls," Sarah said.

Luke wrapped his hand around the neck, holding it firm in order to change the bit. "I've been busy."

"So have I," Sarah countered. How did he make her so angry before she'd even started?

"Spare me," he grumbled, pressing the trigger again. "I have two jobs. You have none. I have two kids. You have none. I have laundry, grocery shopping, and kids' dental appointments. Why would you think I'm purposefully avoiding you?"

"Because you don't want Annie to be my soloist."

"You're wrong, Sarah. I'm not against it. I'm not for it. I think it's too much pressure for a little kid. All of it. She's already got stars in her eyes, and I think you're playing on that dream of hers to get her all excited about something that's not going to happen. Now you've gone and gotten some hotshot Chicago newspaper critic to come to this festival, which only ramps up the ante, as far as I'm concerned. What if she fails?"

Sarah couldn't believe her ears. "What if she succeeds, Luke? Annie has an extraordinary voice. She has perfect pitch. She started to read music with almost no training. She's like a savant. And if she does succeed, what of it?" Sarah paused, noticing the hard line of his lips. He held his drill like a gun. "Is that what you're really afraid of, Luke? That she would succeed?"

He straightened his shoulders and took a step toward her. Beau growled.

With an almost menacing look in his eyes, Luke said, "When you put it that way, *no!*"

Sarah realized she had probably pushed Luke too far. She didn't want to lose Annie as the soloist, but the fact was, she'd never had her in the first place. She could almost hear Annie's dreams crashing down around her. Sarah's heart went out to the little girl. In many ways, Annie reminded Sarah of herself when she was a little girl. Perhaps that was the reason she had championed Annie so much.

As Sarah looked up at Luke, his blazing blue eyes boring into her, she believed she didn't have anything to lose. "No wonder you have problems with your kids. I'd ditch that dictatorial attitude of yours, and fast."

Sarah had struck too close to the mark.

Luke jabbed his finger into his chest for emphasis. "They're my kids! Not yours. You promise both my kids all kinds of stuff. Auditions, play parts, solos and—" he glanced down at Beau "—dogs! What are you really after, Sarah?"

"I just wanted to help Annie. I know what she wants."

"No, you don't. You don't know anything. You can just forget it! That's final!" Luke barked.

Sarah was so angry she was speechless. She opened her mouth to give it back to him, but not a single word traveled from her brain to her lips.

"Oooh!" She lifted both her arms in the air and swatted the empty space between them, spun on her heel and marched back down the drive to her house.

BEAU STARED UP at Luke, cocked his head to the left then turned and followed his master.

Mrs. Beabots, who had been sitting in her white wicker chair on the front porch listening to the whole confrontation, peered over the porch railing and saw Sarah go in her side door.

Luke walked down the drive and stood just below Mrs. Beabots.

"Are you really going to keep Annie from singing?" she asked.

"Maybe I was being too hard on Sarah," he answered, looking into Mrs. Beabots's clear, blue eyes.

"You do that a lot. Why is that, Luke?"

He scratched the one-day stubble on his cheek. "She's always busting my chops. Maybe I do that because she knows me too well."

Luke realized that, in the midst of his arguments with Sarah, she had become a mirror for him to see himself at this point in his life. There was no question his life was a mess. Jenny had been his anchor and her death had capsized his ship. Sarah had burst through his protective bubble and shocked him awake. He didn't like being mentally and emotionally tasered. It was painful and frightening.

So was living in the past.

The past was gone, just a specter of memories. A wife who couldn't hold him or talk to him. A mother of his children who wasn't involved in their lives today.

He'd been wrong to cast such firm, strong lines around Jenny.

"I guess I should go easier on Sarah, huh?"

Mrs. Beabots smiled and said, "Enlightenment is a large pill to swallow. I can't tell you how many times I've choked on it myself."

LUKE WAITED UNTIL the kids were in bed and sound asleep before he picked up the phone to call Sarah. He double-checked the number on the kids' contact sheet from the choir. He dialed three times before he actually let the call go through.

Eating crow was always a tough chew.

"Hi, Luke," Sarah answered. "I saw it was you on my caller ID."

"Oh. Good. Well, I wanted to tell you that I've thought it over and I'll let Annie be your soloist for the festival."

"Thank you, Luke," Sarah said politely.

A very pregnant pause filled the line.

"I want to apologize for the things I've said to you, Sarah. About you not having kids of your own. That was uncalled for. I've always been protective of Annie and Timmy and since their mom died, I guess I've overdone it," Luke said.

"Accepted," Sarah replied. "Luke, Annie has been practicing diligently, and I know she and Timmy would be overjoyed if you came to hear them rehearse."

"I, uh, don't think so. I'll wait till the festival," Luke said, wondering if he should give her a string of excuses or just tell her the truth. He didn't do churches.

Disappointment rattled through Sarah's voice. "Okay, till then. Thank you, Luke," she said before hanging up.

SARAH PRESSED THE end button on her phone as the truth hit her like a bullet between the eyes.

Luke didn't trust her.

It was as plain as that. He resisted just about anything Sarah offered or did outright because deep down, he still thought she had ulterior motives toward his children.

How conceited can you get? Sarah thought. There was only one "ulterior motive' he could possibly have in mind. *He thinks I'm after him. That has to be it.* Sarah knew her wish to help Annie had nothing to do with Luke. Sarah placed the phone on the charger base. She wondered if Luke had always been suspicious of other people and their motivations. Was it something the Navy taught him, or was it a recent perspective he'd developed after Jenny died? Maybe it was only Sarah he questioned.

Sarah had never been anyone's foe. The idea pricked her insides and made her uneasy.

Her eyes fell on the phone. "Maybe we can never be friends, Luke," she said sadly.

CHAPTER NINETEEN

ON SUNDAY MORNING, Luke pulled up to St. Mark's to pick up the kids. He peered out the windshield at the school where the Sunday school classes were held. He checked his watch. *Where are they?*

He had no sooner asked himself the question when he noticed other parents waiting in their cars, as well. He was the only father in line waiting for their kids.

"Luke?" a woman's voice asked, as she knocked on his window.

"Jen..." Luke had to shake his head to dispel his daydream. "Oh, hi," he said, looking into Mary Catherine Cook's face.

"The kids are all in the church. We were practicing for the choir and lost track of time. We're nearly done, if you want to come in and watch." Mary Catherine didn't hesitate and opened his truck door. "It would mean so much to Annie if you did. Timmy, too."

Luke frowned at his kids' teacher. "I could just wait out here."

"You could. But I wouldn't. I have to tell the other parents," she said, then rushed off to the SUV parked next to him.

Luke gripped the steering wheel so tightly his knuckles went white. He watched as Mary Catherine went from car to car and urged the parents to come into the church.

Mary Catherine turned back toward Luke's truck, but he waved her away. "Some other time," Luke yelled, with a forced smile.

Of all the things he could and did do for his children, this was one thing he could not handle.

He hadn't forgiven God for taking Jenny, and he never would. He and his anger and guilt were stalwart bedfellows. They kept him company day and night.

As Mary Catherine held the door open for the parents, Luke heard someone playing the piano and the children singing. Then he heard Annie's distinctive voice as she belted out "My God is an Awesome God."

"I can't do this," he told himself. "I can't…" He felt his breath burn in his lungs and build up heat.

He looked at the church. What was he thinking? How gutless could he be? This wasn't a war zone. There were no snipers or grenades or bomb vests on the children in this building. They were American kids, just singing a song.

But if he could rescue children from a mosque in Baghdad, he could do this.

. He got out of the truck and walked toward the church he'd so expertly avoided since the day he'd followed Jenny's casket outside. He opened the door and heard Annie's voice again. Chills covered his body. He had to hang on to the door latch to steady himself, his knees were so weak.

He didn't understand what was happening. He swallowed the lump in his throat as he recognized Timmy's voice. Slowly, he took a step inside and let the door close behind him.

Luke entered the nave and found a pew to the far left, behind a pillar. Timmy waved to him and Luke waved back.

Luke saw Timmy elbow Annie, but she was singing at the top of her lungs and merely gave an annoyed frown. She did not look Luke's way.

Luke crossed his right leg over his left, and the movement caused the pew to rock back. *What the heck?* He placed his hand on the back of the pew and gave it a slight shove. It rocked again.

Luke got down on his hands and knees to look at the base. It was just as he suspected. The bolt had come off the bracing. When he got back up, he noticed the end piece of the pew was not securely attached. It needed nailing and glue. Not good.

Luke got up and went around to the pew in front of him. There was no cushion on the seat. He glanced across the aisle and noticed only every other pew had a cushion. Looking around the old church he saw water stains on the walls, in the joists and on the ceiling. He'd noticed that the old wallpaper in the vestibule was peeling. The church was old and such things should be expected, he rationalized. He was surprised to discover that he felt concerned about the old building. He had no use for churches or the Gods they espoused.

"They need to do something about this," he mumbled.

The children ended their song as Mary Catherine came back into the church. Luke heard the door open again, and saw several more parents enter the church and sit toward the back to listen to the children.

"Children. Let's sing something for your parents. One last song. We'll do it just as we practiced yesterday. Then you can all go home."

The kids applauded. Annie immediately raised her arm. "Mrs. Cook?"

"Yes, Annie?"

"Can we sing 'Amazing Grace'?"

"That's an excellent suggestion, Annie."

Annie stepped forward and sang the first

lines of the song with the rest of the children performing backup.

He saw Sarah as she accompanied Annie on the piano. She smiled confidently at Annie, who looked back to her for direction. It was the first time Luke had seen a glowing bond of respect and encouragement between Sarah and his daughter. They were mentor and student, and what they'd created was magnificent.

Luke felt a shiver shoot down his spine and cover his back. If Jenny had appeared to him at the minute, he wouldn't have been surprised, because Annie's child's voice was as sweet and as rousing as the thunder of angels' wings.

The song filled the church, with each of the children performing for their parents, who watched with pride and surprise.

Timmy and all the other children sang their hearts out, but none of them could compare to the rare talent that Annie possessed. Luke felt pride filling his body.

Sarah had been right. Annie wasn't just good, she was astoundingly good.

And it scared the daylights out of him. Both his kids' talents and personalities were coming to life, and he was missing the better part of them. The world where he kept Jenny alive and lived with her still was fantasy.

Annie and Timmy had bounced back with

their lives and had moved on. They were resilient. They were stronger than he was, and that frightened him even more. He didn't know how to fix the problem, or if he even could, but he knew he had to do something.

Or he would lose them forever.

When the song ended, the audience burst into applause. Each of the kids went racing off to their parents.

It wasn't until all the kids had left and Annie and Timmy had gone over to Sarah, who gave them each a big hug, that Sarah pointed to the back pew where Luke was standing. "Look who's here to see you," Sarah said with a pleased smile.

Annie squealed with delight and shot down the aisle. She was first to reach Luke.

"Did you see me, Daddy? Did you?"

"Yes," he said, embracing her. "And I thought you were wonderful."

"Me, too?" Timmy asked as he wrapped his arms around his father's legs.

"I thought you were the best little boy up there," Luke said with an impossibly large lump in his throat.

He looked up and saw Sarah walking toward them slowly. "I like being in the choir," Timmy said proudly.

"You like singing?" Luke asked.

"I like everyone watching me."

Annie looked at Luke. "Do you think Mommy saw us singing? From heaven, I mean."

Unprepared for the question, Luke hesitated. "I'm sure she did, and she was just as proud of you as I am."

SARAH REACHED THE family and stood back tentatively. She didn't want to intrude, but felt a glow of happiness for the kids. She was surprised at the soft lights she saw in Luke's eyes, instead of the hard glint he shot her when he was mad, or the cloudy veil of sadness she saw in them at counseling.

"Hi," he said, just as a tear slid out of the corner of his eye.

"Hi, Luke," she replied, realizing he was surely thinking of his wife. Her heart ached for him. Sarah didn't understand why she was more empathetic toward Luke than the others in her grief counseling, but she was. She couldn't control her reactions toward him no matter how much she tried. One minute she commiserated with him, the next minute she wanted to hit him over that blockhead of his. He was the conundrum of her life, and Sarah had always hated puzzles. She liked things well-ordered, categorized and manageable. He was totally the opposite.

She wondered if he thought she was "using"

this situation by intruding on his family time. Did he analyze her every gesture toward him? And if he did, she wondered if he was able to see past his pain and truly see *her*. She doubted it.

"The kids were great today," she said. "I'm glad you got to hear them. Well, I have to get home and feed Beau. I'll see you later." She moved quickly past them and toward the vestibule.

"Sarah," Luke called.

She turned around and faced him. "Yes?" she answered apprehensively.

"Thanks for all your help with the kids," he said with the most sincere smile she'd ever received from him.

"It was all my pleasure," she replied, looking from Annie to Timmy. She turned to leave. Once outside the church doors she exhaled deeply. She hadn't realized that, for some strange reason, Luke had the ability to make her heart stop beating and her breath to stay captured in her lungs.

Luke was more of a mystery to her every time she saw him.

CHAPTER TWENTY

SARAH FINISHED A very productive meeting with a group of volunteers for the summer festival and realized she would have to head straight to the library if she was going to make the bereavement session. She expertly parallel parked her red Envoy in front of the library and grabbed her portfolio of drawings, always paranoid they would be stolen from her car.

She also carried a bakery box of two dozen assorted cupcakes that Maddie had made for her. Sarah never felt comfortable going to any kind of gathering empty-handed. After an emotional session, Sarah was the first to admit she needed a sugar boost.

Sarah entered the meeting room and was surprised that everyone was present, including Luke, who was dressed in a blue-and-white-striped shirt, black slacks and loafers. She also saw a new, young couple who appeared barely out of their teens. Though they sat next to each other, they had turned their bodies away, almost sitting back-to-back. They looked at everyone and everything except each other.

It didn't take a professional counselor to tell Sarah that these two young people had lost a child.

Luke looked up when Sarah entered the room and she knew he watched her as she placed the cupcakes on the refreshment table. She also noticed the friendly smile on his face as she came to sit down. "Hi, Luke," Sarah said, smoothing her brown silk skirt.

"You look nice," he said.

"Thanks." She smiled in return.

Margot started the session by introducing Carla and Jarod Helm. Carla told the group that they had been married nine months. She'd been five months pregnant when they married. Their baby, a boy, had died at home only a week after his birth. The doctors told them the baby had congenital heart disease. Carla's words were caught between a rain of tears and visible anguish that evoked empathy from the entire group. Her story spilled out of her in a torrent, signaling to everyone that Carla probably hadn't vented her grief to a soul—including her husband—since the baby's death. She was forthcoming with details and described emotions that ran the gamut from desolation to wrath.

It was Luke who asked, seemingly nonchalantly, "What was the baby's name?"

"He has no name," Jarod said. "She wouldn't let me name him."

Carla shook her head. "I just can't."

Luke looked taken aback. "But he was your child, and you couldn't possibly be in any more pain than you already are. There's nothing more precious in life than our children. I know. I have two kids, and they are the world to me. Honestly, I didn't know how much they meant to me until recently. You see, I've been lost for a long time. I'm not sure where I am now. I'm not 'found,' that's for sure. But you're both so young. Your life should be filled with laughter and making happy memories and exploring absolutely everything there is about your life together. That's all that ever really counts. I can't imagine what it would be like to lose a child. I lost my wife, and that's been excruciating. Endless, agonizing torture. The only thing that would be worse for me would be to lose one of my kids." Luke took a deep breath.

Sarah looked at the young couple, their rings so shiny and new, their faces without line or wear. They were fresh at this thing called life. They were babies themselves, really.

Sarah's eyes went from Luke to Margot. Margot put her index finger to her lips as a signal to everyone in the group not to interrupt the exchange between Luke, Carla and Jarod.

Jarod folded his arms protectively across his wide chest. "She doesn't want to give the baby my name. That's what's going on," Jarod said angrily. "That's the whole problem."

"What is?" Luke asked.

"Carla never wanted to marry me in the first place. She only married me because she was pregnant. She didn't want *me*."

This time Margot interrupted. "Is that true, Carla?"

"Yes," Carla said quietly, looking down at her hands. A tear fell from her eye into her lap.

Luke shook his head vehemently. "You're lying, Carla," he charged.

Jarod was nearly out of his chair when Sarah put a hand on his arm to halt him. She remained silent and only shook her head. Jarod backed down.

Margot looked at Luke and he nodded, knowing it was time for the professional to take over. "You really started something here, Luke. Seems like you've been paying attention every week."

Luke remained silent and eased back in his chair.

"Jarod, I think it's very interesting that you came to Carla's defense when you thought Luke was attacking her. I would say that's very telling. And Carla, if you didn't love Jarod, you would have already filed for divorce. The baby is dead. You're under no obligation to stay with him."

"I know. My parents want me to see an attorney."

"But you didn't see one, did you?" Margot prodded.

"No."

"Whose idea was it to come here?" Margot asked, looking from Carla to Jarod.

Carla raised her head and glanced at Luke initially, then at Margot. Sincerity filled her eyes. "It was mine. I thought that if Jarod could see that I really do love him, that I didn't just marry him because of the baby, then maybe we'd have a chance. He's angry because the heart disease is from my side of the family."

Jarod turned to Carla and took her hand. "I'm not angry because of that. I'm angry because you always listen to your parents. They tell you I'm not good enough for you because I don't have a college degree...but I can get one. I can get a good job and take care of you."

Tentatively, Carla reached out her hand to Jarod. "I didn't want to name the baby because if you did leave me, I didn't want him to have your name to always remind me of the time we were together."

Jarod wrapped his arms around Carla and hugged her. Sarah surreptitiously glanced at Luke as he watched the young couple. She saw anguish in his eyes, and longing. Again, she witnessed how much in love Luke still was with Jenny. Maybe this was improvement for Luke. His anger had vanished.

Sarah was awed by the direct but deeply empathetic manner in which Luke had spoken to Carla and Jarod. She'd never seen this side of Luke. Taking charge, being the leader, yet displaying a deep understanding of their pain and sorrow.

Luke was a multifaceted person who constantly surprised and perplexed her. He had many depths and layers, and the more he revealed of himself, the more she wanted to know about him. Sarah discovered that she cared what Luke thought of her, and it bothered her that he might think she had "ulterior motives" where he was concerned.

Sarah also realized suddenly that she did want something from Luke. She wanted him to like her. She wanted very much to be his friend. But as she watched him reach over and touch Carla's hand tenderly, she knew that she wanted Luke to reach out to *her*. She wanted to hold his hand and feel his touch. But she wanted him to give it freely.

There was no question that Luke had helped Carla and Jarod turn a corner in their lives. She hoped that after this night they could come together and see that there were real possibilities for their future.

Wasn't that what everyone in the world wanted?

Hope?

Wasn't that what Sarah wanted now, for herself? A future with Luke in it?

CRICKETS CHIRPED IN the shrubs around the library and the cicadas vied for equal time on the summer night's symphony stage as Sarah walked out with Luke, Alice and Margot. Sarah said good-night to everyone and went to her Envoy.

Suddenly, she realized Luke was right behind her.

She turned around and smiled. "What's up?"

Luke shrugged his broad shoulders. "Just thought I'd make sure you made it to your car okay."

"I'm right here in front. Under the streetlamp for protection."

"You can't be too careful these days," he said.

She nodded. "Mrs. Beabots tells me that all

the time. She'd be happier if I had military pepper spray in my purse."

"Want me to get you some?" he joked. "I have a source."

Sarah laughed. "I was kidding."

"I'm not," he said very seriously.

Sarah hit the remote control on her key ring and opened her car door. "You were fairly terrific in there tonight, Luke. So how is that you came by so much insight all of a sudden?"

"Who said it was sudden?" he asked, walking closer.

"I just meant…"

"I know what you meant. You think I'm a dunderhead."

"Yikes. You remember that?"

"I do. It was a first." He laughed. "Here, let me help you with that," he said, reaching for her father's portfolio.

Protectively, she pulled away. "No, thanks. I've got it."

Luke laughed. "What is it? Government secrets? Actually, I know about them, so I would make sure they stay classified."

Sarah exhaled. "No. It's just my drawings. For the festival. You know, the layout of the booths. Just concept drawings."

"May I see them?" he asked earnestly.

"You want to see my drawings?"

"I do. Maybe I can help."

"Okay," she said, going to the hood of her SUV and opening the portfolio. Under the golden pool of light from the streetlamp, Sarah showed Luke her drawings for the booths, the entrance, the dining tent, the area with the carnival rides and the stage for the pageant in which his daughter would be the featured song-stress.

"What materials are you using for the booth designs and the entrance gates?" Luke asked.

"Wood frame and cardboard."

He shook his head. "Let's use Sheetrock. It will stand up much better, and then you can use the booths from year to year. They won't warp like even heavy corrugated cardboard will."

Sarah gazed at him. "*Let's?* As in, you want to help with the festival?"

"Yeah. I do. And I think you could use a good carpenter to build these little storefronts."

"I do need a carpenter."

"Sarah, when I went into the church the other day to see the kids' choir practice, it was the first time I'd seen the disrepair you're talking about. The pew I was sitting in nearly fell over. That's dangerous. There are a lot of little things I can do to help out with the repairs when the time comes. But first you need to raise…"

"A million dollars plus," she groaned as she

put her drawings away. "I know people in town are talking about me, saying I'm crazy to think I can do this, but I don't care. It's the right thing to do. My mother would have done it. And besides, it gives me something to focus on. Honestly, I've never been so...so..." She peered into his face as she looked for the right word, when Luke finished her sentence for her.

"Consumed?"

"Yes! That's exactly it. The ideas are exploding inside my head even in my sleep. It's wonderful!"

"I envy you," he said in a respect-filled tone.

"Then do what you just offered. Help me. You've said a dozen times that I don't have kids and you do. Help me make this even better from your viewpoint. What would you do to draw every kid from the Midwest to our festival?"

"Seriously?"

"Yes. Hit me with it."

Luke scratched the back of his neck and pointed at the drawing on top of the pile she was sliding into her portfolio. "For starters I'd make the entryway more like Cinderella's castle. I'd make it more fanciful rather than an authentic castle. Use a lot of glitter and sparkle stuff that little girls like to see. Girls get both their fathers and mothers to spend money. So I'd increase the number of booths that sell little-girl jewelry, those headbands with ribbons trailing down their backs. Face painting is a must. Put all the little girl booths up front just as the parents come in the gate, so you catch them right away with your dazzle. Little boys just want to ride the rides and be entertained. I'd sell toy swords, capes and maybe felt Robin Hood hats. Timmy loves to play Lancelot."

Sarah was agog. "These are wonderful ideas, Luke, and I hadn't thought of any of them. I can't thank you enough. I'll revise these drawings tonight and show them to you on Saturday. How would that be?"

"Sure," he said, shoving his hands in his pockets while Sarah scrambled with her purse, phone and portfolio and opened her car door. "Sarah."

She looked back at him and saw a very serious look on Luke's face. She couldn't tell if he was angry or sad. "Yes?"

"I want to apologize about some of the things I've said to you. I was cruel. I haven't been… well, myself for a long time. I'm sorry."

"You're forgiven," she said.

"I think you're doing a great job…with the church and all. Not many people would take up the cause like you are," he said.

Luke's eyes drifted to the distance beyond

where Sarah was standing. She knew he was thinking about Jenny.

"Luke," Sarah said, hoping to pull him back to the present. "I think you were remarkable with Carla and Jarod tonight."

"I hope they come back," he said. "I know in the beginning that I thought all this was a waste. But for someone like me, I really needed it." Luke gave Sarah a straight-on look. "You're one of the resilient ones Margot talks about. Margot says I need some private sessions to deal with my yearning…. Sorry. I should have kept that private." He stopped abruptly. "I have to go. My boss's wife is watching the kids and it's their bedtime. I'll see you later." Luke dashed to his truck and drove off before Sarah was behind her steering wheel.

Sarah watched his taillights disappear down Maple Avenue. She couldn't deny it any longer. Luke was more than just a fascinating person to her.

She had come to care for him—deeply—and she wished to heaven she had not.

He was a dangerous kind of man for her. He was in love with someone else—a nearly angelic ghost. If Sarah wasn't very careful, she would spend the rest of her life riding the precipice of unrequited love.

CHAPTER TWENTY-ONE

ON MONDAY MORNING, Luke stood inside the construction trailer listening to his boss, Jerry, who was on the telephone with the owner of the large retail construction job they had all thought would carry them through the winter.

Luke watched as Jerry's face fell. Then Jerry gave him a thumbs-down and finished the call.

Luke was incredulous. "I don't believe it. This is impossible. How can they do that?"

Jerry shrugged his shoulders. "The City Council voted down the new retail complex. They said it would bring too much commerce, too much traffic, too many people to Indian Lake."

Luke wiped his face to hold back his curses. "Stupid, stupid people. We are not living in 1945."

"I know that." Jerry made a guttural sound that hovered on the edge of pure anger. "But they call the shots."

"What does this mean to us?" Luke asked, feeling fear scorch his guts.

"Cutbacks."

"For everyone?" Luke asked.

"Yes. Even me." Jerry slammed his hand on the stained work counter. "And I just signed my son up for Purdue."

"I'm sorry, Jerry," Luke said.

"All we've got is what's on the books to finish out the summer," Jerry said. "Until I come up with a doozy of a brainstorm. I was really counting on this new center. I'm really sorry, Luke."

"I know you are, Jerry. Something will turn up. For all of us. It just has to."

"I don't know about you," Jerry said, "but I'm going to pray for a miracle."

Luke rubbed his chin uncomfortably. "Praying never got me anywhere."

LUKE PUT HIS children to bed and went downstairs. Passing the entry table, he saw the stack of mail that Annie, the organizer, had placed in a neat stack for him. He picked up the stack and went into the living room, flopping into his favorite recliner. Riffling through the bills, he felt every ounce of his former elation sour. Despite his best efforts to pay Jenny's bills on time, he felt as if he was swimming upstream.

The interest on his credit card bills was swallowing up nearly all the payments he'd made on the principal. Though he'd paid the hospital over seven thousand dollars, he was far from paying off his debt. He needed a new truck desperately. In the fall, the kids' tuition would cost over three thousand dollars. Now that Jerry had delivered the bad news about the retail center, Luke would be forced to cut back on their expenses even more. Though he appreciated the universe sending him the extra job at Mrs. Beabots's, what he really needed to do was win the Powerball.

Fat frigging chance.

Luke rose, went to the kitchen, opened his last can of beer and returned to the living room. He stood in front of Jenny's portrait. "I'm doin' the best I can, babe," he said. "But I don't know where to turn anymore."

He looked around at the pretty house Jenny had painted and decorated with her own hands. It was charming and cozy and filled with love. And it was his sanctuary, where his memories of Jenny lived in every room. For over two years, he'd kept her dream that they would be a family in this house going. He felt he owed it to Jenny. She had worked so hard, and so had he. He told himself that Jenny would have wanted him to keep the house at all costs. But the brutal truth was that selling the house was his only hope for his financial problems.

Luke couldn't believe how much his hand shook when he picked up the telephone receiver and placed the call to Cate Sullivan, a Realtor he knew in town. Luke had put off the inevitable as long as he could. He was finally at the end of his rope.

LUKE MET CATE at her office the next day at noon. They had met once before at a fund-raiser walk-a-thon when Jenny was alive. Even then, Cate had impressed him as being aggressive. She'd been handing out business cards to adults and giving kids balloons adorned with her contact information. Other than her apparent marketing skills, he'd heard around town that she was a fair and professional Realtor.

In order to get the best price for his house, Luke was determined to find an ace. Cate fit the bill.

"I know your house well," Cate said, motioning for Luke to sit down. "Jenny hosted a committee meeting there once, and I told her how impressed I was with her decorating talents."

"I didn't know that," Luke said.

"I'm sorry for your loss, Luke. She was a lovely woman. I think we would have been friends if she had lived. Now," she said, taking out a sheaf of papers, "I've run some comps of the area to give us an overall picture of what we can expect." She placed four sheets of statistics and photographs of neighboring houses in front of him.

Luke was surprised. "Our house looks much better than these," he said.

"I know!" Cate replied enthusiastically. "With the new windows you installed and all the things Jenny did, frankly, your house is far superior to what's out there right now. It's not a big house, but it's a doll's house."

"And is that good?"

"Since you want to sell over the summer before the kids start school, I would say it is absolutely a good thing."

Luke struggled to catch Cate's enthusiasm, but as she continued talking about the specifics of listing the house, the lockbox, the advertising campaign and the contracts he needed to sign, Luke began to feel as if Jenny was sitting next to him, holding his hand, urging him to be strong.

Luke's heart was as heavy as stone. Jenny was slipping away from him once again. Once the house was sold, he could not get it back. He would not be able to walk through the rooms and pretend she was there, sitting in her favorite chair, waiting for him to tell her about his day. There would be no more hauntings from his beautiful wife, or night whispers when she came to him in his sleep. He could no longer imagine her touch.

He was losing his dream.

And it was as if Jenny had died all over again.

Luke signed the papers and Cate promised to put the for-sale sign up on the front lawn the next day, after he'd had the opportunity to tell the children that their lives were about to change. Again.

LUKE STIRRED THE macaroni and cheese while Annie emptied a bag of prewashed, premixed greens into the wooden salad bowl.

"How about Ranch?" Annie asked her brother, dumping too much dressing on the greens.

"I hate salad. Can I have graham crackers, instead?" Timmy asked:

"No," Annie said emphatically, with a tortured look on her face. "Graham crackers are for dessert."

"Uh-uh," Timmy said. "Ice cream is for dessert. We got that sugar-free stuff. Low fat. Right, Dad?"

Luke only nodded. "You guys want hot dogs with or without the buns?"

"Bun," Annie said, looking at him as if any other form of presentation was ludicrous.

"No bun," Timmy said. "I have to have room for ice cream."

"Daaaad," Annie groaned as if she thought Timmy should be reprimanded.

Because Luke dreaded what he was about to say to his children he replied, "We should all save room for ice cream tonight."

Luke put the mac and cheese in a bowl and served the hot dogs. Annie placed a spoonful of salad on Timmy's plate. Timmy groaned and pushed it to the far rim, making sure nothing green touched his pasta.

They sat down and Annie lowered her head. Before Luke could say a word, Annie rattled very quickly, "Thank you, Lord, for this food. Amen."

She looked at her father with a great deal of triumph in her eyes. "Pass the ketchup, please," she said.

They ate silently for several minutes while Luke gathered his courage. Finally, he wiped his mouth with his paper napkin and said, "Kids. I have to talk to you about something."

Annie dropped her fork. "You're taking me out of Sarah's play?" she asked, horrified.

"No." Luke shook his head.

"Whew," Timmy said. "I wouldn't want to be around Annie if you did that!"

Luke took a deep gulp of his ice water. "This is much more serious."

Both children stopped eating and gave him their solemn attention.

"What, Dad?" Annie asked.

"First of all, I want to apologize for my short temper over the past months. I have had a lot on my mind, and none of what I've been feeling has anything to do with what you guys have done. I love you both more than you know. More than I ever thought it was possible to love anybody," Luke said, feeling his buried emotions erupt in his chest. "My worries have been about money."

"We know." Annie nodded.

Luke shook his head. "You don't know all of it. When Mom died, there were a lot of hospital bills. To pay them and pay for your school and, well, everything, I have had to use our credit cards. A lot." He looked at them.

They stared back at him blankly.

He changed his tact. "To pay for everything, I'm going to have to sell our house."

"The whole house?" Timmy asked. "My trains and toys, too?"

"No, sweetheart. Not the things in the house. Just the house."

"When?" Annie asked.

"Tomorrow it goes up for sale. I don't know how long it will take to sell. It could be weeks, even months, before we get a buyer."

Annie's expression was granite, but Luke

could see the wheels in her mind spinning as she calculated out the truth from what he was and was not telling her. "Where will we go?"

"We'll find an apartment. Someplace fun for a while. Once I get us back on track, we'll find a new house. And we'll move again. I don't want you kids to go too long without a backyard to play in…."

"We'll have to leave St. Mark's. Right?" Annie demanded. "If there's no money for a house, then it costs too much for St. Mark's. Right?"

Timmy's face spun from his sister to his father. "No way."

Luke nodded, but only once. "I'm afraid so. But you'll still go there this summer for Vacation Bible School. And you'll still go to Sunday school. You can see your friends then." Luke tried to reason, but his excuses sounded patronizing and lame, even to himself.

Timmy was aghast. "I don't want to go to a strange school! Annie knows everybody at St. Mark's! They all like her and they all like me!"

"I love…my school," Annie said, her voice hopping over the tears in her throat. She'd learned to keep her tears out of her eyes when her mother died, by swallowing them. But for some reason, she couldn't choke them back now. Before she knew it, she couldn't see a thing in the kitchen anymore. Her father's face floated in front of her as if she was swimming under water.

Annie felt as if her insides were on fire. She was no longer going to be living in her home and no longer going to her school where she loved her teachers and her friends.

She looked at her father and he seemed to become smaller, as if he were nothing more than a cartoon. Not real. And all of this was not happening to her.

Annie exploded in a burst of anger. "I hate you!" She jumped up from her chair. "I hate you!"

Luke watched as Annie raced from the kitchen, down the hall and up the stairs. She slammed her bedroom door. It was the second time Annie had sought safe harbor in her tent and not in her father's arms.

This time, Luke had no alternative actions that would give his daughter solace. He had to sell the house. Annie would have to deal with a new school and new peers. In time, she would realize that the only real change was that her circle of friends had grown larger, not smaller.

Timmy sat in his chair, fighting tears. "Will we ever move back here?"

"No, Timmy. I'm afraid we won't. I'm so sorry this has to happen, buddy. I'm hoping we can find something in town and not have to move away. I want you to be able to go to Maple Avenue whenever you want."

Timmy sniffed and blew his nose into his napkin.

"Does it bother you a whole lot to leave the house where your mother lived?" Luke asked.

Timmy shrugged his shoulders. "I was only four when she died, Daddy. I don't remember her much." Timmy scooted his chair back, gathered his Spiderman action figures and left the kitchen.

Luke sat in stunned silence. Timmy's unhappiness had nothing to do with Jenny's death and everything to do with the way in which Luke was treating his son. Timmy was crying over the fact that he would have to change schools. Annie was afraid she wouldn't have new friends. His children's fears were rooted in the present and their uncertain future.

It was only Luke who feared leaving Jenny behind.

CHAPTER TWENTY-TWO

EARLY JULY WAS when Indian Lake was resplendent. Down the avenues, the side streets and the winding roads around the lakes, the houses were festooned with flags, red geraniums and blue ageratum. Lawns were lush velvet green before the blazing Midwestern summer heat turned them to toast in August. Flower beds were weeded and mulched and planted with mounds of begonias, impatiens and marigolds. Daylilies and Asian lilies shot up like fireworks and exploded into orange, yellow, crimson and white blooms.

Every Victorian, Colonial and Italianate stucco home sparkled with clean windows that caught summer sun rays in their beveled corners.

On every streetlamp on every street of the downtown area, American flags flapped in the summer breeze.

The lakes were filled with boaters, skiers and fishermen. Across the town, the Fourth of July church bells pealed out the joy of freedom.

Roaring sonic booms exploded over the Indian Lake County Courthouse at precisely eleven in the morning on the 4th of July. Three Air Force F-16 jets flew in formation over Main Street, where thirty thousand local townsfolk and tourists cheered and waved at the pilots. Originating from Grissom Air Force Base in Peru, Indiana, the pilots would fly over the city three times and tip their wings, exciting the crowds.

Sarah stood in the middle of Main Street and felt the thrill of her own deep love of country erupt in goose bumps all over her body. She waved at the planes, and as they soared out of sight, the air filled with dozens of fire engines' peeling sirens. Sarah and the other townspeople hurried to the sidewalks to watch the beginning of the Fourth of July Parade.

She waited for the first few trucks to pass, then headed down the street toward St. Mark's. Today was the summer festival, and she had an impossible number of finishing touches to complete. But no list of chores and obligations would ever keep her from seeing the flyover.

Sarah was filled with excitement as she entered St. Mark's parking lot, which for today was the St. Mark's Summer Festival grounds. She'd followed Luke's suggestion for the entrance gates, and they now resembled the drawbridge to a fairy-tale castle. She'd draped deep blue fabric along the sides and tied these "curtains" back with twisted gold ropes. From the bar that spanned the wide entrance, she'd strung two hundred silver, glittery stars that Isabelle had made. Inside the gates, the grounds looked like a Renaissance village.

The false-fronted booths she had painted and cut out of Sheetrock, as Luke had suggested, formed a wonderland of little fantasy shops. With butcher paper and gold spray paint, Sarah had created a walkway for people to follow through the "village."

Sarah had promised Scott Abbott that she would place his booth next to that of Isabelle Hawks. Sarah and half the town knew Scott was so smitten with Isabelle that he would do anything to be near her. Since Isabelle was one of Sarah's closest friends, Sarah made certain that Isabelle had no objections. Isabelle's ambition was to see her oil paintings hung in a Chicago art gallery someday. She was hoping the summer festival just might draw a gallery owner or two to her booth.

Scott hooked up his cappuccino machine to a portable generator and stacked a mountain of bags of roasted coffee on a sparkling stainless-steel rack. He'd doubled the size of his booth and then tripled it. Sarah wasn't sure if it was ego that urged Scott to have the largest booth, or if all his staging was to impress Isabelle.

Scott had found three authors who lived in the area and brought them in to sign books at the Book Shop and Java Stop booth. He'd rigged up a very large computer screen that flashed the names of the different authors and the covers of their books. As people came in to buy the books or talk to the authors, Scott would entice them to buy a latte.

Maddie Strong's booth was a confection of pink batiste cotton and tulle all whipped up to look like a giant cupcake with mounds of icing. Lester MacDougal had constructed the plywood cupcake bottom and Maddie had painted the wood. Maddie and her new employee, nineteen-year-old Chloe Knowland, used staples and hot-glue guns to whirl the yards and yards of fabric into what looked like a giant mound of pink buttercream frosting. On four tiered displays that Lester had constructed out of plywood and staircase posts, Maddie placed her best-selling cupcakes. Maddie did not have a generator for her espresso machine, and instead chose to sell coffee from tall, stainless-steel carafes.

Helen Knowland, Chloe's aunt, spearheaded the Quilting Bee booth and even Sarah was amazed at the number of quilts and crib blankets that the very small group of women had produced for the festival.

"Oh, most of us have had some of these quilts around for years," Helen explained. "Just didn't know what to do with them. So we dug everything out. We have table runners, placemats, tablecloths, even some aprons that Mrs. Beabots and I made years ago. They fell out of favor for a long time, but the young girls tell me aprons are back."

"It's true," Sarah said, glancing over Helen's shoulder toward the food tent. "Must be the influence of all those cooking shows on television. Helen, I have to check on something."

Sarah walked quickly toward the food tent.

Aunt Emily and Uncle George were hauling huge electric roasters filled with shredded pork. They were going to sell barbecue pork sandwiches along with potato chips, coleslaw and baked beans.

The dining tent had been set up the night before by a professional company Sarah had hired from South Bend. The canvas was red-and-white-striped with a scalloped edge. Sarah had hung baskets of red geraniums, potato ivy, white daisies and tiny blue dayflowers from the tie-down ropes. From the top of each basket she'd hung red, white and blue bows that she and Maddie had been working on until well after midnight.

"People are coming in already," Sarah told Emily.

"I figured that would happen. We're doing fine here. You'd better make sure there's someone up front to collect the entry fee."

"Father Michael and Lester are on duty," Sarah said. "I'll make sure the rides are ready to go. I told them we wouldn't start until after the parade."

Sarah talked to the rides supervisor and was assured that the carousel, Ferris wheel, children's train and the toddler's boat ride were set up.

Sarah walked past the elephant ear cart, the taffy apple booth, the corn on the cob booth and the hot dog cart, which was usually parked downtown during the parade. This year, the owner believed St. Mark's was a better bet for making money.

There were over a dozen booths set up by local artisans—pottery, blown glass and handmade jewelry were all on display. Three booths were selling women's purses, hats, decorated shoes and boots, women's faux fur vests and men's felt hats.

Thanks to Luke's ideas, Sarah had found a young girls' costume maker whose booth displayed princess dresses, tall cone hats with streaming veils, sequined pinafores, glittery sneakers and hundreds of decorated headbands and flower crowns.

Sarah passed the maple syrup booth and quickly put in an order for three bottles. Next to it was a booth with bright ropes of colored lights set against midnight-blue fabric that sold bread-and-butter pickles, pickled watermelon, spiced peaches and even homemade ketchup.

Liz Crenshaw was advertising her grandfather's wine at a very small booth, though by law she was not allowed to give out samples. She handed out elegant brochures announcing that next year, the Crenshaw Vineyards would be selling their first bottles of Pinot Noir, which had been produced three years previously.

Sarah couldn't help admiring Liz's assertive marketing strategies. When Liz paid for the booth, she told Sarah that the Fourth of July was usually a "dead" time for the vineyard. But with this chance to advertise, Liz was hoping to pick up some new out-of-town customers.

Before the parade was even over, the trickle of people into the church parking lot became a stream. Music blared from the calliope inside the round housing of the carousel. People flocked to the Ferris wheel, and as far as Sarah could see, the carnies wouldn't need worry about filling the rides. The lines were already long.

By one o'clock, the dining tent was filled to capacity and all the cakes and brownies were gone. On the north side of the parking lot, now the festival midway, Father Michael sold raffle tickets for a glittering, silver, late-model Chevrolet Malibu that had been donated by Jess Carpenter, owner of Indian Lake Motors. Though the Chevy was used, the chance to win a free car for only ten dollars a ticket was a big attraction. Sarah saw at least a dozen people gathered around Father Michael shoving ten- and twenty-dollar bills at him.

At Maddie Strong's booth, cupcakes were selling fast. Sarah also heard Maddie taking orders for birthday parties and family reunions. Sarah smiled to herself, knowing that her friends were all benefiting from their generosity to her church. It was the way it was supposed to be, she thought.

"Miss Sarah!" Annie called out the moment Sarah entered the school hall. Annie rushed up to Sarah and nearly threw her arms around her. She stopped just short of knocking Sarah over. "I'm...I'm glad to see you," Annie said, clearly putting the brakes on her emotions.

Sarah looked at Annie askance. She had the impression that Luke had warned his daughter not to be effusive with her. Maybe it was just her imagination. At the same time, Sarah saw a little girl who needed female guidance and appreciation. Annie needed Sarah and just the thought of that desire, innocent and guileless, made Sarah's heart trip.

"Do you like my dress?" Annie asked with so much anticipation in her voice, she was breathless.

"I do," Sarah said with an approving smile.

Annie twirled around and let the full skirt of the apple-green sundress fan out around her. Underneath the skirt, three layers of netting kept the skirt full. The bodice had a square neckline and was sleeveless. There was a thick band of red satin around the neck and a wide, red, satin sash at the waist. Annie's shimmering hair was tied up in a ponytail with another red satin ribbon.

"Is it new?" Sarah asked.

"Oh, no. It's the last dress my mother bought for me. She found it at a garage sale and even though it was too big back then, she said I would grow into it. And I did!"

"Yes, you did."

"She was very smart, wasn't she?" Annie said, holding out the skirt and looking down at the red satin around the hem.

Sarah knew the little girl was remembering her mother and all the love they must have shared.

Sarah put her fingertips under Annie's chin and lifted it.

"She would be so proud of you, Annie. Today is your day, and when you get up there on that stage, you sing your best for your mother. She would want you to do that."

"Yes, Miss Sarah. She always liked to hear me sing."

"Remember, if you get nervous, you just look at me. I'll be standing in the wings and will give you a cue if you need one."

"And my dad will be up front," Annie added. "He's already got a seat."

"Really?" Sarah swallowed hard.

"He said he was going to mark it. But he was also going to help Mr. Abbott for a while, too."

"That's good," Sarah assured Annie. "Now, where is Timmy? I want to go over his lines."

"In the bathroom," Annie said and then motioned for Sarah to lean down very close. Annie cupped her hand around her mouth and whispered in Sarah's ear. "He's really nervous, but he doesn't want you to know."

"Poor thing. Does he know his lines?"

"Oh, yes. Backward and forward. And his song is great. It's just that his hat keeps falling off and he doesn't want to look like a dork."

"I'd better see to this."

Sarah and Annie walked toward the men's restroom. There were kids everywhere, going in and out of the restrooms and classrooms, running up the halls and down the stairs. They yelled for their parents and they squealed with the kind of nervous anticipation that children always held for events they just knew they would never forget.

Sarah caught their storm of preshow jitters. Suddenly, it hit her that her name was on the program alongside Debra La Pointe. People would expect a great deal from her. Despite the fact that this was just a children's pageant, she also knew audiences had a tendency to compare even the most amateur performances against those of seasoned and very talented professionals. Sarah swallowed her anxiety and felt her stomach roil. For the first time in her life, maybe she really had taken a too-large bite of this apple.

Sarah had also arranged for a small contingent of the Indian Lake High School Band to play for the pageant. As the folding chairs filled up with parents, friends and tourists, the band played the George M. Cohan Fourth of July favorite, "Yankee Doodle Dandy."

Before the song was finished, every chair had been filled. Sarah noticed that more people came and stood in long lines; some sat on the ground. Mothers held babies and fathers hoisted toddlers onto their shoulders to see over the crowd.

Chills played tag up and down Sarah's back as she stood behind the roll-drop canvas curtain she and Mary Catherine had painted with Valley Forge scenes, an impressionistic version of John Trumbull's famous painting of *The Signing of the Declaration of Independence,* and Sarah's own depiction of Paul Revere's famous ride.

The Children's Choir assembled in the center of the stage and began the program with "The Star-Spangled Banner." When the children finished, they left the stage with proper decorum following Sarah's instruction.

Sarah and Mary Catherine rushed onto the stage and placed a cardboard picket fence, pots of fake flowers and a large cardboard Boston Colonial housefront. Mary Catherine placed a white wooden rocking chair next to the flowerpots.

Next onstage were two children inside a much-rented horse costume. Their entrance, with much neighing and clomping of hooves, elicited uproarious laughter from the audience.

Timmy, dressed in period clothing and his tricorn hat, walked confidently to the center of the stage. He was joined by two other boys in similar costume.

The gist of the story was that Timmy's parents were Revolutionary sympathizers and were great friends of Thomas Jefferson and Benjamin Franklin. The other two boys were from Tory families and had been instructed by their parents not to associate with Timmy's character ever again.

The three boys had been friends all their lives and they were coming to grips with the fact that their parents' politics were not merely points of view, but had created pain and loss. Their world was changing and they were helpless to do anything about it.

Timmy's character, who was the youngest, did not understand why the other boys would be loyal to a king they had never met and who would not come to America to lead them. Timmy's heartbreak was evident when the boys told him that he would not be allowed into their house again.

Timmy stood forlorn and sad-faced, outside the cardboard Colonial house and sang a new, short song written by Debra about lost friends. The pathos in Timmy's little boy's voice was wrenching.

Through Timmy's character, the story revealed the plight of every child who had ever been placed in a situation where they became the victims of their parents' political decisions. It was always the children who lived with the results...good or bad.

Just as she'd been in rehearsal, Sarah was deeply moved by Timmy's obvious passion for his role. He'd always been good, but today he left her breathless. She had witnessed Annie's rare talent, but this was a surprise. A very happy surprise, she thought. When Timmy finished the last notes and walked off the stage, a hush fell over the audience.

Luke, Lester and Mrs. Beabots applauded loudly. Suddenly, dozens of people rose from their chairs and gave Timmy a standing ovation. Louise Railton put her fingers in her mouth and whistled loud enough to break eardrums. Father Michael clapped so hard his arthritic hands would need a warming balm and bandages, but he didn't care.

In the wings, Sarah grabbed Timmy by the shoulders, "Go back out there and take a bow."

"Are you sure?"

"Yes!"

Timmy ran onto the stage and with his very practiced flourish, gave the audience a deep bow. The spectators continued their shouts and applause until Timmy left the stage again.

The rest of the play never sagged. The children had rehearsed their parts perfectly. Not one child forgot his or her lines. The only mishap was when the horse knocked over the picket fence. Sarah felt a flush of pride warm her entire body as she watched child after child execute their roles. There were tears in her eyes when Annie stood beside her and waited for her cue from the band.

Annie took center stage dressed in a white, floor-length dress that had a navy blue tulle overskirt on which Sarah had tacked silver stars and red sequins. In her hair was a crown of white daisies with red, white and blue ribbons falling down her back.

Annie belted out "God Bless America" with a voice as strong as Kate Smith ever hoped to have. Hearing a full-fledged adult voice emanate from a little eight-year-old girl once again prodded the audience out of their chairs and onto their feet with shouts of "Bravo!" and "More!"

Sarah grabbed Mary Catherine and hugged her. "They were wonderful!"

"I saw people texting halfway through the show," Sarah continued. "It's my bet that the reporter over there for the Indian Lake newspaper is going to give the children a glowing review."

The kids congratulated each other, slapping one another on the back. Sarah and Mary Catherine embraced again. "I'm glad it's over, I'll tell you," Mary Catherine said.

"So am I," Sarah agreed.

The parents rushed toward the stage and called out to their respective children. The band continued playing the theme of the play, which was the song Timmy had sung.

Timmy looked up at Sarah just as Luke walked up. "Miss Sarah, do you think I'll be famous now?"

Sarah caught Luke's smiling eyes as he came to stand next to her. "Probably not," she said to Timmy. "It might take a bit more effort on your part."

"Aw, shucks. I was hopin'…"

"Timmy, even if you were famous, it wouldn't last long," Luke said. "You would have to create a performance that was even greater than what you did here today."

Timmy's mouth gaped open. "What? I have to do it again?"

"Uh-huh."

Timmy looked down at his tricorn hat. "Those guys had to fight really hard to make a democracy for us. So I guess if I have to work hard, it's okay."

Luke's shoulders hitched with an intake of breath. "I've never been as proud of you as I am at this minute, Timmy." Luke knelt down and gathered his son into his arms and hugged him close.

Just then, a middle-aged man wearing black jeans and a black golf shirt, carrying a camera case and an iPad walked up to Annie. "Congratulations, young lady," he said with a toothy grin. "It's been a long time since I've heard anyone as good as you are."

Luke stood up instantly and approached the man. "Can I help you?"

The man gave Luke a once-over and smiled even more broadly—if that was possible. "You must be Mr. Bosworth. I'm Alan Freeman. I'm from the *Chicago Tribune.* I got called out to this gig at the last minute, but I have to tell you, I'm glad I took the assignment. Your daughter is amazing."

Wariness filled Luke's eyes as he took Alan's hand. "I think so."

Alan looked over at Annie, who was standing next to Sarah, watching the exchange. "I came out to Indian Lake thinking I was just going to cover the parade and then do a little piece on this fund-raiser you folks have going on here, but I have to say, Annie knocked my socks off. I videoed her performance. She could really have an awesome career ahead of her. How long has she been studying?"

"She hasn't," Luke replied tersely.

"You mean that's—" Alan looked over at Annie, who was now holding Sarah's hand "—that's natural talent. No formal training?"

"No training," Luke said.

Alan took out his business card and handed it to Luke. "I'm going to write a spectacular article about Annie. Trust me. But there's something else I should mention. Every December there's a huge talent show in Chicago. It's underwritten by several universities in town, the papers and dozens of businesses. I'm going to nominate Annie as my choice for the show. All the prizes are scholarships—formal training at ballet, music and acting schools. It's a wonderful opportunity for the kids," Alan said excitedly.

Luke handed Alan his card back. "I didn't give you permission to write about my daughter. I don't want her mentioned in your article. And no nominations for talent shows. Understand?"

"Actually, no. But that's your prerogative." Alan glanced back at Annie, shrugged and said, "Sorry, kid."

Alan walked away.

Annie glared at her father. "You won't let him write about me?"

"You're too young for all this nonsense."

"It's not nonsense. It's what I want. I want to

sing. I want to be onstage making people smile when they hear me sing my songs!"

Luke moved toward Annie, but she dropped Sarah's hand and stepped back several feet. "You don't want me to do anything because Mom isn't here. It isn't fair!"

Annie ran away from them and into the school. Timmy followed after her, yelling her name.

Luke raked his hair with his fingers. "She's too young for a life like that. And the entertainment world eats those kids up and spits them out when it's done with them. That's not the life I want for my daughter."

Sarah could almost see the pain in Luke's heart. "I understand, Luke. I do. Right now she has a dozen emotions going on—from the exhilaration of the audience applause to the fact that a major newspaper wanted to write about her performance."

"And I just invalidated all that for her by sending the journalist away."

"Pretty much. But you have a real point, Luke. Annie is too sweet and so perfect just the way she is to be swallowed up by that kind of big business. And that's what it is. They're capable of eating full-grown adults, body and soul, if they see even a fleck of talent. Annie's talent is limitless. Honestly, a few years of boring, rigorous, disciplined training might take the bloom off the rose for her."

"I hadn't thought of that," he said, and then looked off to the school building where Annie had disappeared.

"Listen, I have to help Aunt Emily and Uncle George in the food tent."

"I'll catch up with you later," he said and walked toward the school.

Sarah hoped Luke and Annie would find a compromise that would be the best for them both.

Sarah continued her rounds of all the booths as the sun set and the lights on the Ferris wheel grew brighter against the darkening sky. The dinner tent was sold out of food before seven-thirty, and yet there were still crowds of people coming by. Word had traveled around town and the lake area that a good time was being had over at St. Mark's. Luke helped Uncle George break down the food tent. Timmy helped Aunt Emily clean up the garbage. Annie made herself scarce, spending a great deal of her time in Maddie Strong's booth. Both Sarah and Luke kept the kids in plain sight while they went about their duties and chores.

THE FESTIVAL WAS officially over at ten o'clock, and the Ferris wheel was going to make one last pass before closing down. Luke saw Sarah at Isabelle Hawks's art booth and went over to her.

"I have it on good authority that if we hustle, we can ride this last go around on the Ferris wheel free of charge."

"I promised Isabelle I'd help put her paintings away," Sarah said, glancing at her friend with soft pleading in her eyes.

Isabelle winked at Luke. "I've got this, Sarah. You deserve some fun after all your hard work."

Luke held out his hand to Sarah. "I want to thank you for what you did for Annie."

She looked at his hand, then up at Luke. "You're welcome. I think. Is she speaking to you yet?"

"Not yet," Luke replied, reaching his fingers toward hers.

She placed her hand inside his palm. She didn't know what she expected, but she didn't expect to experience an odd zing of excitement, nearly a thrill, when they touched. He had big, rough, strong hands that felt as if they could build a skyscraper or move a mountain. They were hands that bathed his children and tucked them in at night. Hands that drew fanciful art designs for her festival and hands that now beckoned her to join him for a simple ride on a Ferris wheel.

Holding Luke's hand bombarded Sarah with

a myriad of emotions. For so long, she had not dared to consider him even a friend. He was too volatile. He was too closed off, too within himself. But that had changed the night of the session with Carla and Jarod. Sarah was drawn to Luke despite the danger and the risk. She knew he'd loved his wife so deeply that not even death had diminished his devotion. But could he love again? Could he love her?

There was no question that Sarah had fallen in love with his children.

Tonight, she felt another shift in her relationship with Luke. There was a sense of calm about him that hadn't existed before. But Sarah was mystified as to whether he was the one changing or if it was her. Had her new awareness of her feelings for him caused this transformation?

Touching him and walking with him, matching her gait to his, oddly, she felt safe. She suddenly felt protected by this man she'd slowly come to know in his pain and anger and through observing his struggle to demonstrate his deep love for his children.

Luke had been generous with his time and skills in helping with the festival. She respected and admired him for that.

She wasn't certain what was happening. Was she falling in love with Luke? In the past few days, working side by side with him, joking with him as they put up the entrance gates, she'd realized that when she rose in the morning, the first thoughts in her head were those about Luke. She knew she'd be seeing him every evening at the school to work on the booths. For weeks she'd stolen a thousand glimpses of him as he worked on Mrs. Beabots's carriage house. This past Wednesday, just before their bereavement session, she'd changed her clothes twice and completely reapplied her makeup, taking extra pains that she normally never would.

Perhaps the answer was right in front of her and she had been so preoccupied with the festival and all her own concerns that she hadn't realized her growing affection toward Luke was very real.

Sarah nearly felt like Cinderella being asked to step inside a magical pumpkin.

"Can't beat a free ride," she said, hoping to divert her thoughts toward what was real, not make-believe.

Luke ushered Sarah onto the ramp and held the carriage steady as she sat. The operator snapped the bar shut, hit the lever and they whisked up to the top of the wheel.

"I love Ferris wheels," Sarah said with excitement trilling through her.

"Yeah? How come?"

"They move you just a bit off the earth and give a new perspective of the world. It's not like when you're in an airplane and not a part of the earth anymore. A Ferris wheel is just a bit off-kilter. A bit abnormal."

"Like a new dimension," he interrupted, looking around. "I see the kids down there with Maddie." He waved to Timmy, who was waving at him. Annie was still mad, and she purposefully didn't look up, even though Maddie was pointing at him.

In the distance, the annual city fireworks display was being shot off at the fairgrounds. Explosions of sparkling colors filled the sky and rained showers of glitter and dying embers down to earth.

Sarah watched Luke's face and saw the reflection of the explosions in his eyes.

"Jenny loved fireworks," he said. "She couldn't wait till the next holiday or someone's birthday so she could have an excuse to light sparklers or fountains. She loved anything that glittered in the sky. Our backyard on New Year's Eve was a pyrotechnics dream. For Christmas every year I'd have to give her a box of fireworks or it wasn't Christmas. I actually proposed to her on the Fourth of July just so she would have all the fireworks she'd ever want."

Sarah's eyes went to the fireworks and she smiled softly. "I would have loved her."

"I still do," he said, finally looking over at Sarah.

"You should, Luke. You should love her all your life. There's nothing wrong with that."

This time when Luke looked at Sarah, she felt as if he was seeing her for the first time and not looking through her or beyond her to some other place and time.

"Thank you for saying that, Sarah. That means a lot to me."

"I think that's what I've discovered in our sessions. The love we have shouldn't die because we've lost our loved ones. I think it stays the same, it's just that we have to get used to the fact that we simply can't hear them when they tell us that they love us back."

Luke's eyes were filled with wonder and appreciation. They blazed with earnest trust and with an openness she'd only glimpsed before when he spoke about his children. She almost ventured to believe that this was the look of love, but of course, it was Jenny he was thinking about.

"I've never heard it expressed that way, Sarah, but it's…well…lovely."

"It's how I feel," she replied sincerely as the

Ferris wheel finished its round and brought them back to earth.

They got out of the carriage and Sarah thanked Luke for the ride. "Thank you for all your help with the festival, Luke. I couldn't have done it without you. I truly appreciate it."

Luke shook her hand. "You're welcome," he said and paused, still holding her hand.

Just then, Aunt Emily walked up with Annie and Timmy. "Look who I found," she said.

Timmy yawned. Annie just stared at her father.

Sarah hugged both the kids. "You guys were absolutely terrific today. No one is going to forget your performances for a long time. You worked really hard and it paid off. Thanks."

"You're welcome, Miss Sarah," they said in unison.

Sarah looked back at Luke. "I think they're ready for bed."

"Yeah," he said. "Well, I'll see you." He hoisted Timmy into his strong arms and took Annie's hand. "Let's go, kids."

BY THE TIME Luke reached his truck two blocks away, Timmy was asleep. Luke put him in his car seat and then turned to Annie.

"Annie. I'm sorry," he said, crouching down

beside her so that they were eye to eye. "I hate it when you're mad at me and I'm mad at you."

"I hate it, too," she said softly.

"Maybe I was wrong about all this. Maybe Sarah was right to encourage you the way she did. It's all pretty scary to me."

"Why?"

"Because…because you are…" He rubbed her arms as he spoke. "Because I don't want to lose you, Annie." Luke grabbed his daughter and pulled her close to his chest. "You're so grown up all of a sudden and I don't know how to handle it." His voice quaked with emotion.

"You won't lose me. I just want to sing, is all," she said.

He held her at arm's length. "I've decided to call the *Tribune* journalist and let him write about you in his article."

"Do you mean it?" Annie asked with a growing smile.

"Yes. I mean it."

"And the talent show?"

"You should have your chance, just like he said. But you have to promise me that you won't be disappointed and brokenhearted if you don't win."

Annie chuckled. "Is that why you're so scared? That I won't win?"

"Well, yes. I don't want you to get hurt."

"Dad. I never thought I would win. I just want to try. That's all. What's the use of having talent if I don't use it?"

Shaking his head, Luke said, "You remind me so much of your mother. That's just what Jenny would say."

CHAPTER TWENTY-THREE

LUKE CAME HOME from work, got out of his truck and felt his guts wrench. Standing in his front yard was Cate Sullivan, his Realtor, with a young couple who was smiling happily as they looked up at his house. The man looked to be about Luke's age and was tall, with very black, straight hair. The woman was pretty, probably in her late twenties, he guessed. She was wearing a bright fuschia sundress.

She was also very pregnant.

"Oh, here's the owner now," Cate said to the woman. "Luke! Come over and meet Mitch and Claudia Green."

Luke swallowed hard and tried to find a smile. "Hi," he said, extending his hand to Mitch.

"We love your house," Claudia gushed. "It's absolutely darling. We've been looking for months," she said, touching her huge belly tenderly. "As you could probably guess."

"Yes," Luke said. He remembered all too clearly when Jenny was pregnant and how they'd looked forward to their new home and their new baby. A pang ripped across his heart, creating a new trench next to the old trenches he'd been struggling to heal for two years.

"There's nothing like it on the market," Mitch said. "I suppose I shouldn't say that since we haven't formally put in our offer."

"It's okay. My wife decorated the house."

"She's really talented," Claudia said and then quickly stopped herself. "I'm sorry. Cate told us about your wife. I'm so sorry."

"Thanks," Luke said, turning away from Claudia's happy glow. He looked up at the roof and then down to the front porch. "So when do you want to move?"

"As soon as possible," Mitch said. "Cate told us you were flexible."

"I haven't even looked for a place for me and the kids yet," Luke replied. "I guess that would be the first thing. Then we can talk about a possession date."

"Sure," Mitch said uncomfortably.

"Luke…" Cate took his forearm and led him away from Claudia and Mitch. "We're going back to the office to draw up the offer. They'll pay your asking price."

"You're kidding."

"No. But they want to move in a month."

"A month," he repeated.

Cate was silent.

"I just didn't think it would happen so soon, I guess."

"I know. But I told you. Jenny did a knockout job. And Mitch and Claudia have been looking for over a year. They don't have time to dicker with prices or demands. That's why they will pay your asking price."

Luke pierced Cate with a steady gaze. "Write it up. Now we need to find an apartment for me and the kids as soon as possible. Something nice. They deserve the best."

Cate nodded. "So do you, Luke. So do you."

THE SCRAMBLE FOR a new home for Annie and Timmy was exhausting, frustrating and impossible, Luke thought as he flipped through colored spec sheets of apartments. There were only two apartment complexes in all of Indian Lake, and they were filled.

Most apartments in town were the upper or lower halves of hundred-year-old homes, which actually appealed more to Luke than a little box in an apartment building or complex. Luke and Jenny had been lucky in that they'd always owned their own house.

"That was then. This is now," he grumbled to himself as he picked up his cell phone and called Cate. He made arrangements for viewings of three apartments in older homes and one three-bedroom house on the south side of town for the next evening.

It was still daylight when Luke drove up to the rental house with Annie and Timmy. Cate Sullivan was already at the property and had unlocked the front door.

"I'm not going in there," Timmy said, looking at the small ranch house that had needed a new coat of paint for about the past twenty years. The front window was boarded up with plywood and the yard had not been mowed for weeks.

"I don't blame you," Luke said. "You kids stay here." He walked up to Cate.

Before he could say a word, she shook her head. "This is a disaster. Don't go in. I'm going to report this to the realty board."

"Doesn't the landlord have any more pride than to let a house deteriorate like this?"

"It's owned by a bank. They don't give a flip."

Luke nodded and put his hands in his back pockets. "It didn't look like this in the photographs."

Cate cocked her head over her shoulder. "There have been squatters here."

"No way."

"Let's go. I'll take care of this." She turned and locked the lock box.

Luke and the kids followed Cate around from one apartment to another. After walking on warped floorboards, seeing bathrooms with no showers, bedrooms fashioned out of former closets and interiors that clearly needed a great deal of Luke's skills to repair, Luke had had enough.

He turned to Cate. "These landlords should be paying me to rent from them."

"I'll keep looking," Cate said.

"Look fast," he replied.

ANNIE AND TIMMY sat inside the tent Annie had put up in her bedroom. Timmy hugged his teddy bear and heaved a very loud sigh. Then he started to cry.

Annie didn't stop him. "It's okay to cry in here because he can't see us."

"I don't want to live in any of those terrible places," Timmy said.

"Dad will find us a nice house."

"Not as nice as Mom's house," Timmy bellowed as his little chest heaved sob after sob.

"No. It won't be as nice as this house. Nothing will ever be this…wonderful." Annie looked out of the little flap door and into her pretty bedroom with its white eyelet curtains and pink walls. "Maybe we should ask Mom to help us find our new home."

"How? She's dead."

"I know that," Annie blurted. "Dead people always help alive people."

"Who said?"

"God did. I think. Anyway, I never felt like Mom was really gone from us. Sometimes, I see her in my dreams."

"Really?" Timmy asked, smearing his tears across his cheeks with the palm of his hand.

"Uh-huh."

"What does she say?"

Annie put her forefinger to her lip to help her remember exactly what it was that her mother had told her. "Not much. But she's there. She told me once that she loved me and you and Dad."

"Well," Timmy replied, "I never saw her."

"Maybe you will someday."

"Not if we move away from here!" Timmy's face crumbled and he started crying all over again. "Ghosts always stay in the houses they lived in. That's what they say in the movies and on those TV shows."

"You're not supposed to watch that stuff."

"I sneaked."

"Oh," Annie said and put her hand on Timmy's little shoulder. "I think the movies are wrong. I think Mom will go with us wherever we are. Besides, we have to take care of Dad.

He needs us a lot. I think he's really sad we
have to move."

"Yeah," Timmy hiccupped. "I think so, too."

"So we have to be brave."

"I don't want to be brave. I want to live in a
nice house and I don't want to change schools."

Annie bit her lower lip and nodded. "Me, too."
Then she put her arms around her little brother
and let him cry into her shoulder. "We're going
to be okay."

"How can you be sure?" Timmy asked.

"Because I asked Mom to help us."

AS USUAL, MRS. BEABOTS had heard the gossip about Luke when she'd gone to Cupcakes
and Coffee Café. Maddie Strong had gotten the
word directly from Cate Sullivan.

"Luke sold his house," Mrs. Beabots told
Sarah as they sat on Sarah's front porch.

"Already? He just listed it."

"Apparently, the couple who is buying the
house is about to have a baby and they needed
to move quickly."

"I wonder if Luke has found a new place yet."

Mrs. Beabots tore off a small piece of the
banana-nut muffin Sarah had baked that morning and put it in her mouth. "Mmm. English
walnuts?"

"And some pecans. I always love pecans." Sarah smiled. "I should call Cate."

"No need. She told Maddie she's having a devil of a time finding something suitable."

Sarah's eyes widened. "This is just awful. The children must be scared silly. Having to change schools."

"Tsk. Tsk," Mrs. Beabots clucked her tongue. "I'm surprised at you, Sarah."

"For what?"

"That you haven't thought of a way to ensure the children's education at St. Mark's for the fall," Mrs. Beabots's eyes gleamed with bright mischief.

Sarah knew exactly what Mrs. Beabots intended. She was going to pay for the children's education. She could make a "donation" as she would call it, for tax purposes, no doubt. Then Father Michael could tell Luke that Annie and Timmy had received scholarships. It was done all the time. In fact, in Mrs. Beabots's day, it was commonplace for an exceptional and talented child to be given an anonymous scholarship. As Ann Marie would say, *that was how it was supposed to be.* Those who didn't understand, and never would, called it "luck."

Sarah jumped up and threw her arms around her friend. "Oh, Mrs. Beabots you are such a love! How wonderful! The children will be so happy."

Mrs. Beabots smiled, but just as quickly, it evaporated into a thin line of concern.

"It's not going to work."

"Why not," Sarah asked.

"If I tell Luke, he'll know it was my money and reject the whole thing. If Father Michael or someone from the church calls him, Luke might turn them down because of his anger against God." Mrs. Beabots snapped her fingers. "You need to be the one to tell him. Coming from you, he might go for it."

"Or not." Sarah frowned.

"I think you can pull it off," Mrs. Beabots said confidently. "Please?"

"Oh, all right. But I don't have a good feeling about it."

"I'll call Father Michael and make the arrangements."

Mrs. Beabots brushed a few errant crumbs from her lavender dress and looked out onto Maple Avenue. "You know, Sarah, I have always loved living in town the way we do. It's a good place for children to grow up. It would be a shame if Luke was forced to move out into the country. Very inconvenient for the children."

"So true."

Mrs. Beabots rose. "Well, dearie, I have work to do."

"Work? What kind of work?"

"Well, not as much as you do. I want to get out those canning jars for you. Those tomato vines of yours are going to be very abundant," she said, hustling down Sarah's front porch steps.

Squinting her eyes suspiciously at her favorite neighbor as she hurried away, Sarah called, "Just what are you up to?"

Mrs. Beabots waved her hand. "I must not dally. No time to lose."

LUKE FELT AS if his life was moving at warp speed. He'd never expected to sell his house so quickly. He'd thought he'd have time to look around for a suitable rental house or an apartment for him and the kids.

Packing had turned out to be an unending task. He had no idea where all their junk had come from. Donating all the kids' baby clothes, furniture and toys to the St. Mark's Children's Fund was a big help. Luke thought he would never get through the endless array of dishes, pots, cooking utensils and holiday decorations Jenny had saved. There was no hope for the majority of their things. He would store everything that was not an absolute necessity until the day came when he and the kids owned a proper house. Then, and only then, he would make the decisions about what to keep and what to trash.

Luke had given each of the kids empty boxes to pack only the clothes that still fit them. The rest of their clothes they were to put in plastic bags for donation.

Luke walked into his bedroom and started pitching the old sneakers, sweatshirts and jeans he would never wear again.

After cleaning out his dresser, he opened the door to Jenny's walk-in closet.

For over two years, he hadn't even turned on the light. The closet smelled musty and close. He fanned the air with his arm.

Every single sweater, dress, pair of slacks and shoes was exactly where Jenny had left it. In her last few months, she hadn't gone out of the house much except to chemotherapy or for checkups. He'd thrown away the clothes she'd worn to the hospital the week she died. But all the rest of her things were still here.

He felt guilty and nearly like a traitor taking her jackets off the hangers and putting them in plastic bags. He decided this process was too slow. He grabbed huge armfuls of clothes and lifted them off the rod and plopped them on the floor. Then he pulled the large black bag around the clothes and tied it up. He found a cream-colored Irish wool cardigan that he'd always hated. Jenny had told him two years ago that she'd given the sweater away, but here it was, tucked into the back of the closet.

Luke didn't realize he was crying until the pain in his chest grew so sharp he actually clutched himself and sank to the floor. "Jenny."

He threw his head back and wailed her name and then shoved his fist in his mouth to stifle his scream. He didn't want to frighten the kids, but he wished to heaven someone would come and keep him from being so afraid.

With tears streaming down his face, he took out another plastic bag and filled it with all of Jenny's shoes until the floor was clear.

He was surprised that her purses, shoes and scarves looked much cheaper and more worn than he remembered.

At the far end of the closet was a tall, narrow lingerie chest that Jenny used for her underwear and personal things. When he pulled out the bottom drawers, he found snapshots. Lots of them.

Sitting on the floor, Luke went through the photographs. There were shots of Jenny when she was pregnant with Annie and later with Timmy. There were at least a hundred photographs of the various rooms in their house, before her design and decoration and after. On the back of each photograph were her notes about paint colors and fabrics, furniture manufacturers and painting processes. If she'd been a licensed interior designer like Sarah, she couldn't have been more precise.

Astonishingly, there was only one photograph of the two of them. It was taken at Buckingham Fountain in Chicago—by a stranger, as Luke recalled. Luke was in his navy dress whites and Jenny wore a sleeveless black sundress. She was as tan as a berry and her long, dark hair fanned around her shoulders as if the breeze had just washed over her. Her eyes literally flashed at him from the photograph, and to this day he'd never seen as brilliant a smile. She was his Jenny…full of life, so willing to love and not care if she ever got a single ounce of it back. She embraced every aspect of life with eagerness whether it was the flowers and herbs in her garden, the special breads she baked for him or the sound of her children playing. Jenny loved it all. And in this picture, he realized he'd seen it that day and he saw it now—she was resplendent with joy.

Joy. That was what he missed most about Jenny.

Joy at seeing the sun sift through the leaves of the Maple trees down the boulevard. Joy at feeling the waters of Indian Lake under his row-boat. That was the lesson Jenny's life had taught him. There was joy all around him, but he had to see it. Appreciate it. Live in it.

He touched her face, but he only felt the slick paper. All around him was a sea of photographs, but it was this one that captured him. It was almost as if Jenny had meant for him to find this picture at this very moment.

"Jenny," he whispered reverently, and was not surprised to see his tear fall onto the photograph. He wiped it away with his thumb.

Often, Luke remembered remarking to his parents and his buddies in the navy that Jenny made him feel alive. It was as if she had enough energy and life in her for two, three—even four people.

Maybe that was why after she died, he'd felt as if he'd died with her.

"Did I do that to you, Jenny? Did I put the burden of my happiness on you?" He looked around her closet at all the things he had not given to the needy, but had clung to as if they would bring her back.

Even in death, he had still put the responsibility of his happiness, his joy, his living, on Jenny. If she were alive, she would not have pulled any punches with him and would have said, "Enough already."

Wasn't that what she was saying here? She wasn't in this closet. She wasn't in the house. She was in his heart, but in the past.

Only *he* could make himself happy.

The problem was that he didn't know how.

CHAPTER TWENTY-FOUR

IT TOOK TWO days for Sarah to rehearse just how she would approach Luke about the scholarships for Annie and Timmy. She'd learned many things about Luke Bosworth, and one of them was that he didn't take charity…for anything. He would rather die first. She had to make certain she could bluff like a gambler and fake her lines as well as any Broadway actor. If she faltered at all, he might turn on her, and then she'd have to apologize to him for not telling him the truth from the beginning. She wanted to back out of the task, but she knew that Mrs. Beabots was depending on her.

When she finally punched out Luke's cell number, her fingers were shaking.

"Hi, Sarah," Luke said, picking up on the first ring.

"Hi, Luke. She paused for a long moment. He had a calming voice most of the time, she remarked to herself. She'd completely forgotten the reason for her call.

"Sarah? Did you want something?" he asked. "I'm on a job and my crew is waiting…"

"Sorry. I can call back later," she said.

"It's okay. What's up?"

"I was just over at the rectory talking to Father Michael about the profit we made…"

"Oh, yeah. Right. How did we do?"

"Really well. Over a quarter of a million. If I can raise another one hundred and fifty thousand, the bank will put up the half a million we need."

"Wow. That's great. Isn't it?"

"It will be when I figure out where the other one hundred and fifty is going to come from."

"You'll do it," he said firmly. "I have confidence in you."

Sarah paused again, marveling at how much his approval uplifted her. She smiled. "Thanks, Luke. Thanks a lot."

"Sure. So is there anything else?"

"Yes. As a matter of fact, the subject of next year's scholarship recipients came up. Father Michael wanted me to call you personally to tell you that Annie and Timmy were selected."

"Selected?"

"Yes. They won the scholarships."

"They never told me they applied for scholarships."

"Well, the children don't exactly apply. The tuition is just given…"

"To needy kids," he said, cutting her off.

"No. Deserving students," Sarah corrected.

"I'm not buying this," Luke said harshly.

Sarah was silent. There was a long pause on Luke's end, as well.

Then Luke continued. "There actually isn't any scholarship fund, is there, Sarah?"

"Sure there is."

"Since when?"

"It's in play from time to time."

"Let me ask you, Sarah. Did you put up the money for the kids?"

"No. I did not," she said firmly.

"Really? Then I know just who did," he said. "Tell you what. You go back to Mrs. Beabots and tell her it was a nice try. But my kids will do just fine in a public school until I can get back on my feet and pay for their tuition at St. Mark's. Got that?"

She heard a deep intake of breath on his end of the phone. She wondered just how much she had embarrassed him with the offer. She knew he was a proud man, otherwise he wouldn't have worked so hard to hold on to his house for the kids like he had. Going to the counseling sessions must have been an even bigger step for him than she'd imagined. "I understand."

"And Sarah?"

"Yes, Luke?" Sarah swallowed hard just knowing he was about to blast her for duplicity. She closed her eyes.

"I'm sorry for jumping to the conclusion that you were behind this scheme. I think it's very sweet of you and Mrs. Beabots to want to do this for Annie and Timmy. It was a really nice gesture. Thanks." He hung up.

Sarah's mouth fell open just as Miss Milse walked into the living room.

"You want coffee?"

"Yes." Sarah smiled. "And I'll take a slice of your strudel, too."

Miss Milse crossed her arms over her chest. "You never want my strudel. Only for special day. That's what you tell me."

"This is a very special day, Miss Milse. I think Luke and I just became real friends."

By early August a summer heat wave had sent the mercury in Mrs. Beabots's garden thermometer into the triple digits. Luke had finished the carriage house and it was time for the final inspection. Along with balancing her accounting book, Mrs. Beabots believed in setting all her records straight.

"I owe you an apology, Luke," she said as she

looked at the new center beam and supporting joists in the ceiling of the carriage house.

"For what?" he asked, wiping his sweaty face with a hand towel he carried in the back pocket of his jeans.

"Trickery," she answered. "About the scholarships for the kids."

"It was too generous," he admitted. "I don't know when I could pay you back."

Lifting her chin, she assessed him with a piercing gaze. "That's what I like about you, Luke. You're a lot like me in many ways. Practical. That's a good thing. Shortsighted and fatheaded decision in this case, but practical."

"Fatheaded?" he chuckled and scratched the back of his neck. "I haven't been called that before."

"Always a first time," she replied. "The other thing is," she said, looking up as he turned on the two new ballasts of fluorescent lights. "Ah! I like that," she said. "Where was I? Oh, yes," she said, tapping her cheek with her forefinger. "Luke, how is the house hunt going?"

"Disaster. Cate hasn't found a thing. I told my boss we need to go into the development business and build apartments and condos for this town. There's nothing here!"

"Ah, but there is. That's what I wanted to talk to you about," she said. She reached into her skirt pocket and pulled out a check. "I think that covers it," she said, handing him the check.

Luke glanced at it. The amount was to the penny that they had agreed upon. He had half expected there to be a small bonus since she was so willing to fund the kids' schooling. "Thanks," he said, folding the check and putting it in his wallet.

"I've been thinking the same thing myself," Mrs. Beabots said.

"Thinking what, exactly?"

"Enterprise!" She beamed brightly.

He shook his head. "I don't get it."

"First of all, I want you to promise you will not take this the wrong way."

"Take what?"

She stuck her finger in the air and wagged it. "No! Promise first," she retorted.

"Fine. I promise," he said. He smiled and crossed his heart. "How's that?"

"Perfect. This is my idea. It's because of your predicament that this idea came to me, so I thought you should benefit from it. I want to turn my third floor ballroom into an apartment that I can rent out to folks like you in the future."

Luke's eyes shot out the carriage house window to Mrs. Beabots's large Victorian house. "Ballroom."

"It just sits there. Unused. It's a waste of space when people like you are looking for a decent home. I seriously doubt that in the future ballrooms are going to come back."

"That could take months. Nearly a year," he said. "Is there plumbing up there?"

"Yes. A bathroom, but it needs updating. And a kitchen, of course. I'll get blueprints drawn up for the layout of the rooms," she said.

"And you want me to do the construction?"

She smiled impishly and answered, "And I want you and the children to live up there while you do the work. Rent free in partial exchange for the work."

Luke stared at her for a thoughtful moment. "We would be in town."

"Yes. Just as you wanted. Annie and Timmy can walk to Sunday school with me. Go up town to shop and to the library. I go once every week, by the way."

"Do you really want to do this? It's a lot of money to renovate like that, plus the inconvenience. The noise," he emphasized. "You're not used to having children around. They can be a handful."

She waved off his misgivings as if they were bothersome houseflies. "Pish posh. You have your own entrance and a back staircase. You come and you go as you please. I had a maid once who lived up there for a year or more, and I barely knew she was around. She was waiting for her husband to get out of prison. Sad story. Anyway. What do you think?"

"I'm not sure."

"About what, Luke? In ten days you're going to be homeless and the kids start school four days after that. Take my deal." She spit in her hand and stuck it out.

He laughed uproariously, spit in his hand and shook hers.

"Good," she said. "Now, let's go up to the ballroom so I can show you just what you've gotten yourself into."

CHAPTER TWENTY-FIVE

SARAH STOOD AT the pulpit after the Sunday service and announced the final profit figures from the summer festival to the congregation.

"I want to thank all of you for your hard work, your time and your money. You all made our first annual summer festival such a success. Also, I am pleased to report that Father Michael and I have met with the bank, and we have a loan for five hundred thousand dollars. This loan is contingent upon our ability to raise the final one hundred and fifty thousand for the renovation. The only way that we can raise this money is directly from all of you. Over the next several weeks, I will personally contact each of you to discuss what kind of donation you feel you can make to the building fund. I hope you don't all run and hide each time you see my name come up on your caller ID, because you will find that I am relentless. It would be best if you take the time now to think about what you can afford before I make that call. Lump sums are always welcome, but I don't expect that from anyone.

"Secondly, I have informed the bank that St. Mark's will continue with the summer festival for the next five to ten years, until we pay back all of the money we borrow. In addition, if the festival continues to create the kind of revenue we saw this year, those funds will be used for the upkeep of the church and school in the future."

Mrs. Beabots sat next to Maddie and Isabelle Hawks as they all smiled at Sarah, giving her approving nods.

Sarah started to walk away from the pulpit when she heard a familiar voice shout, "Sarah!"

She looked out to the congregation and saw Charmaine holding up her hand and then rising from her seat. Sarah's face broke into a happy smile. "Charmaine."

"Sarah." Charmaine stood and looked around her at her friends in the church. "I know I speak for all of us when I say, thank you, for everything you've done for us. Your summer festival was successful because of your creative promotion, your organization, your impossible amount of energy and innovative ideas." Charmaine began applauding and the rest of the congregation and Father Michael joined in.

Charmaine turned back to Sarah. "To show

my appreciation, I am willing to pledge the remaining money, on one condition."

Sarah was dazed as Charmaine announced her pledge. Her boss—her friend—had probably given her the best gift of her life, by letting her go when she did, allowing Sarah to find her purpose in life again. And now she was giving her yet another gift. Sarah almost couldn't comprehend this kind of benevolence.

Mrs. Beabots turned around in her pew and looked at Charmaine. "What's the condition?"

"That Sarah come back to work immediately."

Sarah clamped her hands to her cheeks. "No way! I mean. Way. I mean, yes!" Sarah rushed down the altar steps to Charmaine and hugged her. "This is wonderful! Thank you so much!"

"You see, Sarah? I had to pledge that money. You won't have time to be calling all these people asking for donations. You'll be working." Charmaine smiled.

"Yes," Sarah beamed, a well of tears floating in her eyes. "Yes, I'll be working."

LUKE TRIED TO hire two of his buddies, Matt and Barry, from his construction crew to help him move, but they wouldn't take any money.

"You can buy us some beer at the end of the day," Matt said.

"Besides," Barry said, rolling up his T-shirt sleeves, "when the time comes for me to move again, you'll be obliged to do the same for me."

"True," Luke said. "Sorta like paying it forward."

Barry laughed. "More like a 'marker' from a gambling debt. You have to pay up."

Luke grinned. "Gotcha."

Luke had rented a U-Haul truck to take the largest pieces of furniture and thirty boxes of memorabilia he would probably never open again, but couldn't bear to part with, to a storage unit across town. He'd packed their clothes, the kids' toys, kitchen and bathroom necessities, three metal bed frames and bedding in his Ford F-150. He wanted to keep only the essentials at Mrs. Beabots's house until he got a better idea of exactly what they would need and for how long. As timely as her offer was, it seemed strange to him to think that he and the kids would be living in a construction site until next spring. By that time, new houses would become available, and he'd have Cate Sullivan start looking for him again. He hoped he could find the kind of home the kids wanted—one in which they could all be happy.

Mrs. Beabots hired Lester MacDougal to sweep, vacuum, dust and scrub the back entry and stairs and the entire expanse of the ballroom so that the area was at least habitable when her new tenants came to stay.

She had also enlisted Sarah and Maddie to carry boxes upstairs and help the children get settled in.

"Does Luke know we're here to help?" Sarah asked Mrs. Beabots as she mixed a cup of sugar into a pitcher of homemade lemonade.

"No," Mrs. Beabots answered, taking an apple pie out of the oven and placing it on her wooden kitchen island.

"I thought not," Sarah replied. She took her cell phone out of her pocket and dialed Luke's number. "Hi, Luke. It's Sarah."

"Hey, what's up?" he asked, sounding out of breath.

"I just wanted you to know that Maddie and I are here at Mrs. Beabots's house to help you guys move on this end. Do you need any help over there?"

"Oh, thanks. And no, we've got it here. I guess I'm going to have to get a cleaning crew to scrub up the place, though."

"How about Lester? He'll do it. Or you could borrow my Miss Milse. They could both use the extra money."

"I think I'll need them both," Luke laughed. "The kids drew on the bedroom walls with chalk, which I didn't know until we took their posters down. There's all kinds of stuff like that."

"I understand. What else can we help with?"

"Could I have Barry bring the kids over there and you guys watch them while we go to the storage unit?"

"Why don't I come pick them up? Then you guys can keep loading."

"Good idea," Luke replied.

Sarah handed the sterling-silver spoon to Maddie. "Stir this. I have to go."

"Where?" Maddie asked.

"To Luke's house to pick up the kids and bring them here."

Mrs. Beabots stuck a knife in her pie to check the doneness and stopped midmotion. "You're going to the inner sanctum?" Maddie's eyes whipped to Sarah.

Inhaling a deep, nerve-stilling breath, Sarah replied, "Yes." She rushed to the little mirror that hung by the sink and smoothed her hair. She grabbed a lip stain from her pocket and ran it over her lips, making sure she hadn't smudged it. She stuck her palm in front of her face to check for bad breath. Satisfied, she turned to her friends. "I'm off."

"Good luck," Maddie said and watched Sarah shoot out the back door.

Maddie turned to Mrs. Beabots. "So when

did that happen?" she asked, pointing her thumb over her shoulder.

"Slowly," Mrs. Beabots replied, eyes twinkling. "Ever since she tried to pay for cleaning his kids' clothes after Beau muddied them up."

"I thought he was just a diversion. You know, a summer crush or something to keep her mind off her mother's death. But I can see it's more serious now," Maddie said. She looked up from the lemonade and saw concern scribbled across Mrs. Beabots's face. "What's the matter?"

"I just wish I could read Luke as well as I can Sarah."

THE BALLROOM WAS an immense expanse of honey-colored French parquet floor with high ceilings, exquisite beveled-glass windows that looked out on Maple Avenue and ornate crown molding and framework around faded and water-stained aqua-and-silver panels of French silk wallpaper. Six twelve-foot gilt mirrors hung on the walls, and three Venetian crystal chandeliers were half-covered with white sheeting.

The bathroom at the end of the room was enormous and just as elegant. It had pink-and-gold-veined marble countertops with double white china sinks in a white French provincial vanity. Above the sinks were two gold-framed mirrors. The walls were tiled in white-and-black-veined marble, and a small crystal chandelier hung in the center of the room. There were two toilet stalls, but no tub and no shower.

The actual construction required to divide the area would not be difficult. The old plumbing and electrical system would be the biggest challenges. He would need to hire a couple of his crew—Barry would definitely sign on. He'd need a very good plumber and an electrician to bring the wiring up to code. In the future, everyone who rented this space was going to need proper wiring for DSL, possibly surround sound and even 3D televisions. The kitchen would need a dishwasher, electric stove, garbage disposal and refrigerator at a minimum. All those issues Luke could handle.

Although it had been Luke's lifelong desire to become an architect, the fact was that he did not have any formal training. He didn't want to make even the smallest mistake on Mrs. Beabots's project. What Luke needed was an expert interior designer and architect.

He needed Sarah.

AT THE FAR end of the ballroom, Sarah had tied a long clothesline from a French bronze wall sconce on the south wall to another matching sconce on the opposite wall.

"What's this?" Luke asked Sarah as she picked up a king-size white sheet.

"Timmy's bedroom wall." She smiled, flipping the sheet over the clothesline. "It's not much, but it will have to do for the time being," she said.

Annie handed Sarah a clothespin. "Cool, huh, Dad?" Annie beamed.

"Yeah," he replied admiringly and looked around to see that while he'd been hauling the kids' duffel bags of books and toys up the staircase, Sarah had put together the kids' beds, including their sheets, pillows and bedspreads. She'd started unpacking boxes and had hung their clothes on a rolling clothes rack that he knew had not come from his house. Against the wall, she'd lined up their shoes, backpacks, Annie's purses and Timmy's bike helmet and a long line of baseball caps.

"Dad," Timmy said, coming out of the bathroom and zipping up his shorts. "There's no bathtub in there."

"I know," Luke said. "Mrs. Beabots said we could use her guest bathroom downstairs until I get the new bathroom fixtures installed."

"How long will that be?" Annie asked with a worried look.

Luke turned to Sarah. "That depends on Sarah."

Sarah had just unfurled another sheet and flung it over the clothesline. "Me?"

"I need your help."

Sarah pursed her lips to keep from smiling. "You need my help? Really? Why?"

"I mean I need your expertise to help me design the bathroom and the kitchen. And the living room and the bedrooms."

Annie grinned. "Just say the whole place, Dad."

Timmy walked up and stood next to Sarah. "Can we get a tub big enough to put Beau in?"

Luke shook his head. "What for?"

"So I can give him a bath," Timmy replied, looking at his father as if he was addle-brained.

"That dog is bigger than you are," Luke said.

"Not forever," Timmy replied and walked over to a stack of boxes marked "Timmy's Toys."

Luke looked back at Sarah. "Better figure a six-foot tub."

SARAH SAT AT her drafting table, studying the photographs of Mrs. Beabots's ballroom, the dimensions she'd taken and the initial concept drawings she'd completed. She poured another cup of coffee from her French press and looked up at the summer sky. It was a sultry night, humid and still, without the hope of a breeze.

Sarah had kept the air-conditioning on all day. Fortunately, her parents had installed ceiling fans in each of the bedrooms, which kept the rooms cool in the summer and circulated the warming heat from the furnace in the winter.

She would put ceiling fans in each of the bedrooms in Mrs. Beabots's apartment, she thought, going back to her drawings.

The back staircase opened into the ballroom and the powder room was off to the right. Sarah's concept for the area was similar to a New Orleans style "shotgun" house, but in reverse. She would create a long hallway to the left and all the rooms would be off to the right. The master would be situated next to the bathroom, with a door that opened directly into the bathroom. All the closets would line the outer south wall. There was enough room for three large bedrooms or four small ones. Sarah decided that three was enough for a rental. Between the bedrooms, the dining room and living room would be a large, eat-in kitchen with a great deal of counter space and storage areas. Luke could make custom cabinets, or they could order cheap modular, depending upon Mrs. Beabots's budget.

Because the area was as wide as the entire house, all the rooms had ample space for study or sitting areas. The living room needed to be at the front of the house, where the floor-to-ceiling windows overlooked the treetops along Maple Avenue. Even now, standing at the windows gave a similar impression to riding the Ferris wheel.

Just thinking about that night over a month ago brought a warm glow to Sarah's face that she could actually feel when she touched her cheek. She believed Luke turned a corner that night in his quest to put his grief behind him. Until that night, for a good deal of time, Luke's mind and heart had been so filled by memories of his wife, that there hadn't been room for anyone else.

"Not even his children, sometimes," she mused. "Especially not for me."

Glancing out the window at Mrs. Beabots's house, she realized that the lights in the ballroom were still burning. On this side of the house, the stained glass was placed at normal window height, and did not start at the floor. Peering at the window, Sarah was certain she saw Luke standing alone, looking out. She raised her hand to wave, but realized he probably couldn't see her seated this far away from the window.

Then he walked away and the light went out.

Sarah smiled to herself as she went back to her drawing, penciling ceiling fans into each bedroom. It was amazing to her that a few months ago she felt as if she was living in a cave—alone, dark and frightened. She'd lost her job and had been confused about almost everything in her life.

On Monday, she would be going back to work. Her world had been put back together again, yet it had been permanently altered. She'd dug down deep inside her heart and discovered that she had just as many flaws as the next person. Luke had accused her of being needy, and the truth was, she had been just that. Especially in her relationship with James. She had also come to truly care for Annie and Timmy and she was genuinely happy that they lived next door to her now. She looked forward to being able to see them whenever she wished.

She also realized Luke was growing more and more important to her. What she felt for him was different than anything she'd ever experienced. She felt enormously happy when he was happy. Ever since the festival, she noticed that he hadn't displayed anger about selling the house, his move, giving away his wife's clothes or even the fact that the kids were going to public school. These were enormous hurdles for any family, yet Luke faced each one head-on. The kids seemed happier and more resigned to the idea of making new friends in a new place.

No doubt living at Mrs. Beabots's house had brought some of the comfort and stability that one of the hovels the wretched rental market in Indian Lake could never provide.

In a few days school would start. Summer was nearly over, and Sarah had to admit that as her life moved forward, there probably would never be a more propitious time in her life. She'd made many changes of her own that summer. She hoped that she'd become a better person. She was trying. Perhaps, she thought, that was all any one person could ever expect of themselves…that they could just keep trying.

CHAPTER TWENTY-SIX

SARAH'S FIRST DAY back at work was filled with welcoming hugs from her coworkers and a closed-door meeting with Charmaine.

"I've met with a couple, Emma and Ralph Collingswood, from Atlanta, who are moving here and want to open an aromatherapy shop," Charmaine said, handing Sarah a folder with the couple's business plan, photographs of storefront designs they wanted to emulate and a budget sheet.

"This is going to be tight," Sarah offered as she looked over the paperwork.

"That's exactly what I said. I told Emma that the only way she could get this kind of work done was to hire us. Between my contacts in Chicago and your network of friends in the estate auction business in this area, we might be able to find the kind of antiques she wants to create the look of a turn-of-the-century apothecary shop she wants."

"Did they buy this property on Main Street, or are they renting it?"

"Renting. It's a ten-year lease and they got it for a steal."

"Did you use Cate to broker the deal?"

"Absolutely. With the kind of money the Collingswoods will put into the building, the landlord should be doing flips."

"I would think. So when do you want me to meet with the clients?"

"Tomorrow. Nine in the morning. We're doing a Skype conference. I'll introduce you then. I want you to get started on the drawings. That gives you time to check out the building today, see the city engineer and schmooze him a bit. Apply for the permit. You know the drill."

"When do they want to have the grand opening?"

"May first."

"Opening day of tourist season."

Charmaine winked. "You got it."

Sarah closed the folder. "I'll get on it," she said and started to rise.

"There's one more thing." Charmaine stopped her. "I want to know what you're going to do about the church."

"What about it?"

Charmaine held up her finger, whirled her Italian black leather swivel chair around and stuck a pod of caramel macchiato coffee in her Keurig. "Want one?" Charmaine asked.

"I'm good, thanks. So tell me what you mean."

Charmaine whirled back around and looked Sarah squarely in the eyes. "I had a meeting with Jerry Mason over the weekend."

"Luke's boss."

Charmaine raised an eyebrow, but continued. "Yes, well. Jerry has had a rough summer. The city council squashing the new retail center didn't help anybody, especially for the fall and winter. Fortunately, for us, I got on the phone and secured several jobs out of Chicago. But Jerry depends on the building that is going on right here in Indian Lake. So I was thinking, now that it looks like you've nearly got the money secured for the church, that you could give the bid to Jerry's company."

Sarah smiled. "I thought of the same thing."

"You did."

Sarah nodded. "Actually, I thought of it when Luke and I were working on the festival together. I just wasn't sure how long it would take or if I could pull that much money together. Thanks to your generosity, we can go forward with the renovations. Jerry's company absolutely fits the bill. The Church Council asked for three bids. One was from a firm in Gary. Another from one in Chicago. They were both way over our budget. I figured since Luke knew how much money we had nearly to the dollar, he and Jerry would bid appropriately."

"When are you sending this information over to Jerry?"

"I faxed it an hour ago," Sarah said with a gratified smile.

Charmaine took the cup of steaming coffee from the Keurig and sipped it. "I can't tell you how happy I am that you're back, Sarah."

"I'm glad to be back," Sarah replied. "And not just physically."

"That's what I meant," Charmaine replied perceptively.

WHEN SARAH PULLED into her driveway, she was surprised to see Timmy sitting on her front steps with his arm around Beau.

She got out of the car and walked up to them. "Hey, guys."

"Hi," Timmy said, stroking Beau's head. "I bet you're wondering what I'm doing here."

"That did cross my mind," she replied.

"I came to ask you for a job."

"What kind of job?"

"I was thinking I could walk Beau every day for you. Brush him. Stuff like that. After school, you know?"

"I see. And how much would you charge me for this?"

Timmy shrugged his thin shoulders. "Twenty five cents a day. When I get bigger, I could give him a bath, too. Once my dad puts in a bathtub." He pointed to Mrs. Beabots's house. "I've decided to be a vet'narian. So this job would be important for my future," Timmy said earnestly.

Sarah hid her smile behind her palm. She nearly had to bite her lip to keep from laughing. The little boy had clearly thought of every pitch he could.

"I think it's a fine idea," she said. "What does your dad think about all this?"

"I haven't asked him." He looked at her pleadingly.

Sarah instantly understood what Timmy was up to. "And you want me to go to him and ask him about this job for you. Is that right?"

Timmy looked sheepishly at his sneakers. "Yes," he answered quietly.

Sarah looked at Beau, who was smiling as Timmy continued stroking his head. She glared at the dog. He ignored her. "You're not helping, Beau."

Beau let out a bark.

Sarah folded her arms across her chest. "All right, Timmy. I will ask your dad for you. But don't blame me if he says no."

"I won't, Miss Sarah!" Timmy squealed. "This is going to be great!" He hugged Beau around the neck so tightly Sarah was afraid her dog would choke.

Sarah sat in a red-velvet Victorian chair in Mrs. Beabots's front parlor. The house had two parlors, one of which was always kept behind locked doors and added to a growing mystique that Sarah believed her elderly friend purposefully perpetuated. Thus, this smaller, but still elegantly appointed room was where they usually gathered for tea or coffee.

Timmy sat on the floor petting Beau, which was, without question, Timmy's favorite pastime. Annie sat on the red-velvet French settee poring over a stack of songbooks Sarah had loaned to her.

"I'd give anything to play the piano," Annie sighed.

"And I think you'd be a natural, Annie. You have a good ear, but you're also learning to read music very well. Mrs. Cook commented on it just last Sunday. Playing the piano would help you in the years to come. I could teach you, if you'd like."

"You would?" Annie's blue eyes flew open. "That's like a dream come true!"

"I'd be most happy to do that," Sarah assured her, and continued pouring tea for herself and

Mrs. Beabots. "We will have to ask your father first."

"I'll ask him myself," Annie replied confidently.

"Sarah," Mrs. Beabots said, placing a crocheted tea cozy over her English Rose teapot to keep the liquid warm, "would you mind checking the sweet potatoes for me?"

"Not at all," Sarah said, rising and going to the kitchen.

Because Luke wouldn't have a kitchen installed in the ballroom for several months to come, a microwave was his only means of warming up food for his family. Mrs. Beabots had offered to make the evening meals for everyone. Luke had agreed on the condition that he pay for the groceries and for her hours of labor.

Mrs. Beabots accepted. Again, with her spit handshake.

"The potatoes need another twenty minutes or so. I brought a casserole of creamed corn. It's bubbling nicely," Sarah said, coming back to the living room. She took a cup of chamomile tea off the tea tray and handed it to Mrs. Beabots.

Annie instantly looked up from her songbook with a grimace. "Creamed corn? Not regular?"

Sarah smiled. "I make my own creamed corn. I roast the corn and then cut it off the cobs. The rest is a secret, but I make it with whipping cream and a bit of sugar."

"Don't tell Dad about the sugar," Timmy warned. "He'll throw a fit."

"It's only a tablespoon. Just enough to bring out the flavors. I made a double batch," Sarah said.

"It'll be perfect with my pork roast and baked apples," Mrs. Beabots said, floating a paper-thin slice of orange in her tea.

Just then, they heard the sound of Luke's truck pull up and his door slam.

Timmy looked at Annie and then at Sarah. "Dad's home," he said with a quaking voice and a great deal of wide-eyed apprehension. "Maybe we should wait till tomorrow to ask him."

"Ask him what?" Annie whispered to her brother, but Timmy was already standing at attention as Luke came in the front door.

"I saw all of you sitting in here through the window when I pulled up, so I came in this way. I hope that's all right," Luke said, looking at Mrs. Beabots.

"Perfectly fine, dear," Mrs. Beabots said.

Luke looked at Sarah, "Hi," he said with a wider smile than Sarah thought he'd intended. Or had he?

"How was your day?" Sarah asked.

"Brutal. This heat is a killer. Reminds me

of…never mind." He looked at Mrs. Beabots. "Mind if I take a shower before dinner? Believe me, everyone here would appreciate it."

Mrs. Beabots nodded. "Supper will be ready in about half an hour."

Luke started to turn away.

"Dad!" Timmy said too loudly and too anxiously.

"Timmy? What is it?"

"I…er…uh…Sarah wants to give me a job."

"A job?" Luke's eyes tracked from his son to Sarah, who was smiling at Timmy and not looking at Luke.

"What kind of job?" Luke asked.

"Walking Beau every afternoon after school. Giving him a treat and brushing him. She's going to pay me twenty-five cents a day."

Luke took a long, purposeful moment before saying, "I assume this would include Saturday and Sunday since the dog has to be walked every day. That would mean you would earn a dollar seventy-five cents a week."

"Yeah, I guess so."

"And why do you need this money?" Luke asked.

"To save up for vet'narian school. It's for my future," Timmy said with a series of little nods as if assuring himself his negotiations were going well.

"I see," Luke replied, scratching his cheek. He turned to Sarah. "When did he come to you with this idea?"

"Today," Sarah answered honestly. "I told Timmy he had to ask you first."

Beau had scooted over to Timmy's side, propping himself directly under Timmy's hand. Timmy was stroking the dog's head without even knowing it. Sarah watched Luke observing his son. She had given Luke a perfect opportunity to ease Timmy into the responsibilities of owning a dog. Luke wanted Timmy to have a dog someday, but she knew he also wanted Timmy to understand the importance of that decision.

"Okay, Timmy. I will agree to your taking the job, but you have to promise that in bad weather, you don't go far from this house. Just to the corner and back."

"Okay." Timmy finally allowed delight to explode all over his face. "So I can start tomorrow?"

"If it's okay with Sarah," Luke said.

"Fine with me. Miss Milse will be at the house all day. So whenever you want to come over."

"We start school next week, but for the rest of this week, I could come over two, maybe even three times to take him out," Timmy rattled excitedly.

Sarah laughed. "As many times as you want, Timmy."

"Yes!" Timmy plopped down next to Beau and hugged the dog. "Did you hear that? I can see you anytime I want."

Luke smiled at Sarah and mouthed the words, *Thank you.*

Annie jumped up, holding her songbooks. "Dad, I was thinking of asking you if Sarah could be my piano teacher."

"Your what?" The smile on Luke's face faded as if it were melting wax.

Sarah saw it and reflexively braced. Something was wrong. The air in the room suddenly filled with tension.

Mrs. Beabots put her teacup down. Her eyes went to Luke and then to Annie. She glanced at Sarah and gave a quick warning shake to her head.

Sarah remained silent.

"Piano teacher," Annie answered innocently. "She's really good and maybe she could teach me on Saturdays or something. I really want to learn…."

"When I can afford a real piano teacher, we'll get one, and not until then. Understand?" Luke said firmly, enunciating each and every word—though Sarah noticed he did not growl.

"But Dad," Annie started to argue. Luke cut her off.

"Not now, Annie."

Sarah quickly realized that Luke thought she had overstepped her bounds with his kids again. She didn't know if he believed she'd put Timmy up to his request, but suddenly everything had gone awry. It was up to her to set him straight. Because he needed setting straight.

Sarah rose and faced Luke. "Whatever you want, Luke. That's fine. Just so you know, it was not my idea to hire Timmy. He came to me. He does want this job. Can he still have it?"

"Yeah. Sure. I guess."

"As for Annie, I offered to teach her. I think the discipline of piano lessons would be good for her. I don't expect to be paid. However, you're right. I'm not a piano teacher. So the decision is up to you if you want to wait and get someone who is truly qualified."

Sarah turned to Mrs. Beabots. "I need to go. I have a new project at work and I'll be up till midnight working on it." She leaned over and kissed Mrs. Beabots on the cheek.

"Good night, dear," Mrs. Beabots said.

Sarah walked past Luke, who avoided eye contact. "'Night," he said.

Timmy jumped up and raced to Sarah. "Thanks for everything, Miss Sarah," he said. "Can Beau stay for a while? I could bring him over after supper."

"Only if it's okay with your dad."

"Fine," Luke grumbled, crossing his arms over his chest.

Sarah went straight to her study. She opened her blinds and looked out at Mrs. Beabots's house. The lights were on in the dining room, indicating they were sitting down to supper.

For half an hour, Sarah moved papers around her desk, checked her emails, texted Maddie and looked up several auctions on line for items she could use in the aromatherapy shop.

Finally, she dropped her head in her hands. "Ugh. Luke! Can you be any more mule-headed?" she said out loud. What was so terrible about letting Annie have piano lessons? Nothing. This was all about Luke. Luke and his precious pride.

For the first time in her life, Sarah wished she'd become a psych major in college and not a designer. Maybe then she would know what the heck to do with Luke. Sometimes she just didn't understand him.

Or maybe it was that she *did* understand him and his motivations, but she didn't want to face the real truth.

Luke had encircled his heart and his life with chains that he didn't mind keeping locked and in place. Obviously, he'd grown comfortable in his self-imposed prison. She'd hoped that with the sale of the house he was moving forward with his life, and putting not only his grief behind him, but also his unnatural suspicion that she, in particular, was some kind of psycho child stealer.

Tonight, Luke had shown her that his dark side was still lurking in him somewhere.

Sarah didn't think she'd been wrong to offer to teach Annie the piano. Even now, knowing Luke's reaction, she'd still make the offer. At this point, Sarah had to face the fact that she and Luke were going to be neighbors—for a time, anyway—and that was all. She was willing to acknowledge that Luke was still climbing out of his grief. However, she believed he'd come to see her as a real friend over the past weeks. Even Mrs. Beabots had commented that when Sarah was around, Luke smiled more and was less tense. He'd told Mrs. Beabots how much he appreciated all Sarah had done to help during his move. He exuded high praise for her design ideas for the ballroom renovations. Sarah noticed that since the end of their counseling sessions, Luke smiled more, laughed more and generally appeared to be in brighter spirits. The fact that the summer festival and their Ferris wheel ride coincided with the end of their sessions with Margot had not entered her calculations until now.

Maybe Luke's uplifted outlook had nothing to do with her. Maybe he had progressed to that state of resilience that Margot spoke about, and his transition was simply nature taking its course.

Maybe she and Luke could only be acquaintances.

Annie, on the other hand, might just wind up being the real reason they were all brought together by fate in the first place. Sarah had championed Annie and her talent, and had helped Annie stand up for her passion to sing. Through Sarah's efforts, Luke had been forced to recognize his daughter's needs.

Annie had her whole life ahead of her. Luke had his reasons to want to protect his kids and that was fine. But to Sarah, stifling creativity and talent was close to unconscionable.

Sarah looked over at Mrs. Beabots's house and saw the third-floor lights go on. It was getting late and the kids were undoubtedly on their way to bed.

She didn't realize she was staring. She saw Luke stop at the window and look over at her. She sat up straight, feeling his eyes on her. She got up and went to the window, so that he could see her.

Luke immediately walked away.

Sarah picked up the phone and dialed Mrs. Beabots. "Hi," she said. "I thought I'd come over and get Beau."

"Luke said he'd bring the dog over. Timmy and Annie are getting ready for their baths."

"Tell him that I know he's got a lot to do. I'll come get Beau. I'll meet you on the front porch." Sarah hung up. Before she left the room, she slowly closed the blinds.

CHAPTER TWENTY-SEVEN

GOLDEN SUNBEAMS SKIMMED the placid waters of Indian Lake like tiny sprites as Annie and Timmy rode the bus to their new school. Their first terror, of waiting for the bus, was behind them. The new bus route allowed for the school bus to pick up four kids at the corner just down from Mrs. Beabots's house. On the first day, Luke had walked them to the bus stop and made certain they understood the routine.

The other two kids were younger than Annie. She was happy not to have to face older kids at the bus stop.

Annie was overwhelmed by the huge school. A large expanse of land held walking trails, a volleyball court and a regulation soccer field with bleachers for the parents to watch the competitions. The school building itself was filled with sunshine and natural light that streamed in through clear glass ceilings and skylights that ran along the hallways. The classrooms were cheery and the kids all sat at tables rather than individual desks like she had at St. Mark's.

There was an enormous television screen in the front of her class and over a dozen computers at stations on the right side of the room. The teacher had decorated the walls with posters, artwork and stickers for the school's September Reading Month projects.

Mrs. Geary was a tall woman with a caring, soft, but firm voice. She seemed to smooth her blond, chin-length hair a lot.

Annie was assigned her place at a table in between two boys who kept looking at her out of the corner of their eyes instead of just looking right in her face. Annie decided she didn't like either of them. She hugged her reading book and kept her eyes on the teacher, afraid to make a move right or left.

At lunch, Annie found Timmy and helped him go through the lunch line and pay for his food.

They sat at an empty table near the doors. "I don't like it here," Timmy said, opening his carton of milk and inserting a straw. "The teacher put me next to a creepy girl. She keeps pinching my arm."

"Tell the teacher. She'll make her stop."

Timmy looked at his sister with a horrified expression. "And become a tattletale on the first day of school?"

Annie agreed. "You're right. Wrong move. Pinch her back."

He shook his head. "What if she goes crying to the teacher? I'm toast."

"Right." Annie thought for a long moment as she munched on a turkey sandwich. "Let's ask Sarah what to do."

Timmy brightened. "Right after school, okay? We can call her at work from Mrs. Beabots's phone."

"Okay."

FOR OVER TWO weeks, every day at three-thirty, Sarah received a phone call from either Annie or Timmy about another crisis they faced at their new school. Sarah assured them that all these problems would be ironed out as time went on, and many of them were.

However, by the sixteenth phone call in as many afternoons, Sarah began to see a pattern forming. She immediately went to Charmaine.

Sarah tapped on Charmaine's office door and went in. Charmaine looked up from her computer. "Oh, Sarah. I was just going to call you in. Did you get those Frank Lloyd Wright stained-glass panels we looked at?"

"I lost the bid, as you can imagine. But I found three replicas, same colors, same size, made by a guy up in Traverse City. They're stunning. And a fraction of the cost. They're being shipped tomorrow."

"Good. Also, what's going on with the church bid?"

Sarah beamed. "Jerry Mason won the bid. I just got the call from Father Michael. I thought I'd give Jerry a call when we finish."

"Excellent." Charmaine smiled as she considered Sarah. "I know this look." She wagged her finger. "Something's up."

"I'd like to know if I could start leaving the office at three every day. I'll still work at home. You know I will."

"I'm not ever worried about you getting the job done. Quite the contrary. I worry that you often work too much. So why do you need to leave early?"

"Annie and Timmy are having a hard time adjusting to their new school. They call me every day when they get home with some problem that they have."

"Shouldn't they be calling their father?" Charmaine asked with a raised eyebrow.

"They should. Many times he's on a job and can't talk. I know they talk to him when he comes home. But I get the feeling they don't want to tell him some of these things."

"Such as?"

"They're scared, Charmaine. Intimidated. Even terrified of bullies."

"That's a real problem—certainly more so than in my childhood. Even cyber-bullies. It makes me cringe."

"I told Luke about it, and though he's talked to the kids and told them to report any incidents to their teachers, it's not enough."

"And what is?" Charmaine asked.

"I was thinking if I was home so that they could stay with me instead of with Mrs. Beabots, where they mostly just stay to themselves, it would be better for them. We could talk things out and they'd have…"

"…a mother?" Charmaine offered with pointed accusation in her eyes.

"A friend, Charmaine."

"Sarah, I think you're treading on dangerous ground. I know you love these kids. I know you want what is best for them, but if you do this, you run the risk of really making Luke mad. I think you're setting yourself up for even more heartbreak."

Sarah inhaled deeply. "I've thought of that, but these kids are so darling, so precious, I'm willing to face Luke's wrath. They aren't possessions. They're human beings, and right now, they need me."

Charmaine folded her hands on the desk and

peered at Sarah. "Know what? I agree with you
If it was me, I'd do the same thing. I'd face the
devil himself if I thought I could help them out
I remember being that little and that scared i
grade school. I think it's a treacherous place. If
had kids, I'd homeschool." She chuckled. "Any
way," she waved her hand in the air. "Go. Tak
the time. Once you think the kids are settled in
then you'll come back to the office."

"Absolutely," Sarah assured her.

LUKE WALKED INTO the construction office i
time to hear Jerry say, "Thanks so much fo
letting me know the good news, Sarah."

Luke waited until Jerry hung up the phone
"Sarah Jensen?"

"Yeah." Jerry grinned and actually rocked
back on his heels. "We got it."

"Got what?"

Jerry laughed. "Sorry. I didn't say anything
to anyone before this because I was afraid i
might not happen. We won the construction bi
for St. Mark's renovations!" He slapped Luke'
hard upper arm. "We're saved for the winter
buddy!"

Luke looked at Jerry suspiciously. "I didn'
know we were in the running. There were some
much bigger outfits than us."

"Yeah. And they bid big, too. Since you tol

he about that summer festival, I contacted
harmaine Chalmers and she put me in touch
ith Sarah, who went to the pastor or board or
omebody and we got the job."

Luke rubbed the back of his neck, wondering
hy he felt strange about this good news. This
neant his crews would have work through the
inter. Barry and the other guys who were help-
ng him with the ballroom could now use that
noney as secondary income. This meant that
y next spring, when the church was finished,
uke would have enough money to move the
ids to their own home. More important, he'd
e able to afford the tuition at St. Mark's again.

Luke was aware that Annie and Timmy were
aving a difficult time in their new school. Ini-
ally, he wanted to chalk it up to first-week jit-
ers. Then he started hearing Timmy whisper
 his sister about the "big kids" and Annie told
Mrs. Beabots that there was a group of girls in
ne fourth grade who called themselves "Mean
iirls."

Luke had never broached the subject about
ullies with his kids. He had no idea if they
new how to defend themselves, what to do or
ot do. This new landscape was suddenly just
s frightening to Luke as it was to the kids.

He wondered if this was payback from the
niverse for his pride in turning down Mrs.

Beabots's "scholarships." He hoped not. H
didn't want his kids to have to pay for his fool
hardiness.

"This is really good news, Jerry. This coul
make a real difference in my life."

Jerry beamed joy. "You're telling me? I can'
wait to call my wife. I think I'll take her out fo
burgers tonight to celebrate."

Luke bit his bottom lip. Simple reaction
Wanting to share joy with someone you love
But Luke didn't have anyone to call or share
burger with. Jenny was gone.

Suddenly, Luke wondered if it was alway
going to be like this for him.

Moments of joy came so seldom in life, an
to not venerate them was somehow wrong.

He thought of Sarah. She was the one who'
made this all happen. He knew her well enoug
by now to know that winning this bid had ev
erything to do with Sarah and little to do wit
their expertise as a construction company.

Sarah was giving Luke another gift. Sh
hadn't told him about the bid or the possibil
ity of Jerry winning it. She hadn't asked for a
accolade or pat on the back. She just took car
of business. She helped out a friend.

He needed to thank her.

Luke looked at his watch. "Jerry, I know it'
only a little after four. Do you mind if I knoc

off early? I thought I'd stop by Sarah's office
and thank her from both of us. Heck. All of us!"

"Great idea, Luke," Jerry said, picking up the
phone. "I'll see you tomorrow."

CHAPTER TWENTY-EIGHT

SARAH SAT ON the piano bench next to Annie and went through the scales with her. Annie had tinkered around with the piano at the church through the summer and had taught herself a few rudimentary songs.

"Very good. Let's try something a bit more difficult than 'Twinkle, Twinkle, Little Star.'" Sarah flipped through the pages of her very first piano music book. The pages were worn and the binding coming apart, but Sarah didn't care. With the turn of each page she remembered her mother sitting on this same piano bench teaching her just as she was now passing on her skills to Annie.

Timmy sat on the floor playing tug-of-war with Beau, who had a thick, tied rope clamped in his teeth.

"Beau did really good on his walk," Timmy said. "I scooped his poop and put it in the bag and then put it in the poop barrels on the boulevard."

Sarah sucked in a horrified breath. "Timmy

Bosworth! You did not cross that street all by yourself!"

"No! Annie watched me. Besides, Miss Sarah, can cross by myself. I'm in first grade now."

Shaking her head, Sarah scolded him, "I don't care. If I'm not home, you ask Mrs. Beabots to watch for you. Okay?"

"Okay," Timmy replied guiltily.

Sarah placed her hands on the keys and halted. She spun around on the bench. "Just how far down Maple Avenue did you walk?"

"Only one block and then back, just like I promised Dad," Timmy said defensively. "I heard him when he asked Mrs. Beabots to watch out for us. He said he didn't want us to be kidnapped."

Annie shivered. "Snatched. That's what Mom used to say. You can't be too careful."

"Hmm," Sarah mused. "I think from now on, I better go with you when you walk Beau. If you promise never to go farther than either corner, that's okay. Maybe I should buy you a cell phone so you can call me if there's trouble."

"Seriously?" Annie asked.

Sarah lifted her chin and pretended to peer at the sheet music. "I think I need to look into these things. I'm not used to having kids around. I can already see there are all sorts of dangers."

Annie looked up at Sarah. "You really car
about us, don't you, Miss Sarah?"

Sarah's eyes welled as she put her hand o
Annie's head and smoothed her hair. "Of cours
I do. I couldn't love you more if you were m
own," she said.

Impulsively, Annie threw her arms aroun
Sarah's neck and hugged her tightly. "I'm s
glad because I love you, too."

Timmy didn't look up from his play wit
Beau, but he'd heard every word of the conver
sation. "I love you, Beau," he said and kisse
the dog's head.

LUKE HAD JUST reached the bottom step of Sar
ah's porch when he looked up to the open fron
windows and saw Sarah sitting at her piano wit
Annie.

Luke had stopped at Sarah's office and wa
told by the receptionist that Sarah had gon
home early that day. He'd thanked the pleasan
woman and had driven away, thinking of jus
how he should thank Sarah.

As he approached the house, he was sur
prised to hear the sound of his children's voice
coming from inside. He'd thought they woul
be at Mrs. Beabots's, helping her with dinne
or watching television.

At first, Luke smiled, hearing Timmy's gig

gles as he played with Beau on the floor. Luke could see the dog lick Timmy's cheek and then pick up one end of a large rope, flinging the other end at Timmy, urging his friend to play.

Then he heard a few plunks on the piano, a missed key and a few bars played perfectly. He heard the muffled sounds of Sarah's voice as she spoke to Annie.

But it was the distinct and reverberating echo of Annie's words that caused Luke's internal protection devices to engage. "I'm so glad because I love you, too."

Luke peered through the screen and watched his daughter wrap her arms around Sarah. Sarah's back was to him, but he distinctly saw Annie's joy-filled face.

Jealousy gripped Luke in an excruciating vise. His anger stormed from its cage, free and unfettered as it had never been before. Luke felt as if he could tear the door right off its hinges.

He should be the one his daughter was hugging. He should be the one making his son laugh. He should be the one they sought out for everything. He didn't know why the kids were here and not next door, waiting for him. Why did they need Sarah and not him? Why was she better for them than he was?

Luke went to the door and banged his fist on the wood. "Annie! Timmy! You come out of there right now!"

STARTLED BY THE banging, Sarah jumped. She looked at a horrified Annie. "I'll take care of this," she said, touching Annie's cheek reassuringly.

"Okay," Annie said, already starting to shiver.

Timmy sat stock-still on the floor and watched as Sarah walked to the door.

Miss Milse came rushing from the kitchen with a very large rolling pin in her hand. She clomped up behind Sarah while Sarah opened the door.

"I want my kids," Luke fumed, looking past Sarah at Miss Milse.

Miss Milse raised the rolling pin high enough so that he could see it.

Annie scrambled off the piano bench and rushed over to Sarah, standing next to her. "We're here, Dad," Annie said bravely.

"Exactly. Here and not at home. You and Timmy go next door. I have to talk to Sarah."

Timmy hugged Beau one last time and slowly trudged past Sarah and out the door. As he reached the top step he turned around. "Bye, Miss Sarah. Thank you for letting me play with Beau."

"You're welcome, Timmy," she said.

Annie looked up at Sarah. "Thank you for the lesson," she said and then glared at her father. Quickly, she raced across the porch and down the steps to her brother.

Luke glared at Sarah. "Can we get rid of the bouncer, please?" he said, motioning toward Miss Milse.

Sarah turned around. "It's okay, Miss Milse." She turned back to Luke. "He won't be staying long."

"You're right about that," Luke said.

"What's this all about? Now my house is off-limits to them?"

"In a word, yes. You and your house. I saw that little display you had in there with Annie. I was right all along. You were using my kids. You keep inching your way in bit by bit." He threw his hands up in the air. "This was all a mistake! I should never have moved next door. I guess I wasn't thinking straight at the time. I definitely should have rented out of town."

Sarah stood her ground, matching his laser looks with some of her own. "Are you finished?"

"Just stay away from my kids. You got that?"

"I got it. But now you get this, lunkhead. I don't care what you think you heard or if you heard everything correctly. I'll spell it out for you. I love your kids, and whoa! News alert. They love me back. You can't change that. But as you so distinctly put it, they aren't my kids. They're yours. So I will abide by your rules and not allow them into my house. You, however, will be the one to tell Timmy he can't play with Beau anymore. You tell your talented daughter that she has to wait to learn the piano. By the way, most kids these days aren't up to the discipline, but she's wise enough to know she will be rewarded in the end. And then you can abide by *my* rule," she continued, feeling indignation and power mingle in her veins. "You don't come here, either. Ever. You got that?"

"Fine by me."

"One last thing, Luke. I just want to know what it feels like carrying around that iceberg inside your chest that you call a heart. It must burn something fierce!"

Sarah slammed her front door and threw the dead bolt.

CHAPTER TWENTY-NINE

OCTOBER GILDED ALL of Indian Lake in an extravagance of bronze, amber, crimson and gold, casting an iridescent shawl of sunset hues from misty dawn's light to evening's shadowed, streetlamp glow.

Rather than walk Beau past Mrs. Beabots's house every night after work and risk being seen by Luke, or worse, catching a glimpse of the children, whom she missed terribly, Sarah stole the last of the day's light by walking the beach along Indian Lake. She watched the sun set through the amber maples and towering oaks and felt the warmth of the Indian summer sun on her face. Soon the days would be so short she'd go to work in the dark and come home in the dark. But for now, she and Beau enjoyed these stolen moments alone.

It had been over a month since her argument with Luke, and for all that time, she'd watched him come and go from the house. On the weekends, she'd often caught Timmy waving to her from Mrs. Beabots's kitchen window. Annie had been a bit more brave and had surreptitiously put notes in Sarah's mailbox.

Sarah didn't know how much longer this strange and stupid attitude of Luke's would last. Sarah was still involved with the children's choir, and she saw the kids every Sunday for practice, which was wonderful for all three of them. Sarah felt like a divorced parent only allowed to visit her children once a week. She marveled at those who were able to withstand that kind of emotional torment.

She supposed that in Luke's mind, this little bit of contact was not to be avoided or feared.

As Sarah walked among the cattails and falling leaves, she realized that because of Luke's presence in her life, she'd faced her greatest fear of all.

Rejection.

Of all her demons, Sarah had been most vulnerable to rejection. She'd learned to deal with clients who didn't like her ideas, and even Charmaine when she quashed one of her projects. Both were accomplishments toward her well-being.

Luke, however, was another matter. She'd come very close to losing her heart to him.

Who are you kidding, Sarah? she thought,

picking up a gold leaf. *You can't stop thinking about him.*

She looked sadly across the lake. But he didn't want her. Not as a friend. Not even as an acquaintance.

The setting sun touched her face with warm, amber fingers. Thinking about the days to come, Sarah felt her expectations spring to life once again.

You are such a hopeless romantic, Sarah.

In November, the construction work for the church would begin. She would be forced to see Luke from time to time on the job. Thus far, she'd only communicated and worked with Jerry on the church project. Luke had been able to remain distant, so far. It wouldn't be long until he was forced to talk to her, though. As heartbreaking as it was, that project could be Sarah's last hope.

But hope for what? Another shot at rejection? *Oh, Sarah. You've got it bad.*

Sarah pulled Beau's leash to bring him away from the water's edge. "Let's start heading home, Beau," she said, and looked out at the sunset one last time.

Sarah supposed that in a way, she should be proud of herself. She'd actually lived through Luke's rejection. That was something, wasn't it? She hadn't fallen apart. Hadn't gone into a depression. She hadn't lost her mind.

What she had done was come face-to-face with a new and more vicious fear.

She was in love with a man who was never going to love her back.

SATURDAYS AND SUNDAYS had become two mind- and body-numbing days for Luke as he, Barry and Matt worked on the ballroom. They'd divided all the rooms according to Sarah's blueprints. The frameworks were finished, Sheetrock hung, the walls floated and puttied. Matt had installed a six-foot-long bathtub and tiled a walk-in shower area that finished off the new bathroom. The kitchen was taking shape. Mrs. Beabots had decided to purchase modular cabinet units, which made Luke's job a great deal easier. The new wiring allowed for ceiling fans in each bedroom and an electric fireplace unit to be installed in the living room.

Once the cooler nights of October hit, both Annie and Timmy liked sitting next to the electric fireplace reading their books.

Luke had just finished hanging the doors on all the bedrooms when he walked down the hall in time to see Timmy looking out the window onto Maple Avenue.

"You guys about ready for bed? I got the doors up," he said with a smile.

Annie closed her book. "Can I finish this after my bath?"

"Sure," Luke said, noticing Timmy was watching something outside with great interest.

"Timmy? Bedtime."

"Okay," Timmy replied and turned around. He was wearing his favorite dog pajamas, but as he walked toward his father, Luke noticed the pajamas were suddenly several inches shorter. "Did those shrink?"

"Naw. I grew," Timmy said and walked away.

Curious, Luke went to the window and looked down the street. Then he saw what had caught Timmy's attention. Sarah was getting out of her SUV with Beau. She went around to the back of the vehicle, opened the door and took out a beach towel. She wiped the dog down and rubbed him dry. She shook out the towel, put it back in the car and closed the door. Then she walked into her house.

Luke also noticed that Sarah didn't look up at Mrs. Beabots's house. He was surprised that he felt very disappointed.

MRS. BEABOTS CARRIED a china plate piled high with oatmeal-raisin cookies as she climbed the steps to her house. It was nearly Halloween, and this year she had cajoled Luke into driving her and the kids out to the pumpkin farm to buy the pumpkins and mums she wanted to decorate her front porch.

The children had loved the hayride and the romp through the corn maze. Because Mrs. Beabots took her pumpkin-buying quite seriously, she asked Luke if he would pull the little red wagon through the rows of gray, white, Cinderella, orange, yellow and green pumpkins so she could make her selections.

When she'd finished, Mrs. Beabots had bought no fewer than a dozen pumpkins, a half dozen mums, a bale of hay and three sets of corn shocks, which she would tie around the lamp-post in the front yard.

As Luke loaded all of the pumpkins in the truck, he had asked, *Do you buy this many pumpkins every year?*

Goodness, no, she'd said. *I cut back this year.*

Annie and Timmy had flung their hands in front of their faces and giggled.

How did you get them home before I was around? There's a whole truck bed full of stuff back there, he said as he settled in behind the steering wheel.

I have friends, she'd replied. *This year, you're my new friend.*

New flunky you mean.

That, too, she'd replied.

MRS. BEABOTS LOOKED at her pumpkins and decided the one she'd placed closest to the door was the one she'd give the children to carve for Halloween.

She unlocked the door and went in.

Slipping off her sweater, she was surprised to find Luke sitting in her parlor.

"Is it all right that I came down here?" Luke asked. "I was just going over these wallpaper samples for inside the molding inserts you gave me."

Placing the cookies on the table between them, she sat down.

"Sarah picked out the samples," she said flatly.

He looked at the cookies. "She baked those, too, didn't she?"

"Yes. For the children. They have reduced sugar, applesauce and oatmeal. You can't object to those." She sniffed.

"No, I guess not." He looked down at the wallpaper samples, but didn't see them.

Mrs. Beabots said, "Luke, ever since your breakup, or whatever the dickens you want to call it, Sarah hasn't felt comfortable coming to my house. That's not right, Luke. She's my friend. She's been my friend all her life. I miss her."

He looked at his hands, feeling like an errant child. He didn't understand why he should feel this despondent. He'd only been protecting his children. Hadn't he? He wanted to do the right thing at all times. He remembered that when he was in the navy, doing right and being right had seemed so simple. Easy. Life back then had been like looking at cut crystal. Now, every blasted thing was muddled in confusion.

"You're right. This is your home and she should be welcome here. I'll make myself scarce."

Mrs. Beabots clucked her tongue and threw Luke a sharp look. "You're a fool, Luke Bosworth."

"Excuse me?"

"Do you think I don't see you sneaking peeks at Sarah's window every night when you help me with the dishes? Do you think I don't see you watching for her in the morning before you go to work? I see you take the cell phone out of your pocket and stare at it like it's going to talk back to you. I've seen when you dial a number on that thing and then don't call anyone. I can tell you one thing, young man, dead people don't use telephones."

"Dead..." he repeated and suddenly realized her inference. She was talking about Jenny. "No, they don't."

She leaned forward. "I think it's Sarah who occupies your mind more than you'd like to admit."

"She must think I'm a jerk."

"Believe me, she does. So do I."

"What?"

She smiled. "Well, you were. But that's not who you really are. Luke, you are a fine person and your children need you to be their guidepost in life. They will learn everything from you. I don't believe for a minute that this stubborn mule you've decided to be lately is you at all. I can tell you one thing. Life is nothing but change and challenge. A body no more gets through one set of problems when it's time to cope with another. But—" she wagged her finger at Luke "—I can tell you this. You're going to miss your entire life if you don't jump in and get wet."

"As I remember it, I did that once."

"So where's all that courage?"

"I guess I've been afraid."

"I'd venture you're correct. Nothing wrong

with being afraid, so long as it doesn't freeze you in your tracks. That's where you are now. Frozen."

"Funny. That's what Sarah said to me."

"Astute girl. Always was." Mrs. Beabots cocked her head to the right and smiled.

Luke glanced at the plate of cookies. "So Sarah made these for the kids?"

"Uh-huh."

"May I?" he asked.

"Help yourself," she said, holding the plate out to him. Luke munched on the cookie. "It's not like the ones I remember my mom used to make," he said after three bites.

"Of course not. There's not enough sugar or butter, if you ask me. Sarah altered the recipe to make you happy."

Luke nodded solemnly. "I think I get it."

"I should hope so," Mrs. Beabots replied.

ON FRIDAY EVENING, Luke walked with his kids down Maple Avenue and then turned west on Apple Lane and walked down two blocks to Rose Street, where they found Louise Railton closing up The Louise House.

"Hello, Louise," Luke shouted as he and the kids raced up to the tall, slender woman in her mid-forties.

Louise's infectious smile filled her face as

she turned away from the pretty aqua-blue door to the white, steep-gabled house. "Hello there," she said.

"Is it too late?" Luke asked, looking up at the front porch with its wicker furniture and fifty-year-old metal, ceiling-mounted swing. "You were just closing up."

Louise patted Luke's hand reassuringly. "I haven't washed the dipper yet. Still time for a scoop."

"Yes!" Timmy said as they all scooted inside.

Louise led the way into the candy shop and vintage-looking ice cream parlor. The Louise House was a child's delight. An entire wall was filled with enormous glass canisters of every conceivable candy—jelly beans, licorice, anise drops, homemade horehound drops, lemon drops and sour candies. Louise was a superb chocolatier, and in the glass case facing the jelly beans and hard candies were her super creamy caramels, truffles, chocolate-covered nut clusters, coconut-and-chocolate "nests" and dark-chocolate-covered dried blueberries, cherries and raspberries.

Behind the chocolates case were upright freezers filled with pink-and-chocolate-brown-striped containers of Louise's ice creams. No one in town knew precisely the secret to Louise's extra creamy ice creams. She told the tourists the recipes had been in her family for generations.

Mrs. Beabots had told Luke about The Louise House. After her husband, Raymond's, heart attack over twenty-five years ago, the Beabotses had been forced to sell the Rose Street Grocery, which they had owned nearly all their adult lives, to a very young Louise Railton.

"Have a seat," Louise said, pulling out a dainty wrought-iron chair with her signature pink-and-brown-striped seat cushion. "You all can be my guinea pigs. I have a new flavor I want to try out. No charge."

"Cool!" Timmy said.

Louise went to the freezer and pulled out a plain white container, picked up her scoop and dug into the ice cream. Taking out three crystal, fluted ice cream dishes, she deposited a small lump of white ice cream into each one. "I call this Magic Mountain," Louise said, turning around and taking a tall green-and-purple-felt hat off the hat rack. It had ribbons trailing down the back in every imaginable color and there were opalescent sequins forming a hat band around the brim. "This is my Fairy Queen hat. I made it myself. What do you think?" Louise asked, coming around the counter and setting the ice cream on their little round table.

"Does it help increase sales?" Luke asked as he looked at the preposterous hat.

"Evidently." Louise sat in a chair across from them and plopped her elbows on the table, resting her chin in her hands. "Be honest."

In unison, Luke and the kids dug into the ice cream. It was a creamy, vanilla-and-cinnamon-flavored frozen custard with bits of macadamia nuts and chunks of white chocolate. Luke had to close his eyes, the taste was so good.

"Does this have a lot of sugar?" Annie asked Louise.

"Heavens, yes," Louise replied.

Timmy looked at his father. "Why are we eating this?"

"Because I'm a lunkhead when I'm not being a dunderhead."

Annie looked at Timmy, who scrunched his shoulders and watched while his father closed his eyes again and ate the ice cream.

Annie put her forefinger to her ear and whirled it around, indicating that she thought her father was nuts. She finished her ice cream in two more bites.

Luke laughed at Annie and said, "After this,

I think we owe it to ourselves to go see the sunset at the lake."

"I love the lake," Timmy said, licking his spoon.

Annie nodded. "The stars are so pretty over the lake."

"Then the lake it is," Luke said.

They took the short drive down to the water and climbed out of the car.

LUKE TOOK OFF his work boots and socks, stuffed the socks inside the shoes and tied the shoelaces together. He carried his shoes in one hand while holding Timmy's hand with the other as they walked along the shore of Indian Lake.

"It's really pretty here in the fall," Annie said, staring at the setting sun. Marbling the azure-blue sky were ribbons of lavender, rose and amber. The sun was huge on the horizon, looking like a ball of flame that would set the earth on fire. "We should come out here more often," Annie said. "I had the best summer ever at the beach with Captain Redbeard and Mrs. Taylor."

"Me, too." Timmy picked up a smooth rock and tossed it back in the lake. "The only thing that would make it better..."

Timmy looked expectantly at his father.

"It's okay, Timmy. I know you miss Beau. I've been thinking about that."

"Really?" Timmy asked.

"Is it Beau you miss or just that you want a dog of your own?"

Timmy hung his head. "I miss Beau."

"That's what I thought," Luke replied.

The sun moved lower and the shadows from the trees around the lake cast long, wide, deep purple streamers over the water, the beach and Luke.

He stopped abruptly and looked at the light and shades as day transformed into evening and night began to fall. For more than two years he'd lived in the shadow of Jenny's death. But there was an even darker shadow in his life. It was of his own making. His own decisions. He had chosen this joylessness. He had chosen to feel this emptiness. He had no one to blame for this emptiness but himself.

Timmy picked up another rock and skipped it over the lake water. It bounced three times. "Hey, Dad! Did you see that? I got three skips!"

"Excellent, Timmy. Just excellent," Luke exclaimed.

At that moment, they all heard a dog bark. Then the dog barked again.

Timmy stood stock-still for a moment and then took off in a run. "Beau! Beau!"

Luke looked off toward the darkness that fell over the cattails. He heard the dog bark again.

Beau came crashing out of the cattails and nearly jumped on Timmy, who squealed in delight.

Luke's eyes scoured the cattails but he couldn't see anyone.

Suddenly, Annie yelled. "It's Miss Sarah! Sarah!" Annie raced into the dark.

Then he saw her and he thought his heart had gone into ramming speed. He should have been surprised to see her, but he wasn't. He had a strong feeling that fate would continue placing them in each other's paths until he realized he had been falling in love with Sarah for quite some time.

Sarah wore a long, white skirt and a dark jacket as she emerged from the edge of the tall grasses. Annie raced up to her and hugged her. Sarah enveloped Annie in her arms. She seemed genuinely thrilled to see her.

Luke watched as Sarah crouched down to pull Annie even closer. He knew that Sarah was aware of him watching her, but in this moment, Sarah didn't care about his reaction to her demonstration of love for his daughter.

Sarah was being Sarah. Loving and open. Kind. Giving.

Luke knew that Mrs. Beabots had been right. He'd been a fool.

Luke walked toward Sarah, who stood still, stroking Annie's head.

EVEN IN THE shadows, Sarah could see Luke's blue eyes blazing at her, but this time she saw a look she hadn't seen before. Her breath caught in her chest. She didn't dare hope. Her hand started shaking and she felt that her knees would give way and she would just melt right into the sand.

"Annie," Luke said, "go play with your brother for a minute. I want to talk to Sarah."

"Okay, Dad," Annie said, looking from her father to Sarah and back to her father. Annie smiled and then ran over to Timmy and Beau.

"Sarah," Luke said as he moved a few steps closer to her. "I owe you an apology…again." He took a deep breath and shook his head. "No that's wrong. I owe you about a thousand apologies. And they're all from the bottom of my heart."

"I'm listening, Luke."

He smiled wanly. "Thanks for not calling me a dunderhead again, because I really am. And

a jerk. I was pretty awful to you, Sarah. And
was very wrong."

"About letting me see the kids?" she asked.

"About everything. When I saw you with
the kids at your house that day when you were
all so happy, I was shocked because I hadn't
heard them laughing like that in a long time
I watched from the porch and I couldn't think
of a happier picture than you and Annie hugging. Then you told her that you loved her. And
I knew it was true. And she told you that she
loved you. I was so jealous, Sarah. So mighty
crazy jealous."

"But why, Luke?"

"Because I wasn't part of any of it. I felt like
you'd stolen my family, but the truth was that
I'd given them away. I neglected them…here
in my heart. You were right about that, too. I'd
let my heart turn to ice from sheer lack of use
You showed me that, Sarah."

"I wanted to be your friend, Luke. Sometimes
it's not easy to be a friend."

"Especially to me."

"I wouldn't quite say that."

"Well, I could use a friend. A best friend,
really."

Sarah had spent a great deal of her life deal-
ing with her fears. She had a choice right here

nd now to choose them or choose another path.
he threw her fears to the wind and asked, "Is
nat all you want, Luke? To be friends?"

He moved closer, never taking his eyes off
er. "No. It's not. I want the full ride. Top of the
erris wheel and all."

"It could cost you a lot," she said.

"Don't have much. Just my heart. And it's got
emperature malfunctions."

Sarah smiled and soft lights filled her eyes.
I bet I could fix it."

"I know you can," Luke said.

Sarah was mesmerized by the love glowing
n Luke's eyes. If she ever saw a firework again
he knew it would never compare to this. She
oped she wasn't just dreaming. If she was, she
oped she wouldn't wake up. Ever.

Luke moved closer and took Sarah's hand in
is. He squeezed it and then pulled her hand to
is lips and kissed it. "I also thought I should
ell you that we broke a rule tonight. We had
ce cream."

"Sugar? Before bed?" She chuckled. "That
s a breakthrough," she teased lightheartedly.

"I was thinking about breaking some other
ules," he whispered, his voice lowering an oc-
ave and his eyes peering so deeply into hers
hat Sarah felt he had just touched her soul.

"Which ones?"

"All of them," he said and pulled her into his arms. He smoothed her hair with his palm and cradled her face with his hands. "I love you Sarah."

Sarah's eyes welled with happy tears, and when they cascaded down her cheeks, he caught them with his thumbs. "I love you back, Luke."

When Luke kissed her, Sarah was very, very certain that the wishes she'd made on the star had not been in vain.

Her wishes had all come true.

* * * * *

THE SHORES OF INDIAN LAKE
continues with HEART'S DESIRE.

LARGER-PRINT BOOKS!

GET 2 FREE
LARGER-PRINT NOVELS
PLUS 2 FREE
MYSTERY GIFTS

Love Inspired

Larger-print novels are now available...

YES! Please send me 2 FREE LARGER-PRINT Love Inspired® novels and my 2 FREE mystery gifts (gifts are worth about $10). After receiving them, if I don't wish to receive any more books, I can return the shipping statement marked "cancel." If I don't cancel, I will receive 6 brand-new novels every month and be billed just $5.24 per book in the U.S. or $5.74 per book in Canada. That's a savings of at least 23% off the cover price. It's quite a bargain! Shipping and handling is just 50¢ per book in the U.S. and 75¢ per book in Canada.* I understand that accepting the 2 free books and gifts places me under no obligation to buy anything. I can always return a shipment and cancel at any time. Even if I never buy another book, the two free books and gifts are mine to keep forever.

122/322 IDN F49Y

Name _____ (PLEASE PRINT) _____

Address _____ Apt. #

City _____ State/Prov. _____ Zip/Postal Code

Signature (if under 18, a parent or guardian must sign)

Mail to the **Harlequin® Reader Service:**
IN U.S.A.: P.O. Box 1867, Buffalo, NY 14240-1867
IN CANADA: P.O. Box 609, Fort Erie, Ontario L2A 5X3

**Are you a current subscriber to Love Inspired books
and want to receive the larger-print edition?
Call 1-800-873-8635 or visit www.ReaderService.com.**

* Terms and prices subject to change without notice. Prices do not include applicable taxes. Sales tax applicable in N.Y. Canadian residents will be charged applicable taxes. Offer not valid in Quebec. This offer is limited to one order per household. Not valid for current subscribers to Love Inspired Larger-Print books. All orders subject to credit approval. Credit or debit balances in a customer's account(s) may be offset by any other outstanding balance owed by or to the customer. Please allow 4 to 6 weeks for delivery. Offer available while quantities last.

Your Privacy—The Harlequin® Reader Service is committed to protecting your privacy. Our Privacy Policy is available online at www.ReaderService.com or upon request from the Harlequin Reader Service.

We make a portion of our mailing list available to reputable third parties that offer products we believe may interest you. If you prefer that we not exchange your name with third parties, or if you wish to clarify or modify your communication preferences, please visit us at www.ReaderService.com/consumerchoice or write to us at Harlequin Reader Service Preference Service, P.O. Box 9062, Buffalo, NY 14269. Include your complete name and address.

LILPDIR13R